"From its seductive first pages, *The Last Mona Lisa* carries us along on an utterly irresistible time-jumping, continent-leaping tale of intrigue and family secrets, obsession, and the ineffable power of art itself. I could not put it down."

—Megan Abbott, bestselling and award-winning author of *Dare Me* and *The Turnout*

"This is a terrific read—compelling, intelligent, fascinating, and deeply satisfying. It was a book I did not want to end."

—Peter James, UK #1 bestselling author of the Detective Roy Grace series

"A riveting novel, weaving the real-life 1911 theft of Leonardo's masterpiece into a nail-biting contemporary drama where billionaire collectors, art historians, book collectors, and INTERPOL engage in so many double and triple crosses you're left wondering until the last page whom to trust and whom to fear. *The Last Mona Lisa* is like a master class in how to create a deep understanding of art history while making a seamless thriller."

—Sara Paretsky, *New York Times* bestselling author of the V.I. Warshawski series

"*The Last Mona Lisa* is a pacy, seductive international thriller of the first order. With its seamless blend of action, intriguing maze of family secrets, and the gripping, emotional journal entries of a long-dead art thief, this is a transporting novel, made all the more captivating because of the true story at its heart. Don't miss it!"

—Lisa Unger, *New York Times* bestselling author of *Confessions on the 7:45*

T0036378

"Astonishingly, Jonathan Santlofer is a brilliant writer of fiction and nonfiction—and a superb visual artist as well. All his skills come together in *The Last Mona Lisa*, and the result is wholly satisfying."

—Lawrence Block, bestselling author of more than fifty novels, including *Eight Million Ways to Die* and *A Walk Among the Tombstones*

"It's hard to imagine another writer who could pull off a feat like *The Last Mona Lisa*, with its combination of thrills, history, and insider knowledge of the art world. A singular achievement by a terrific writer. Really stunning."

—Laura Lippman, *New York Times* bestselling author

"A deliciously tense read that mixes a present-day hunt for the truth with a real-life historical heist to page-turning effect!"

—Ruth Ware, #1 *New York Times* bestselling author of *One by One*

PRAISE FOR *THE DEATH ARTIST*

"A crime novel that is savage and erudite, layered in wit, satire, and psychosis—in short, a chilling read."

—*USA Today*

"Santlofer's insight into the passion at the heart of great art brings this evocative thriller to richly impastoed life."

—Page Turner of the Week, *People* magazine

"A rollercoaster...a sure sense of pace and engaging literary style."

—*Plain Dealer*

"Brisk...inventive...compelling."

—*Washington Post*

PRAISE FOR *COLOR BLIND*

"Smart, lurid, and fascinating, with layered prose and a wealth of detail...vivid and realistic characters who weave their way through the fast-moving plot."

—*Library Journal*

PRAISE FOR *THE KILLING ART*

"Entirely believable... Unsettling... Mr. Santlofer may become even far better known for his writing than for his paintings."

—*New York Times*

PRAISE FOR *ANATOMY OF FEAR*

"A riveting story of a serial killer, a police sketch artist who gets involved in the murders... A tense, psychologically nuanced story that is never less than compelling... The quality of Santlofer's art and the way it becomes a galvanizing force in his prose is stunning."

—*Pittsburgh Tribune*

"Santlofer sure knows how to tell a story! His writing is fluid and vivid, and the illustrations just add this whole other dimension to the suspense, especially toward the end, when things get really manic."

—*San Francisco Chronicle*

PRAISE FOR
THE WIDOWER'S NOTEBOOK

"Wrenching, heartbreaking, intense, and emotional—but valuable too: we're all approaching the age where this will happen to us—or to others because of us—and understanding that it can be dealt with is consoling. I don't know how Santlofer found the fortitude to write this, but I'm deeply grateful he did. I think the world is a better place with this book in it."

—Lee Child, #1 *New York Times* bestselling author of the Jack Reacher series

"Jonathan Santlofer's stunning *The Widower's Notebook* raises all the blinds on immense and sudden loss, bringing light to all its dark corners. In so doing, he offers a deeply moving, often funny, always big-hearted portrait—not just of grief but of a long and rich marriage brought to vivid life and of a mighty father-and-daughter relationship both tested and enduring. A true gift."

—Megan Abbott, bestselling and award-winning author of *Dare Me* and *The Turnout*

"Deeply moving…beautifully written… It is such an achievement, like running uphill against a strong wind."

—Joyce Carol Oates, National Book Award–winning author

"This chronicle of devastation is devastating, a deeply powerful and unflinching report of how painfully and strangely life continues in the wake of a sudden, tragic death."

—Andrew Solomon, National Book Award winner

ALSO BY JONATHAN SANTLOFER

The Last Mona Lisa
The Death Artist
Color Blind
The Killing Art
Anatomy of Fear
The Murder Notebook
The Widower's Notebook: A Memoir

Anthologies as Editor
The Dark End of the Street (with S. J. Rozan)
Inherit the Dead
The Marijuana Chronicles
It Occurs to Me That I Am America

THE LOST VAN GOGH

A NOVEL

JONATHAN SANTLOFER

sourcebooks
landmark

For Nico Joy Thompson
and his parents Doria Santlofer & Douglas Lyle Thompson

Copyright © 2024 by Jonathan Santlofer
Cover and internal design © 2024 by Sourcebooks
Cover design by Laura Klynstra
Cover images © Vincent van Gogh "Self Portrait" (1889)
Public Domain/Wikimedia Commons, Anan

Published by Sourcebooks Landmark, an imprint of Sourcebooks
P.O. Box 4410, Naperville, Illinois 60567-4410
(630) 961-3900
sourcebooks.com

Cataloging-in-Publication Data is on file with the Library of Congress.

Printed and bound in the United States of America.
VP 10 9 8 7 6 5 4 3 2 1

"What would life be if we had no courage to attempt anything?"

—VINCENT VAN GOGH, Letter to Theo Van Gogh,
The Hague, Thursday, 29 December 1881

"The past is never dead. It's not even past."

—WILLIAM FAULKNER

"Art is the lie that enables us to realize the truth."

—PABLO PICASSO

PROLOGUE

August 1944
Paris

He could get shot for what he was doing.

Windows shut, shades drawn, the room stifling. One lamp on as he applied a thin wash of glue over the tracing paper. Then, he laid it onto the painting and flattened it with a soft rag so it molded to the surface, taking on the impression of every brushstroke below. This part was crucial, the paper a divider, a layer between the old and the new.

While he waited for it to dry, he shook a Gitanes out of a crumpled blue pack, placed it between his lips, and took a drag, the smoke harsh, the taste bitter.

Harsh and bitter, *he thought, like the past five years.*

A moment to fiddle with the dial on the cheap Bakelite radio he'd outfitted with an antenna so he could pick up the BBC, on occasion American music, his favorite. Though it was a criminal offense to listen to foreign radio stations, he didn't care, and it no longer mattered. His good luck tonight, the King Cole Trio, the lead singer's voice smooth as silk despite the static. He sang along, mimicking words he didn't understand, "It's only a paper moon..." then tested the painting's surface: still not dry. According to the company's claim, the new thermoplastic glue would create a strong bond that could be easily removed in the future.

Below the translucent paper the image appeared ghostlike and one he would never forget. Of all the pictures he had painted over, this was the most important.

When he touched the surface again, the glue was dry. He applied a layer of water-based white paint over the paper, creating a clean surface, then propped the canvas onto an easel. He thought about painting a Rouault-like clown or a simple design, then slipped a photograph from his wallet, a picture of his wife, Josette, taken five years ago before the world had erupted, her face dramatically lit, half of it shrouded in darkness.

Gitanes between his lips, he poured linseed oil into a small tin and added a few drops of cobalt drier. Though he knew it would eventually make the paint crack, saving time now was more important. Sorting through his remaining tubes of paint, he arranged small blobs of pigment onto his makeshift palette: mars black, titanium white, burnt umber, Naples yellow, a dollop of precious Venetian red from an almost squeezed-out tube, a sprinkling of marble dust over them all to speed drying further.

He shifted the lamp closer and worked fast, using his largest brush to paint a dark wash of black and umber to fill in the shadow side of the face. For the light side, he mixed white and Naples yellow and laid it on quickly. With a small, pointy brush he added a few deft strokes indicating the nose, eyes, mouth, then mixed vermilion with more white to make pink and filled in the lips, trying to capture Josette's hopeful half smile.

The radio was all static now, but he did not stop to fix it, lost in the painting, creating shadows beneath the nose and chin, the slightest sugges-tion of eyelashes, working quickly, the thought of another bonfire not only possible but probable, artillery fire in the distance growing louder.

A few broad strokes across the forehead and on top of the nose to make them stand out, then lighter highlights at the corners of the lips and a thick dot of white to create a convincing tear in her eye, something not in the photograph, but Josette had cried so many times in the past four years he could paint it by heart.

After that, he was finished. No reason to labor over a painting that would one day be destroyed. *He turned it around, painted 1944 on the back, dried his hands and set the painting in front of a fan.*

A moment to play with the radio's dial, this time to find the resistance station and his instructions, in code, about where to deliver the painting.

1

The Present
Stanfordville, New York

The Antique Barn was two floors crammed with old furniture, baby carriages, vases and crockery, lamps, stacks of moldering books, magazines, and moth-eaten clothes, a heady mix of mildew and dust in the air. But here, among the junk, was the object Tully had been hired to find.

A few people were milling about, poking through other people's discards, while he perused a table littered with old political buttons and fished a pack of Juicy Fruit out of his pocket.

"Help you?" the old guy asked. In his seventies, thinning hair in a ponytail, flannel shirt, denim overalls, the top half festooned with iron-on patches and pins—Grateful Dead, Jefferson Airplane, Joan Baez, Jimi Hendrix, rainbows and peace signs—a living Woodstock museum.

"How much for that one?" Tully indicated a McGovern/Shriver button.

"Oh, that's a good one," the old hippie said. "Couldn't part with it for less than ten bucks."

Tully offered five and they compromised at six. He tapped his baseball cap and fake mustache to make sure they were still in place and asked for a bag.

"Will cost you a nickel," the old hippie said. "Whole state's gone green, y'know."

"Can't argue with that," Tully said, adding a big smile.

"I'm Cal," the old hippie said and offered his hand, nails cracked and dirty, and Tully shook it though he did not want to. Then, he invented a wife, and a home they were decorating "forties style," and asked Cal if he had any paintings from the era.

Cal led Tully to the second floor, where he pointed out several framed landscapes resting on the dusty floor; not what Tully was looking for.

"The wife has her heart set on a portrait," he said. And when Cal said he'd just sold one, Tully tried not to curse, told himself to chill, and asked, "What did it look like?"

"Uh, a portrait of a woman, mostly in black and white."

"Darn," Tully said. "Sounds like the kind of picture my wife is looking for."

"It was nothing special," Cal said, "but the woman who bought it liked it."

The woman who bought it.

"Someone you know?"

Cal hiked up his overalls. "Nope. But I know her friend, local gal, comes in all the time, decorator, outfitted half the homes in the area with Antique Barn bric-a-brac."

Tully was trying to think of a way to get more information that would not arouse suspicion when Cal said she'd bought a lamp too. "Made out of a McCoy," he said, going into a riff about the early 1900s pottery company in Ohio, how the pots had taken on the owner's name, and the various colors: "mustard, teal, off-white."

Tully added the requisite "uh-huhs," then asked if he had any more of the pots, and when Cal pointed some out, he bought two—one green, the other mustard yellow. As Cal wrapped them, Tully talked more about his invented wife and the house they'd just bought that "needed decorating" and wondered aloud about "that local gal, the one who'd helped so many people in the area."

Cal rummaged through a stack of cards beside the cash register and handed him one.

Sharon MacIntosh, INTERIOR DESIGN.

Damn, Tully thought, *I love small towns.*

Cal even offered to give her a call, his cell already out.

Tully folded a new stick of Juicy Fruit into his mouth and listened while Cal told Sharon that he had a new customer for her.

2

The Present
Bowery, New York City

Late morning sun filtered through the floor-to-ceiling windows, across my palette and over half-finished paintings leaning against the walls of my Bowery studio, new work for an upcoming exhibition, my first in four years at the Mattia Beuhler Gallery, one of the best galleries in New York. A second chance, and one I never thought I'd get. But I did, thanks to my friend Jude, the art critic and auction expert who knew everyone in the art world, and who had personally brought the gallerist Mattia Beuhler to my studio and lobbied hard on my behalf.

My new paintings were a mix of figures, interiors, and parts of the city I saw through my windows, a change from the abstract work I'd been known for, but I was still searching for something that would take them to another level and set them apart.

I dipped my brush in bright cadmium red and outlined a nude figure that filled most of a six-foot canvas. I wasn't sure what Alex would make of it. Though she had posed for the painting, I'd reworked it so many times you couldn't tell. She complained I could have used anyone as the model, but that wasn't true. For me, there was no one like Alex.

A year had passed since we'd met in Italy, a crazy time, and I was happy to be back in New York, even happier that Alex and I were living together. Well, not quite. She spent most nights here but had kept her Murray Hill apartment as an escape hatch.

A glance back at the painting, at the way I'd scumbled paint across the face so it was unrecognizable and mysterious, and I wondered for a moment if there were things about Alex I still didn't know. Not that I was an open book; I didn't let many people in, a fact every one of my ex-girlfriends had pointed out. But I wanted to know everything about Alex, to be with her all the time, and I missed her when she wasn't around. Like now, when she was visiting her mother, which she did every other week, at a memory care facility in Stanfordville, New York, two hours north of the city.

Another hour of painting, then I stripped off my plastic gloves, dumped my brushes into coffee cans filled with mineral spirits, and changed out of my paint clothes. By the time I'd washed up and put on a clean shirt, I heard the freight elevator's gate creak open and Alex calling "I'm home," words that never failed to thrill me.

I wrapped my arms around her, and she rested her head against my chest.

"Missed you," I said, noting the strain on her face. "You okay?"

"My mother," she said. "Sometimes she doesn't know where she is or who I am."

I hugged her tighter and she let me, but after a minute stepped out of my embrace and forced a smile. "Sharon sends her regards to the handsomest man in New York," she said, and I asked if she was seeing someone else. Alex laughed, then went on about her old friend Sharon being too young to be living alone in "that isolated old house" and asked if there was someone I could fix her up with. "What about Ron?"

"You want to fix her up with a self-involved, narcissistic artist?"

"Now who'd be crazy enough to do *that*?" she said and patted my cheek.

"Ha!" I said, then noted the stuff beside her suitcase and asked what it was.

Alex raised the lamp and explained it was made out of an old McCoy vase, "and apparently *very* collectible, according to the antique store owner, an old hippie with a story for everything."

"And that?"

Alex knelt to remove paper and plastic from a painting, then brought it into the living room and set it up on the long dining table. It was a small portrait of a young woman, half her face painted white against an almost black background.

"What do you think?" she asked.

The brushwork looked assured, and the artist had painted a believable glint in the woman's eye. I turned it around. No signature. Only a date, 1944, though it looked older, the stretchers cracked, the linen canvas badly stained. "The hippie store owner didn't tell you who painted it?"

Alex said he didn't know, just that it was part of an estate sale. "It only cost twenty-five dollars, and I like it, the brave look in the woman's eyes."

"It's okay," I said.

"High praise," she said, adding that Sharon had to stop her from buying me a zoot suit.

"God bless her," I said, and made the sign of the cross, what remained of my Catholic upbringing.

An image of Holy Name Cemetery, Jersey City, a soggy spring day less than a year ago, standing at my father's grave site, arm around my mother, small and fragile, leaning into my six-foot frame, the new pastor from St. Mary's Star of the Sea giving a two-minute eulogy that proved he'd never met my father, "a humble man, who loved his family and friends."

I took a closer look at the painting, pointed out it was badly cracked, and suggested Alex have it restored, if she cared about it.

"I'd like to find out more about it before investing in it," she said, then asked how my work had gone while she was upstate. We went into my studio where she pointed out things in the paintings she liked and others not so much, always with tact, but I listened. She had a good eye and was a professional, only a few credits shy of a doctorate in art history.

After that, we ate my famous eggplant parmigiana, one of the few things I cooked, Alex with a glass of wine, while I drank Pellegrino. Then Alex brought the antique store painting into the bedroom and balanced it on top of the television, and we got into bed, turned on the Criterion Channel and watched an old film noir, one of my favorites, *Out of the Past*, a story of how the past can come back to destroy the present.

When it ended, Alex talked about the visit to her mom and the sadness came over her again. She poked the tattoo of the Bayonne Bridge on my upper arm, and I made a muscle and the bridge expanded and she laughed, something that still, after more than a year, gave her a kick. I'd gotten the tattoo at fifteen, along with the words *Kill van Kull*, the name my posse and I stole from the waterway beneath the bridge where we drank beer, smoked weed, and plotted trouble.

I put my arms around Alex and kissed her, and we slipped out of our clothes. Light through the blinds caught her hair and the golden down on her cheeks, which I caressed while she played with the curls on the back of my neck and said I needed a haircut. Then we made love, taking our time, and fell asleep in each other's arms.

I didn't know if it was two minutes or two hours later when Alex woke me, talking in her sleep, something she did when she was upset. Clearly, the time with her mother had been rough. I stroked her cheek and whispered, "It's okay," and when she rolled over, rubbed her back until her breathing was even again. I checked the bedside clock, almost three in the morning, got up, went to the bathroom, and on the way back accidentally brushed against the television and knocked the painting to the floor.

Alex bolted up.

I whispered, "It's nothing," and she went back to sleep, but I was wide awake. I scooped the painting off the floor, brought it into the living room and propped it up on the wooden table. Other than the noise of the city, sirens, garbage trucks, cars horns and alarms, it was as quiet as it ever got on the Bowery.

I noticed again how badly the painting was cracked, and when I touched a lower corner, a square of paint fell off. I leaned in, squinting, trying to make out what lay beneath.

3

The next morning I found the painting where I had left it and examined the area I'd accidentally chipped off last night. In the light of day, I could see there was some sort of paper under the paint, and though I was tempted to pick off more, Alex was at school. I left it alone and busied myself with notes I was making for a lecture on Cézanne. He was an artist I loved even if he had been an anti-Semite and on the wrong side of the famous Dreyfus case. If you had to choose artists you liked based on their personal lives, there'd be few left to admire. Every few minutes I eyed the painting, and as soon as Alex came home, I showed her the exposed spot.

She leaned in for a closer look. "So, you think there's something under the painting?"

I didn't know but asked if she was willing to find out. She thought a moment, said she'd wasted twenty-five dollars before, took a few pictures of the painting "to remember it," then told me to go for it.

We brought the painting into my studio, where I chose my sharpest palette knife, held it over the painting, hesitated a few seconds, then slid it under the paint at the bottom corner where the piece had already fallen off. It easily popped off another square of paint, and the two of us crowded in for a better look.

"Hold on," Alex said, then returned with a magnifying glass, which she held over the exposed spot. "There's paper there for sure," she said, and told me to keep going.

I worked the knife under the paint and more cracked off. Alex took another picture, and I continued working to remove about a quarter of the paint.

Now, with the lower half of the woman's face gone, we could see the layer of paper clearly. It was thin like tracing paper, painted white.

"Someone went to a lot of trouble to do this," I said, and getting back to work too fast, skimmed off not only more paint but some skin from my knuckles.

Alex winced and led me into the bathroom where I washed off the blood and she applied Neosporin and a couple of Band-Aids. When she pointed out I'd gotten blood on my T-shirt, I took it off. She patted my back and said, "How's it going, Mona?" referring to the tattoo of *Mona Lisa* that filled most of my back, something I'd gotten in honor of my great-grandfather and his infamous theft.

I put on a new tee and went back to work, this time careful to scrape *away* from my hand. It was slow going, over an hour to remove the rest of the woman's face, but the white paper was fully exposed, bumpy and filled with ridges.

"There's definitely something under that," Alex said, and urged me on.

I found a longer, flatter palette knife, worked it under the paper, and managed to lift it up.

4

"It's another painting!" Alex said, both of us staring at the few inches I had exposed, mostly deep blue with flecks of green, the paint thick.

I got my palette knife under the paper again, but this time when it tore, I put the knife down and used my fingers, tugging gently, and lifted off a small piece, about an inch square, before it tore again. I repeated the action, tearing off bits of paper inch by inch. It was slow and laborious, the torn paper often trapped in the paint below, but I kept going, Alex beside me, taking pictures and egging me on until the bottom half was exposed.

"Are those cows?" Alex said.

I tugged off a few more inches of paper, both of us holding our breath as I revealed a man's jacket, vest, and a shirt painted in heavy, expressive brushstrokes, the style immediately identifiable but...

"Keep going," Alex said, taking another picture, and I could see her hand was shaking.

I tore off more paper until there was only a large, jagged swath concealing the top third of the painting. Then I set it upright on the table, sat back, and we both looked—gaped is more like it—at a portrait of a red-bearded man with a gaunt face and haunted eyes, all too familiar.

"It can't be," Alex said. "Can it?"

I said I didn't know and got back to work, removing the last bits of paper to reveal the hair, a lighter shade of red flecked with yellow and green, each hair thickly painted as if sculpted.

A few pieces of paper clung stubbornly here and there, but the image was fully exposed—face, beard, a swirling blue background with a strip of earth and two small, crudely painted cows at the bottom.

"Do I dare say, Van Gogh?" Alex said, looking from the painting to me. "It's not possible, is it?" She took another picture, then laid her phone down and slid my laptop over, tapping away on the keyboard, then turned the laptop around.

"Here," she said, "every known Van Gogh self-portrait, by year and where they are now." One by one she enlarged them, going through all thirty-eight, then read the caption under the last one aloud. "This may have been Van Gogh's last self-portrait, painted in 1889, collection of the Musée d'Orsay, Paris." She looked up. "*May* have been."

I looked from the portrait on the screen to the one sitting on the table in front of us, a remarkable similarity.

"It's not signed with his familiar Vincent," I said.

Alex reminded me Van Gogh, like many artists, didn't sign his paintings until he was sending them off to an exhibit or selling them, so many were left unsigned. She examined the painting, running her magnifying glass over every inch while listing various Van Gogh attributes and facts, referring to it as "late style, if you can call anything by Van Gogh *late*, since he died at thirty-seven." She went on about how much work he'd made. "Over two thousand artworks in his lifetime, most of them in just one decade, *seventy* in the last months of his life!" she said, citing letters Vincent wrote to his brother Theo, and asked if I'd read them, and insisting I must.

I made a note to read them while Alex went on studying the painting, tapping her lip, and talking about Vincent's death.

"He shot himself, didn't he?" I asked.

"That's the commonly held belief, but no one knows for sure. There were no witnesses, the gun wasn't found until the nineteen-sixties, *if* it's the gun, plus Vincent's easel, his canvas, and paints were missing that day as if someone cleaned up the scene."

"Are you suggesting he was murdered?"

She said it was one theory, the others accident or suicide. "But that's not it. I'm thinking about his funeral, which was described in a letter by his young artist friend Émile Bernard."

Alex sat back and closed her eyes. "Vincent's body was laid out surrounded by a halo of yellow flowers, along with his latest canvases, landscapes and still life paintings and two self-portraits." She opened her eyes. "That's it, *two* self-portraits!" She tapped the picture on the laptop screen. "This one, and another one which has never been found. Either the painting got lost or someone took it." She looked back at our newly uncovered self-portrait. "Could this be it, the lost Van Gogh?"

I didn't want to be a downer but suggested it could be a forgery.

"Then why hide it under another painting? That's going to a lot of trouble for a forgery," she said, and she had a point. "There's something else about Van Gogh forgeries, something I recently read or heard, but I'm too distracted to remember."

I told her I was sure it would come to her, and we talked about getting the painting authenticated at one of the auction houses. I even suggested *Fake or Fortune*, the BBC show that investigated artworks and their provenance.

Alex gave me a look. She wanted no part of a television show or the attending publicity, saying she'd stick with an auction house and would call one in the morning. "Give me one night to dream it's the real thing."

"Sure," I said, though another thought slid into my mind: *What if it turns out to be stolen?*

5

Still in her nightie, a cotton minishift, blue with white stripes, no makeup, hair wet from the shower pulled back in a ponytail, Alex looked about sixteen. As opposed to me in boxers and an old tee, not yet showered or shaved.

She already had her cell to ear. "That's great," she said. "See you later, and thanks." She laid the cell on the table and turned to me. "It's all set."

I put my coffee mug down, rubbed a hand across my eyes, still struggling to wake up. After last night's discovery, I had downloaded the nine-hundred-page Van Gogh biography by Steven Naifeh and Gregory White Smith, along with a book of the artist's letters, and had ended up reading till I fell asleep only a few hours ago. I asked what she was talking about, and she told me she'd just gotten an appointment at the Lower East Side Auction House through a connection, a friend in her PhD program.

"Jennifer. You've never met her, or you'd remember. She's very pretty, smart too. We've recently become friends," she said, talking fast about Jennifer doing some work-study at the auction house, which was new and cool and how it was just next door to the old Eldridge Street Synagogue, only six or seven blocks from the loft, though I'd never been. "Jennifer put me in touch with the post-impressionism specialist at the auction house, a Ms. Van Straten, who's willing to see me this afternoon." She went on about walking the painting over when she got back from class, after stopping at her apartment to get her mail.

I managed to interrupt and offered to bring the painting over now, before my class, but she turned me down.

"I want to be there when she tells me I have an original Vincent Van Gogh," she said, and asked if I'd wrapped it.

I took the painting into my studio and measured it, approximately twenty-by-seventeen inches. Staring at Van Gogh's face, I covered it with a sheet of glassine paper and a layer of Bubble Wrap, then found a tote bag, slipped the painting in, and stuffed more of the wrap around it for added protection.

Alex emerged all dressed up, silk blouse, black slacks, high heels. "I think people take you more seriously if you're dressed well." She raised a foot to show me a red sole. "My one and only pair of Louboutins," she said, which meant nothing to me. "They're going to cripple me, but they look good."

I agreed and leaned over to stroke her leg.

She gently removed my hand. "I've got to get to school, and I'm meeting Jennifer for coffee before class." I showed her the canvas tote bag, and where I'd hide it behind a painting when I left for school. I didn't like leaving it out where anyone could see it. I'd only had one break-in since I'd lived here but didn't want to take a chance.

"You look tired," Alex said and ran her hand along my cheek.

I admitted I'd been reading about Van Gogh half the night and babbled on about his father and grandfather being pastors and how he had studied to be one and failed, and about his life and struggles, though I didn't say how much I related to this artist whose parents didn't get him or support him and what his art meant to me. All things Alex already knew about Van Gogh and about me—my life, my drinking, my juvie record, the path of self-destruction I'd been on and what I might have been had I not found art.

"'Do right and don't look back, and things will turn out well,'" I said. "Van Gogh to his brother Theo, in a letter. I've read about thirty."

"That leaves only two thousand more," Alex said and smiled, then wrapped a scarf around her neck and said she'd call after the auction house specialist "lets me know if our Van Gogh is real or a fake."

6

If only every case were this easy.

Tully stared at the road, the Taconic Parkway, one curve after another, the trees a pale-green blur in the morning light. He was feeling good, the information gleaned easily. He unwrapped a stick of Juicy Fruit and popped it into his mouth like a reward, a habit developed after he'd quit smoking for the fourth or fifth time.

Sharon MacIntosh had turned out to be pretty—long, shiny hair, baggy jeans and a loose denim shirt that failed to hide her figure.

"Sorry for barging in," he'd said, adding a practiced smile. He was wearing a new costume, wire-framed John Lennon glasses, a David Crosby mustache, no baseball cap, his sandy-gray hair mussed up to look boyish, everything to appear less threatening, including his stance, to which he'd added a slight slump of the shoulders. The acting classes had paid off.

"Cal tells me everyone up here swears you're the best," he said, and Sharon smiled, listening as he lied about the home he'd recently bought in Red Hook, a town close by but not *that* close, a detail he'd googled on his drive over, and how he wanted to "outfit it all in Early American," adding that he was divorced, with no kids.

After the house tour she'd made coffee, and they sat at her kitchen table and she asked questions about his new home and took notes on answers he made up on the spot. He brought up McCoy pottery, recapping a few facts, thanks to Cal, and how he was looking for vases that could be made into lamps.

"You're kidding!" Sharon said. "My friend, Alex, just bought a McCoy lamp from Cal."

His turn to say, "You're kidding? I have a friend named Alex who collects McCoy. Could it be…?"

"My Alex is short for Alexis," she said, taking the bait.

"No way! So is *mine*!"

"Alexis *Verde*?"

"No." Sad face. "Alexis *Berkowitz*. But still, it's a coincidence. I mean, that they both collect McCoy pottery. Does your Alex live up here?"

"In the city. Murray Hill," she said and asked if he knew where that was, and he said no though he did, while she explained it was on Manhattan's east side, the midthirties, and he smiled, enjoying how he got people to tell him things he hadn't even asked. Then he went out to his rental and came back with the two McCoy pots.

"I bought these for Alex, Berkowitz, not *Verde*. That was the name, right? Like green in Italian?" A confirming nod, and now he had the spelling. "But you've been so nice I want you to have one."

Sharon demurred but when he insisted, she chose the green one and offered him another cup of coffee, but having gotten what he'd come for, he said he had to get going. She reminded him to email the pictures of his new house and he promised he would.

Two hours later, car parked in an open lot, he was back in Manhattan watching the Murray Hill building, the address easily found on the internet, but no sign of Alexis Verde.

He had already tried the doorman, who confirmed that Verde lived there but was not home. Now, from across Thirty-Second Street, he stared at the building, watching as one doorman ended his shift and another took over. Then he saw her, a blond coming down the block, and pulled up the pictures he'd found on Facebook and Instagram. He took a few steps closer, hovering behind a bus stop partition, and watched as she headed into the building's circular drive where she stopped to chat with the doorman. He observed their pantomime, her animated smile, the doorman's flirty grin before she disappeared into the building. He would give it ten minutes, then present himself to the new doorman, his speech for Alexis Verde prepared: *"an old friend of Sharon's, just saw her upstate…"*

He was about to cross the street when she came out of the building sorting through a thick stack of envelopes and magazines. She was even prettier than her pictures, slender and stylish, the kind of girl who would not give him a second look, right now a good thing. She headed uptown on Lexington Avenue, and he followed, the street crowded, easy to keep a few people between them.

He watched her put half the mail into her bag and dump the rest into a trash bin, then head uptown. He let her get ahead, then tugged on plastic gloves and fumbled the mail out of the trash bin, getting a disgusted look from a well-dressed woman as he thumbed through ads and generic solicitations to "Occupant" until he found one with Alexis Verde's name, all he needed to be sure it was her. He dropped the rest back into the trash and picked up the trail, watching her stride across the street, elegant in black pants and high heels, a pale-gray scarf around her neck trailing like smoke.

The traffic light turned against him, but he kept going, dodging cars and taxis, but when he got to the other side, she was gone. Eyes raking the street, cursing, he sprinted to the corner where he caught a glimpse of her heading into the subway.

A few feet away from her on the platform, he watched her through the corner of his eye, waited till the train pulled in and she got on. It was only half-full, but she stood, and he did too, his back toward her but he could smell her perfume, he was that close. The train jerked into a station, and when he lost his footing, she reached out and asked if he was okay, her voice deeper than he expected, just audible over the screeching metal doors opening and closing, the train starting up again.

He nodded, then moved away, didn't want her to remember him though he'd added sunglasses and a different baseball cap to his costume. He stared at an ad with a colorful rainbow, DR. JONATHAN ZIZMOR, CLEAR BEAUTIFUL SKIN, unconsciously touched his cheek and felt the pockmarks, seized by a memory of teenage jeers so hurtful he almost lost her when she got off at the next stop.

On the street, squinting despite his shades, the sun high in the sky, people walking at a clip, and so was she. He took in the hodgepodge of Bowery buildings, new, old, cast-iron with impressive facades and ornate details, slowed to weave between lunchers and brunchers crowding a café in front of the Bowery Hotel, had a passing fantasy of sitting here across from the blond rather than tailing her.

She paused for a quick look into a glass-fronted building, and when he got there, he did the same, noting the name, the New Museum, and glanced up at the modernist ziggurat tower. It reminded him of one of his favorite community college courses, History of Western Art, a survey of the greats.

Alexis Verde crossed the street and he followed, waiting a few yards away while she got her key into the graffitied door of a large brick building. When the door closed behind her, he checked the buzzers—no names, just numbers—then walked away, giving her a few minutes to settle in.

At the corner, he watched two young guys exchanging drugs for cash in front of the Bowery Mission, then headed back. He was about to hit all the buzzers, was rehearsing his story about her friend

Sharon when the door swung open, and it was *her*, the two of them face-to-face. He backed up but she'd gotten a good look at him at the same time he'd seen the canvas tote bag over her shoulder, something she did not have before and just the right size for a painting.

"May I help you?" she asked.

Tully shook his head, stroked the mustache to make sure it was still in place, walked away, and did not dare look back.

A moment to think. Then he was back in front of the Bowery Mission, signaling the two young drug dealers, telling them what he wanted them to do, "get the bag," indicating the blond now halfway down the block, handing them each a fifty-dollar bill and promising the same if they retrieved the bag.

Then he waited, twice exchanging his Juicy Fruit for a fresh stick, and checking the time again and again. It was exactly seventeen minutes before they returned with the bag.

"Where *were* you?" he asked.

One said they'd had to wait for the right place. The other, striking a hip-hop pose said, "Had to let the body hit the floor, man."

"*What?* Is she"—Tully swallowed—"okay?"

"She wouldn't give up the fuckin' bag," one of them said.

"She's in an alleyway just off…" said the other.

Tully gave them each the other fifty, his mind spinning as he watched them take off. Then he dipped a hand into the tote bag, felt along the edge of something rectangular and solid, tore at the Bubble Wrap just enough to see an edge of canvas.

The subway to Queens was crowded, Tully standing, the punk's words washing over him again.

Had to let the body hit the floor, man…

Jesus, had they killed her? This was not what he'd intended. He found people, didn't kill them. He gripped the overhead strap, the tote bag clenched to his chest. He couldn't be blamed, could he? He only told them to get the bag, not to kill her!

Back at his small Long Island City office, he took the painting out, peeled back a few more inches of Bubble Wrap, and stopped short. This was not the painting he was after. *Shit!* Did he get the wrong picture? How was that possible? He stripped off the rest of the Bubble Wrap, turned it over to compare the back with the photo he had received: a match, the date, 1944, even the stained canvas.

Same back. Different front. *What the fuck?*

Tully sat a minute, thinking again about his History of Western Art class. It had been a long time ago and he didn't remember much, but this artist was unforgettable, a household name and one he knew. A quick internet search confirmed it. None of the paintings an exact match, but similar.

He fished an old pack of cigarettes out of a desk drawer, lit one, and took a drag. Stale as shit, but he didn't care; he needed time to think, to figure this out.

He slid a comic book off a stack, "Jimmy Olsen," the first in a series. Cost him almost four hundred dollars on eBay, more than he'd ever spent on a single comic but worth it, the collection he imagined one day as his retirement fund. But right now, it didn't matter.

Comic book trembling in his hand, he looked back at the painting and took a couple of cell phone pictures, a plan taking shape in his mind.

7

Alex lay on the couch while I held an ice pack to her cheek, her eye going purple.

"If I'd been there, they'd be dead!" I'd never killed anyone, though right now I thought I could. I kept the ice pack on her cheek while she explained again how a good Samaritan couple helped her up and walked her home, and that she was fine, but I could not stop thinking what could have happened.

"I'm *okay*," she said. "I know the bad boy in you is just dying to break someone's neck, but calm down."

I blew out a breath. "If anything ever happened to you, I'd…"

"I'm *okay*," she said again, a finger to my lips. I took another deep breath and for the third time said we should call the police.

"And say what? That I was attacked, and the perpetrators took what *might* be a very important painting, which, by the way is possibly a forgery or maybe even stolen. Do *you* want the police looking for the painting?"

I saw her point but thought she should at least see a doctor.

"The little punk punched me is all. I swear if there weren't two of them…"

"Yeah, you're tough."

"But how did they know what I was carrying?"

"It could be a simple mugging," I said.

"They took the canvas tote bag but not my Prada bag. Come *on*, they had to know *something*."

A good point: How did a couple of punks on the Bowery know which bag to take?

"I don't care that some little thug punched me. Well, I do, but that's not the point. It's that I wanted to be the one who found this legendary painting."

I tried to console her by suggesting it could have been a forgery and not worth much.

"Then why did someone *steal* it?" she said, another good point. "Do you think that's it, our discovery gone for good?"

Maybe yes. Maybe no, and I had no idea how to find it. Then I had a thought. "Hang on," I said, scrolling through my phone log till I found the number.

"Who are you calling?"

"Someone who's good at finding things."

8

John Washington Smith leaned back in his ergonomic chair, the only new item in the Midtown Manhattan office and a nod to his bad back, the result of injuries sustained on the last job. Well, not exactly a job. In fact, he'd gone AWOL, something the general secretariat at INTERPOL would have fired him for had he not been successful and almost died.

Hands flat on the cigarette-scarred desk, Smith took in the two hardback wooden chairs and worn leather love seat left by the former tenant, the only furniture in the space selected *for* him.

Framed above the desk, his diploma from John Jay College of Criminal Justice, an INTERPOL citation for his twenty years as an art theft analyst, and his private investigator license, State of New York, good for two years, one almost gone.

Outside the one window, Times Square billboards, a flashing Coca-Cola sign, and the incessant noise of taxis, buses, cars, and endless construction, a hotel being erected just across the street. Though Smith had grown up in Manhattan, he still wasn't used to the racket after the dead quiet of INTERPOL headquarters in Lyon, France, and the one-room studio apartment he'd moved into after his divorce.

But right now, he was thinking about the call from Luke Perrone. The last time he'd seen him, Smith was losing consciousness and close to death. The assignment had ended successfully, the painting in question returned and no one the wiser, though he'd gotten no thanks, only his old job back until he realized he no longer wanted it and bargained for this.

He took a sip of his Starbucks Caffè Americano and typed PERRONE into his smartphone calendar, then erased it. Better not to have a record. He'd made it sound as if he was doing Perrone a favor, squeezing him in, though in fact he had no appointments if you didn't count his daily workout at Equinox, then drinks with a woman he'd met at the gym.

Only his third date since moving back to the city a year ago, and though he liked to think of himself as independent and needing no one, something he had learned early growing up in Manhattan's Baruch Houses project, lately he'd been lonely. He even missed his INTERPOL office, the analysts and agents, every part of the world represented, all religions and colors, so that no one seemed to notice he was Black. Odd, that here, in one of the most racially diverse cities in the world, he was feeling different, a persistent topic of discussion growing up with his single white mother, his father having died just after his third birthday leaving only a hazy memory of a dark-skinned man who'd held his hand as he learned to walk and a smattering of phrases that played in his mind, like *No wahala*, Nigerian slang for "No worries."

He finished the coffee, crushed the cup, and hurled it into the trash.

Perrone hadn't told him much: "a painting, possibly valuable, possibly a forgery, possibly stolen." *Possibly.* A word he didn't like. He prided himself on making decisions, on taking action.

He scanned a few laptop folders—old INTERPOL cases, personal contacts in the art world, above and underground, links to art theft databases—and opened one, the Art Loss Register, an up-to-the-minute news source of stolen art and antiquities. He skimmed an article about the recovery of a bronze sculpture stolen from a Swiss museum twenty years ago, one of his first cases though he'd received no credit. Typical INTERPOL. Analysts worked to get all the intel, then turned it over to local law enforcement who got the glory, something he should have gotten used to but never had.

A second article on the site caught his eye: police in Spain intercepting a group of forged paintings, the fence and the buyers killed in the arrest, three dead, identities withheld, all trafficking in stolen art, a high-risk game that he knew from experience often ended in disaster.

If Perrone had stumbled on an important forgery or a stolen masterpiece, he was likely diving into those same dangerous waters, something he should know about from his last venture. Was he willing to go there again? Was Smith? No question. He had been since the moment he'd agreed to this position. They were grooming him for something big, or so they said, but so far, the assignments had been few and relatively small—intercepting stolen art at docks and airports, following a trail of dark money for a commissioned theft.

Patience, they'd told him. Not his strongest suit.

Up from his desk, he wrapped his hand around a twenty-pound barbell, did a dozen curls, the conversation with Perrone replaying.

Barbell down, he reached for his cell, hesitated, then chose the burner. He had to let his employers know about Perrone and his *possibly* important painting.

9

The next morning Alex and I were huddled together on a worn leather love seat in Smith's office, one room in a Times Square office building with water-stained walls, a cracked linoleum floor, and a window that looked out on billboards and a blinking Coca-Cola sign five stories high. Quite a comedown from international art theft and forgery, but I knew INTERPOL had not valued Smith the way they should have, and I couldn't blame him for leaving. We hadn't spoken since he'd first set up shop in New York a year ago, an awkward call where we talked about grabbing a beer but never did. Too many bad memories and too much baggage to pretend we were old pals when we never had been, though his had been the only name that came to mind when I thought who could help.

I had filled Alex in on the way over, the pros and cons, and she thought it was worth a shot. Now we told Smith how Alex had gotten the painting, what we'd discovered under it, and how she'd lost it. She showed him the cell phone pictures she'd taken during the unveiling of the painting, and Smith skimmed through them.

"I'm sending these to my phone," he said before Alex could say yes or no, then handed the phone back. We had yet to hire him, and his presumption annoyed me.

Alex took off her sunglasses to tell him about the mugging.

"Quite the shiner," he said, pushing his own glasses, the gray-tinted wire frames I remembered, up the bridge of his nose, a familiar gesture. He still looked as if he spent too much time at the gym, his rolled-up shirtsleeves showing off ropy muscled arms, his neck thick. His hair was cropped to a shadow on his skull, his sand-colored skin with a few more lines than I remembered.

"The muggers," he asked. "Can you describe them?"

"One white, one Black, both young, though it happened so fast. They came up from behind me and grabbed the bag. When I didn't let go, one of them punched me."

I winced.

Smith asked if they'd said anything, and Alex said no, then, "Wait, after the punch, I was on the ground, they must have thought I was out, and I heard one of them say, 'Let's get back to the mission.'"

"The mission," Smith repeated.

The only mission I could think of was the Bowery Mission, practically across the street from my loft, and Smith made a note.

"Okay," he said when we'd finished. "A few obvious things to check out. One, this mission, then the upstate antique place, though I'm not sure what that will tell us because the guy obviously didn't know what he was selling, or he never would have sold it. Two, the woman at the auction house. We need to know who she told about Alex coming in with the painting. Did she know what you were bringing in?" he asked and Alex said no, but he pressed. "You must have said something."

"Only that it was a painting in her area of expertise."

"So, you didn't say *who* the painting was by, but you narrowed the field." He made another note, then asked how many post-impressionists there were, though after twenty years as an art analyst at INTERPOL, I thought he must know.

"Basically five," Alex said, and named them, "Van Gogh and Gauguin, Cézanne, Seurat, and Toulouse-Lautrec."

"All well-known artists, hard to come by, and big-ticket items." Smith put a cigarette between his lips.

"Still haven't quit?" I said, picturing him in the Paris hotel room behind a cloud of smoke.

"Yeah, I did. You mind?" he asked and lit it, not waiting for an answer. "So, those punks who attacked you… It's likely they were paid to snatch the painting, and I hope so. If they were just a couple of random street kids, they would be pissed when they opened the bag and saw it was a painting, worthless to them, and they'd dump it. Could be incinerated by now."

"Jesus," Alex said.

"Didn't mean to scare you," Smith said, "but we can't rule that out."

"So what do you suggest?" I asked.

"I suggest those kids were told to get that bag, and whoever they delivered it to is the one we're after, though he or she could be long gone."

"So you're saying we've got *nothing*?" Alex asked, a throb in her voice.

"No. They may be gone but we all leave something behind." He asked Alex to tell the story of the attack again, but to start earlier. And she did, from the moment she picked up the painting in the loft until the punks punched her and took it away. Smith took more notes and stopped her several times for specifics—exactly where she was when they'd attacked and if she had noticed anyone before or after. Alex couldn't remember, then she did, a guy in front of our Bowery building.

"He was hitting the buzzer or about to. I asked if he needed help. I don't remember what he said and didn't think much about it. I was excited about getting the painting to the auction house."

"Can you describe him?" Smith asked, instructing her to try to picture the moment.

Alex closed her eyes. "Yes, I can see him…late thirties, early forties, wearing sunglasses. He was kind of nondescript... Wait, he had a mustache, I can see him stroking it and... Wait, he was wearing gloves. Latex gloves!"

"So, he came prepared," Smith said.

"But no one knew about the painting," Alex said. "It had been hidden under another painting until *we* uncovered it."

"Doesn't mean no one knew about it." Smith folded his hands on his desk. "Okay, we can try to find this guy. Also, talk to the antique place and the specialist at the auction house, and maybe track down the punks who took the painting. If they were dealing drugs in front of the Bowery Mission, it wasn't the first time and probably not the last. So..." He scribbled something on a pad, then held it up. "My day rate, plus expenses."

I was taken aback. Not by the rate—it seemed fair—but by the speed of him accepting our case, though it was why I was here, and what I wanted, wasn't it? "What sort of expenses?" I asked.

"Travel. Food. Lab tests."

I asked if he had a lab and he said he had the use of one, then peered over his glasses, gave me a look, and asked if that was okay with me, his tone sarcastic.

A part of me wanted to say *no*. I remembered what it was like to work with Smith, though back then he had not given me a choice—he'd threatened to destroy me if I didn't cooperate. Now I *did* have a choice. We could walk away and pretend I'd never called him. I glanced at Alex for an answer to Smith's questions about his expenses, and she read my face, returned it with a look that said, *why not?*

I could think of a dozen reasons, but Smith spoke before I did, addressing Alex, not me.

"Perrone tells me you're an art historian and an expert in the field."

"On my way," she said.

"So, off the top of your head, who would you say has the most information about Van Gogh's paintings?"

"Off the top of my head, the Van Gogh Museum, in Amsterdam."

Smith turned back to his computer and started typing. I asked if he was looking up curators at the museum. "No," he said. "I'm checking flights to Amsterdam. Coach or business class?"

Alex, eyes wide, looked at me, then back at Smith. "Are you serious?"

"Are *you*?" he said.

She asked when we would go and Smith held up a hand, then enumerated on his fingers. "We need to go upstate, check out the Bowery Mission, follow up on the muggers, and try to track down your gloved stranger. Five, six days, say a week to be on the safe side. That puts us at a week from Tuesday. What do you say?" His fingers were poised on the keyboard, I could see he was anxious to do it. *But why?* Were we his only job? "What about your other jobs?"

"Just finished one and don't start another for three weeks. Should be enough time." I tried to read his face—not easy, his eyes hidden behind the tinted shades—and I guess he read mine. "I don't have to do this, Perrone. I'm doing you a favor."

Really? I didn't know favors to be Smith's style.

"I have school," Alex said, "and a job."

I added I was teaching too and making paintings for a show.

"So, neither of you are willing to take off a few days to pursue what you just said could turn out to be one of the greatest art discoveries of all time?" Smith steepled his fingers and sat back. "Hey, I can go by myself if you like."

No, I didn't like. If Smith discovered anything, I wanted to be there, and I knew Alex did too. I gave her a look.

"Well, these days I do almost everything for Estelle virtually," she said, speaking of the private art dealer she worked for part-time.

"And my school is almost all independent study, so even if we discovered nothing about the painting's whereabouts, I'd get to see places Van Gogh lived and worked, which would be great for my thesis." She looked back at Smith. "How long do you think we'd be in Amsterdam?"

"Depends," he said.

"On what?" I asked.

"On what we find. If there are leads we need to follow."

"What do you think?" Alex asked me, though I could see she was excited, that she wanted to go.

I took another moment to weigh my teaching, my coming exhibition against seeing all those Van Gogh paintings and whether I wanted to do this. We had already ruled out the police and we couldn't pursue it alone. I looked at Smith sitting back, arms locked behind his head, a cool pose, but could feel him waiting, wanting us to say yes, but I was having second thoughts. Then Alex squeezed my hand and gave me a nod and I thought, *What the hell, a trip to Amsterdam. How bad could that be?*

10

Smith wrapped a hand around one of his barbells, did a dozen fast reps, adrenaline pumping as he digested what Perrone and his girl-friend had just told him, just shown him.

Only a few years ago, Leonardo's *Salvator Mundi*, another "lost" masterpiece, had been found, and while that painting's veracity had been challenged, it still sold at auction for a whopping $450 million, something INTERPOL regretted they had not been part of, something every art collector regretted not being part of, whether they believed in its authenticity or not.

And now the lost Van Gogh. The stuff of fairy tales and fantasies? Not quite. Every art analyst at INTERPOL knew the story of the painting being at the artist's funeral, then disappearing, though it had never been proved.

Smith set the barbell down, his mind firing.

Back at his computer he checked the Art Loss Register, this time for Van Gogh. There were no reports of any paintings missing, but a small drawing from a private collection had been identified as a Van Gogh, and two paintings formerly considered forgeries had been newly authenticated. Also, a story about a Van Gogh painting of olive picking, which had supposedly been sold "under the table" by New York's reputable Metropolitan Museum of Art. The transaction having taken place in the seventies but just coming to light, the painting owner's heirs claiming the museum had sold the painting quietly because it knew the illicit circumstances surrounding the painting's original sale: stolen from a Jewish collector. Like most Nazi-looted art, there was a bill of sale, for 50,000 Reichsmarks that had gone into the Jewish collector's bank account, which was then blocked and confiscated.

Smith made a note of it, then scrolled through the pictures he'd taken off Alexis Verde's phone and placed them in a file. Using 7-Zip, he encrypted the email, created two passwords, then sent it to his supervisors.

They called him back in less than a minute.

11

We had decided to divide and conquer, Alex upstate to the Antique Barn and to see her friend Sharon, Smith and I to the Lower East Side Auction House. Having Smith beside me was like a time warp and flashback to Paris, though on the Bowery there was no smell of freshly baked baguettes or the muffled sound of church bells. Here, garbage trucks grinding, manhole hole covers rattling, and people, lots of them: old, young, Black, white, Latin, Asian, workers and walkers and runners, some heavily tatted and multiply pierced, straight, gay, and trans.

Our first stop, the Bowery Mission, was just past the modern glass-fronted New Museum, Manhattan's only institute of contemporary art, the dream-child of Marcia Tucker, former Whitney Museum curator who'd been fired for her radical thinking: putting women and people of color in museum shows! I'd met her at a party in Soho when I was fresh out of art school, a brash twenty-one-year-old ready to take on the art world. Marcia was in her sixties then, a legend, wildly charismatic, brilliant, funny, and flirtatious. I noticed her tattoos and, still drinking at the time, did not think twice about lifting my shirt to show her *Mona Lisa* on my back. A week later, she sent me a book, *Heavily Tattooed Men and Women*, for which she'd written the introduction, the first serious analysis of tattoos as art and the likely cause of the tattoo craze that swept the art world, and the rest of the world soon after.

She was gone now, but I couldn't help thinking about her as I geared up for my show, wishing she were here for advice.

Smith doubled back, cuffed me on the shoulder, and woke me from my reverie. The Bowery Mission was just a few yards away, its red double doors looking freshly painted, the brick front so clean it looked scrubbed. There were a few older men huddled outside and a CityMD van parked out front; otherwise it was quiet.

I was scanning the street for young men who fit the description of Alex's attackers when the mission's doors opened and a distinguished-looking man with dark skin and steely-gray hair introduced himself as the mission's pastor.

Smith asked if he knew of any drug dealers who might being using the mission's sidewalk as headquarters.

"Drugs? Here? On the Bowery? In front of the mission?" The pastor laughed. When I told him how Alex had been mugged and one of her assailants had said something about "the mission," his laugh died, but when I described the guys, he said, "They could be anyone."

"You have *no* idea?" Smith asked, and the pastor's face closed up.

I tried another approach, asking him about the mission and how long he'd been there, and he talked about Christian values and serving the hungry and homeless, and we shared a laugh about the building's history as a coffin factory, which seemed ironic. Then Smith got tough and flashed his PI license, and that was it.

"Could be anyone," the pastor said again, and disappeared behind those red double doors without another word.

"I guess patience and goodwill do not fit in with his Christian values," Smith said, but I guessed he was protecting his flock the way AA shielded its members, something I understood and valued.

We hung around awhile to see if any punks fitting Alex's description showed up, but the mission's sidewalk remained empty, like word had gone out, and it probably had. It struck me that finding two random guys on the Bowery was next to impossible, and I said so. Smith wanted a coffee, so we took a small detour over to Mott Street, the heart of Little Italy—cafés, restaurants, Dean Martin crooning through speakers onto the street—and picked up espressos at 12 Corners, which we nursed, walking along the Bowery to the approach ramps to the Manhattan Bridge. I pointed out that its arches and colonnade had been based on St. Peter's Square in Vatican City, and Smith called me *professor*, making it sound like a dirty word.

Across Canal Street, dodging several lanes of converging traffic, we headed into Chinatown, another world of markets, restaurants, vegetable and fruit stands, and more music, but here Chinese pop was blasting into the air.

With its slightly Moorish Gothic facade, the Eldridge Street Synagogue stood out like some majestic mistake. For a moment I was back in Florence in search of my great-grandfather's diary. I glanced over at Smith and wondered if he felt it too, but he'd already moved past the synagogue in search of the auction house.

It wasn't until we were up close and read the sign, LOWER EASTSIDE AUCTION HOUSE etched into a small brass plaque, that we found it. The plain, low building looked like a garage, one level with double steel doors. I pressed the intercom, gave my name, peered into a security camera, and heard the doors click open.

The reception area was in glaring contrast to the neighborhood, white walls and polished concrete floors, Eero Saarinen tulip chairs, the desk a thick slab of white marble, the young woman behind it in a gray tunic, a ring through her bloodred lip, the only color in the room. She asked for an ID. I gave her my driver's license. Smith used his old INTERPOL badge, which surprised me.

When she pointed out we were a half hour early and that Ms. Van Straten was busy, I decided to kill time at the synagogue next door.

Smith, already folded into a tulip chair checking emails and texts, declined to join me.

Outside, I had the weird feeling of being watched, stopped a moment, and scanned the street. But other than passersby walking fast, most with headphones or on their cells, there was no one.

12

Sharon's old Victorian house was lovely, but looking across the wooden table at her friend, Alex thought she could never live by herself in the middle of nowhere.

She had already been to the Antique Barn and talked to the old hippie, who remembered her and the painting. She'd gotten him talking, and he'd told her about a guy who'd been in wanting something just like it, and how he'd not only told him about selling the painting, but about Sharon and where she lived, and had sent him over to see her!

"About decorating," Sharon said. "He's recently bought a house and is decorating it, a nice guy. Though I haven't heard from him, and I thought I would."

So that was it, Sharon liked the guy. Alex wanted to shout, *Sharon, you're in the middle of nowhere and you let a stranger, a man, into your house?* Instead, she told her friend the truth, at least part of it—that the black eye was not "an accident" but that she'd been mugged, the painting stolen.

"Oh my God. How awful. Thank goodness you're okay."

Alex brought her back to the guy, the one supposedly decorating his house, and Sharon provided a description, the same description as Cal, both a match for the guy she'd seen in front of her building.

"Why steal an antique store painting?" Sharon asked, pinning Alex with a look. "What are you not telling me?"

Alex was itching to tell her friend the truth but held back. The fewer people who knew about the painting, the better.

"There must have been something about it," was all she said, bringing Sharon back to the guy who had sweet-talked Cal into getting information about her as nonchalantly as possible.

"He gave me that," Sharon said, indicating the greenish-colored vase on a sideboard in her dining room.

"Have you touched it?"

"Not really. Why?"

Alex asked to borrow it and Sharon, again suspicious, asked what was going on.

"Better if you don't know," Alex said, but promised to tell her later. Then she wrapped the vase and tucked it under her arm.

Outside, getting into her car, Alex said, "If you hear from that guy, let me know," again with as much innocence as possible.

"Should I be worried?" Sharon asked.

"Oh no," Alex said, and started the car. "Nothing to worry about at all."

There was little traffic on the Taconic, and Alex was making good time, distracted by the newly budding trees that bordered the highway and listening to music, a Spotify mix Luke had made for her. She was singing along when her cell phone rang.

"I thought we had a deal about when to call," she said.

"A *deal*? Is that how you see this?"

Alex sighed. Had this been a mistake? What she had been asking herself since it began. "We have an arrangement, that's all. How are you feeling, any better?"

"Not really," he said. "I just wanted to tell you that you can depend on me."

"I'll call you tomorrow," Alex said, "at our arranged time," and disconnected, focusing on the road through tears, which she swiped away, ridiculous to be crying, to let her emotions get the better of her.

You can depend on me.

She could only imagine what Luke would say to that, the look on his face, the judgment. Why she hadn't told him, though she wanted to. In fact…

She hit autodial, listened to the ringtone, then disconnected. No, she wasn't ready.

A moment later he called back. "Did you just call me?"

"Must have been a butt-dial," she said.

"But such a cute butt."

"*Please*," she said.

"Are you okay?" he asked. "You sound funny."

Luke could always read her. She should tell him, and she would, later.

"I'm fine. Driving, that's all."

He asked how it went and she told him about the vase.

"I'll tell you more when I see you."

"Love you," he said.

"Love you too," she said, feeling a shiver of guilt about not telling him. But she was protecting him, wasn't she?

The words brought her back a year, how she had believed she was protecting him then and how it had almost gotten them both killed.

13

Inside, the synagogue was a letdown. I'd expected grandeur but the entry room was dull, low tin ceiling, fluorescent lighting, industrial-sized heating ducts. A middle-aged woman in a patterned overblouse asked if I'd like a tour, and though I wanted to say no, it seemed inescapable.

The first stop, a side room with old posters in Hebrew and Yiddish, reminded me of Russian constructivist or degenerate art posters, which I might have looked at longer had the guide not urged me on, leading me and three women to the ark, the only beautiful part of the room. She pointed out a carved spittoon and detailed the early Jewish migration from Germany, Russia, and Poland, talking about persecution and pogroms, then directed us into a narrow, low-ceilinged stairwell, indicating original woodwork and wallpaper while I concentrated on not hitting my head.

But the upper floor was another world. Large and open, with a high vaulted ceiling, everything bathed in natural light along with beautiful tulip-shaped lamps and an enormous chandelier. I looked over the rows of elaborately carved pews, and it took me back to Bayonne's St. Mary's, wedged between my parents, smelling my mother's powdery perfume and the beer on my father's breath. I managed to shake off the memory to take in one of many marble pillars, which on closer inspection was not marble at all.

"All faux?" I asked.

The guide nodded. Tucking her hair behind an ear and smiling, she explained how the immigrants wanted to build the most lavish synagogue they could, but marble was too expensive and so they had hired craftsmen to fake it. I was making a mental note to try something faux in my own paintings when she opened the ark.

"The original velvet," she said. "With room for twenty-four torahs."

I studied more faux marble and a faux painted curtain, all trompe l'oeil, French for *trick of the eye*, a way to convince the viewer that what they were seeing was real when it was not. The idea of it felt oddly ironic, as if I were missing something.

The guide pointed out the rose window and I glanced up; it was modern and unlike anything else in the synagogue.

"Kiki Smith," she said, a contemporary artist I knew. She explained there had been no pictures of the original window and so an artist had been employed to do something new. I took in the huge blue circle and stars, and thought of something Van Gogh had said that I'd just read.

When I have a terrible need of—shall I say the word—religion, then I go outside to paint the stars.

I was taking a picture of the rose window, still thinking of Vincent's words when I felt it again, more than being watched, almost touched, felt a shiver, and turned, surveying the synagogue, which was quiet and practically empty.

14

You watch him head up the synagogue stairs, taking in his lanky stride, the skinny black jeans and Chelsea boots, the well-worn leather jacket, like the hippest guy ever, like the world owes him a living.

Inside, it's hot, radiators hissing, sweating in your jacket but you can't take it off, nor the cap pulled down to your shades, keeping your distance, watching, listening, the guide going on about original floors and woodwork "twenty years to renovate," and smiling at him. *Is she flirting?* Does she think he would give her a second look? You move closer, just behind him, could almost put your hands on him, fingers twitching in your pockets.

"All faux?" he asks the guide, and you follow his gaze and see the wood has been painted to look like marble, and he turns, and you turn but not fast enough, and for a moment you are face-to-face, his eyes big and dark and *piercing.* But you will not be describing his eyes, just what he's seen, what he is doing.

You step back, hear the guide say, "Note the etched doorknobs," and for a crazy moment you consider prying one loose and taking it with you. Then you run your hand along the smooth wood of the pews, head down but watching him, wondering: *Has he come in here for a reason? Is there something here you should know about, report back?*

He looks up at the stained-glass window, blue and dappled with stars, and takes a cell phone picture and you pretend to do the same, but you're taking a picture of him.

When he heads down the tight, angled stairs, you slip in behind him thinking how easy it would be to give him a push. But you are only here to watch. Then you follow him out into the sunlight, stopping to make a note when he goes next door, as you imagined he would. This time you do not follow, knowing you will hear the details later.

15

I met Smith back at the auction house, where we followed the young woman with the bloodred lips down a wide white corridor, open cubicles on either side, people hunched over computers, and at the end, a large theater-like room with an empty stage.

"The auctions are completely virtual," she said, and was about to say more, then looked past us and stopped.

A woman in a black sleeveless tunic stood in the hallway.

"Anika Van Straten," she said. "How do you do?" She extended an arm for a firm handshake, a silver cuff circling one of her biceps and a dozen bangle bracelets clinking. She cut a glance at the receptionist. "That will be all," she said, and the girl turned away so fast she almost fell.

The antithesis of the blond auction-house girls uptown, Van Straten was dark—dark eyes, dark brows, dark hair pulled back from her face, striking and handsome. Somewhere in her forties I guessed, though she felt older, her eyes world weary.

"Yes, we are almost totally virtual," she said, picking up the conversation, her English clipped, an accent I couldn't identify. "This room could be a bidding room if we had in-person auctions, but we do not. Nowadays, it is just for show."

"The art biz, showbiz, same thing," Smith said.

"I could not disagree more," Van Straten said, lancing him with a look. "Art is very serious business, and I cannot imagine it is thought of as 'showbiz' in INTERPOL's art theft division."

Smith ignored her comment and asked how long she'd been working been here.

"Less than a year," she said, turned, and we followed her down the hall. "It is temporary. I was hired to help the auction house get to the next level."

"Van Straten," Smith said. "Is that German?"

"No. Dutch. Why?"

"No reason," he said, making it sound like he had a dozen reasons.

Van Straten's office was stark—white walls, a Lucite desk, on it a laptop, a cell phone, a large glass ashtray, and nothing else. Behind it, a gray-mesh swivel chair, which she took, gesturing at two matching chairs for us, ones that did not swivel. She folded her hands, strong and crisscrossed with veins, in front of her and listened while Smith told her about the mugging, the reason Alex had missed her appointment, the reason we were there.

"I see," she said. "I was surprised when Ms. Verde did not show up, annoyed she had wasted my time. Now, I understand. Most upsetting." Though her expression revealed no upset, impossible to read.

Smith asked if she had logged the appointment into her calendar, and she said she didn't use one.

"I jot my appointments down on Post-its." She indicated a few on her desk. "Then I dispose of them. It is simpler."

And leaves no record, I thought. But if she didn't like paper, why not use a virtual calendar?

"Did anyone else know Ms. Verde was coming to see you?" Smith asked.

"Other than Jennifer, who put us in touch, no one. My assistant has been on vacation so I spoke to Ms. Verde myself. But it was very brief. She said she had a painting to show me. Do you know what it was?"

"She didn't tell you?"

"Only that it was something in my field, so I presumed a post-impressionist painting, Van Gogh or"—she cleared her throat—"Gauguin or Lautrec." Her hands remained folded on the desk, but looking through her Lucite desk, I noted one of her feet was jiggling.

"So, other than you, no one knew Ms. Verde was coming in?" Smith leaned forward, plucked a Post-it off her desk, then stuck it back.

"I already answered that. Why?"

"Because she was attacked, of course, and I'm looking into it."

"INTERPOL is looking into it?"

"No," he said. "I'm just a friend."

"And you think that her attack had something to do with her appointment *here*?"

"We're just checking all of Ms. Verde's appointments on the day of her attack."

"I see." She looked over at me. "And you, how are you connected to this?"

"I'm a friend of Ms. Verde's too."

She studied me a few seconds, then slipped on a pair of reading glasses, turned away, and started typing. "I see you are an artist with an upcoming exhibition at the Mattia Beuhler Gallery, of all places."

"What do you mean by that?"

"It is an impressive gallery, that is all." Her eyes shifted between me and her computer screen. "Do I know your work?"

"Not if you have to ask," I said, and half laughed.

"I can see you mix abstraction and figuration and some German expressionism, no?"

I told her Beckmann and Kirchner had been an influence, and she peered at me over her glasses. "So, you are a fan of Entartete Kunst?"

"Degenerate art."

"Ah, you know it."

"I teach art history, so yes, I know it, the term, the exhibition in…" I tried to come up with the date.

"1937," she said. "About 650 objects, paintings, sculptures, prints, all confiscated from German museums by the Nazis, over 2,100 plundered works of art on display with derisive text and slogans scrawled on the walls around them—*an insult to German womanhood, the Jewish longing for the wilderness, the Negro becomes the racial ideal of a degenerate art!*" She stopped and took a breath. "You are lucky to be making your art now, Mr. Perrone. You might have been fired from your teaching position, forbidden to exhibit or to sell your artwork, and like the degenerate artists, forbidden to produce any art at all."

I said I knew I was lucky, and she went on about the exhibition.

"It was a sensation you know. The German people lined up, over two million people in the first six weeks. Unlike the other, concurrent exhibition, *Große Deutsche Kunstausstellung.*"

"Great German Art," I said.

She gave me an approving nod, and when Smith started to say something, she talked over him.

"Yes, the state-sanctioned show, a tedious exhibition of portraits and landscapes, images from German mythology that few bothered to see. Ironic, is it not, that the Nazis expected people to detest the *degenerate* work, and some did—it is reported that a few even spat at the artwork—but they came to see it in *droves*. In the end, the Nazis helped make the art they loathed become famous." She slid a pack of Dunhill cigarettes out of her bag, dark red and lined with gold. "Do you mind?" She flipped the pack open and offered them up. Smith took one and she produced a lighter, antique-looking, brass or gold.

Smith leaned forward for the light. "Der Römer?" he said, reading the engraved writing off the lighter.

"It was a…gift," she said, snapped it closed, and dropped it back into her bag.

"What happened to the work in the degenerate art show?" I asked.

"Much of it was destroyed. In 1939, the Nazis burned nearly five thousand artworks in the courtyard of the Berlin Fire Department. In 1942, more artworks were destroyed in a bonfire on the grounds of the Jeu de Paume in Paris."

"You're quite the expert," Smith said. "I thought your area of expertise was post-impressionism."

"Much of the influence for degenerate art, for German expressionism, originates with Van Gogh, who *is* my area of expertise."

Smith asked again who at the auction house might have known Alex was coming in.

"Only me," she said.

"Only you," he repeated, then said he enjoyed the Dunhill, thanked her, stood up, and that was it.

Outside, we had to shout to be heard over a construction crew breaking up the sidewalk.

I brought up Van Straten's first guess that Alex was bringing in a Van Gogh, and Smith agreed but didn't think it was damning.

"There are only five in the group, so one out of five isn't a bad guess."

"She brought him up again when she mentioned degenerate art," I said.

"*Mentioned?* It was a fucking master class."

"But interesting," I said. "Also interesting that she knew which department you were in at INTERPOL and that I had a teaching job. She did some snooping."

"Everyone does," Smith said and took a moment to do some of his own. "Der Römer. Her lighter. Made in Frankfurt, Germany, in the 1940s. Very rare, according to Google." He looked up from his phone. "And I can tell you one thing… She's not Dutch."

"And you know this how?"

"Twenty years at an international organization like INTERPOL, you get to know accents, Perrone. I'll figure it out if I meet her again. In the meantime, I'm going to dig deeper, see what I can find on her." He checked his phone again and said he had to go. When I asked where, he said, "You're not my only client."

"I thought we were," I said, but he'd already turned away and the jackhammers had started up again.

16

Copies of their IDs duplicated and sent on, Anika Van Straten sagged back into her chair, tugged off her boots, and massaged her feet. How many more years could she do this, the thought accompanied by a barrage of images—salt mines, storage units, checkpoints, border controls, Homeland Security, a picture of her grandfather brought to his knees. She sat up straighter. *As many years as it takes.*

The images were replaced by the men—the INTERPOL agent Smith and the artist Luke Perrone with his show at the Beuhler Gallery—and how they figured into this, something she did not yet know. And the girl, Alexis Verde, and the mugging.

She lit a cigarette, ran her thumb over the lighter, the etched name Der Römer. Not a gift, as she had said, but something she'd taken, a talisman, a reminder, though she was neither sentimental nor superstitious.

She played with the bangles on her arm, annoyed with herself for talking too much, nearly letting on that she had suspected, *knew*, what Alexis Verde was bringing in and, worse, allowing herself to be drawn into that conversation on degenerate art, showing off, foolish and not worthy of her, discretion and restraint always paramount.

The burner vibrated on her desk, and she read the text: pix received details pending.

Pending for too long, she thought. She erased the text, then called Dispatcher. She needed him to be ready, *just in case.*

17

Jennifer decanted the red cabernet into the glass pitcher and set it on the table, everything in the Upper East Side townhouse perfect, though she was picturing another apartment, one in Amsterdam, the paintings that came and went, everything temporary, and she worried that she was temporary too, though she was making sure she was not, doing what he asked.

She took a moment to arrange the silverware on the linen tablecloth just so. He had taught her to like beautiful things.

She thought of Alex and her discovery, *a painting in our area*, their conversation replaying in her mind, asking what it was, pressing, probing, teasing. *An old master? No, you said in our area. A Cézanne watercolor, like the ones we saw at MOMA? Oh, Alex. You can tell me.*

Again, Alex had refused, though Jennifer could feel her weakening, wanting to tell.

Lautrec? Gauguin? Something from Tahiti or Martinique? Am I warm? You can tell me that much, Alex. Who am I going to tell? It's just between us.

Though ultimately Alex did not tell her, she'd said enough: not Cézanne, not Lautrec, not Gauguin. So, who was left? Seurat or Van Gogh. And she knew from conversations that Alex was not a fan of Seurat.

At that point, Jennifer knew what to do. First, she connected Alex to the auction house, then she told *him*. Making herself indispensable, invaluable.

And just now, a second call from Alex asking about the previous call. *Did I tell you what I was going to show the auction house?* and Jennifer, acting distracted, as if she had forgotten all about the first call, as if it were unimportant, while Alex went through it again, and she had reported every word of it to him.

Keep doing what you are doing, he'd said, and she promised she would.

Silverware in place, table set, she took in the wall of framed black-and-white prints, Max Beckmann, Ernst Barlach, Otto Dix. *All degenerates.* All valuable. When she left here, she would take them with her.

At the sound of the key turning in the lock, she took a glass of wine and hurried to the door.

"Dearest," she said.

Anika Van Straten leaned in for a kiss. "I can taste the Burgundy on your lips."

Jennifer offered her the glass of wine. "Here, have a sip, so we can taste the same."

Anika did, and they kissed again, passionately this time.

"So," Jennifer said. "How was your day at the auction house? Tell me *all* about it."

18

Alex was pacing, excited from her trip upstate but defensive from my question.

"I did *not* tell Van Straten *what* I was bringing in. I simply said an artwork, a painting."

"Okay," I said. "But I think she knows."

"Then someone else told her."

I did not ask who but waited for Alex to come up with a name, and she did.

"Jennifer. She's only other person who knew."

"You told her what the painting was?"

"No. Of course not. I just said it was something important. I'm sure I did *not* say the artist's name."

I pushed and asked what she had said "exactly."

"Stop interrogating me!"

I stood back, hands up in peace. "'There is nothing more artistic than to love others.' That's Van Gogh speaking."

Alex sighed and said I was becoming obsessed "and annoying."

I apologized. Told her it was okay. But was it? Had a chain of events already begun? Were there dozens of people who knew about the painting, all of them willing to mug someone to get it? Or worse?

"Maybe I *did* say too much to Jennifer," Alex said. "I'm going to call her and feel it out."

I asked her not to, but she disappeared into the bedroom to make the call.

"Jennifer doesn't know. She hardly remembered the call," she said when she came back, thinking about her friend from the Institute. How she had noticed Jennifer from afar for months, but it was only a few weeks ago they'd started talking. They'd bonded almost at once, Jennifer interested in just about everything Alex had to say.

"Good," I said, and changed the subject back to her successful trip upstate, how she'd gotten a description of the man from Sharon, the same as the one the old hippie at the antique store had supplied, and very much like her own of the guy in front of our building. Plus, the vase she'd gotten from Sharon, which Smith had already sent to the lab for fingerprints.

I kissed her cheek and told her she'd done well.

"Don't be patronizing."

"I'm not," I said, but maybe I was. I asked if the antique store guy had said where he got the painting.

"He said he bought the contents of several houses at once but hadn't met and didn't know any of the original owners, that it was all second- or third-hand—relatives, children, grandchildren clearing out houses through different real estate agents. He started to get a little suspicious why I was asking. I said because I liked the painting I'd bought so much, I wanted another, and he said he'd keep an eye out and that was it."

One more time I said it was obvious that whoever sold the painting didn't know what it was, *if* the painting turned out to be real. Alex believed it was and that her fading black eye was proof, at least to her. "And your friend Smith took the case," she said. "So he must believe it too."

Did he? I wasn't sure. "Hardly my friend."

Alex shrugged. "The bigger question is how did a Van Gogh portrait that disappeared over a hundred years ago make its way to upstate New York?"

19

August 1944
Paris

When it was dry, the artist wrapped the painting in clean rags, slid it into a specially constructed wine crate with a false bottom, added a few bottles of cheap Bordeaux and two books, Céline's Mort à Crédit *and Malraux's* La Condition Humaine, *his choices and ironic, the first author an anti-Semite, the second an outspoken resistance fighter. Then he found four other half-empty wine bottles, filled them to the top with water, jammed corks in and put them in a sack.*

Outside, the air was hot and moist, the Tuileries gardens overgrown, lampposts unlit as he made his way toward the Seine. Distant gunfire and blasts of pineapple grenades mixed with intermittent bolts of lightning that set his skin shivering and lit up the darkness for split seconds, trees, statues, groups of German soldiers suddenly there, then not. Somewhere nearby, members of the United Resistance were gathering, arming themselves for battle when the city was liberated. Until then, he moved fast. Passed l'Orangerie, the building dark though he could picture Monet's monumental murals of Waterlilies *inside, the paintings too large for the Nazis to steal but they would have no trouble destroying them. It was well known Hitler had ordered Paris blown to bits rather than surrender it, dynamite planted under Notre-Dame, Les Invalides, and every one of the city's cherished monuments. The artist touched the cross at his neck and prayed the Allied troops would be here in time to prevent it, though right now his concern was to save the one painting under his arm.*

Across the Pont des Arts in the dark, careful where he stepped, the metal bridge pitted from aerial bombardment. Waiting on the other side, a group of German soldiers, pistols tucked into belts, submachine guns and sniper rifles resting against the bridge railing. He greeted them with a nod and handed over the sack of wine. Clearly exhausted and resigned to their fate, they did not thank him or search him, or ask for ID, or what was in the crate under his arm. He moved quickly past them, cutting between buildings, darkened homes, and old Parisian hotels.

At the wide rue Jacob, a barricade, more German soldiers, a commanding officer on a walkie-talkie, pacing nervously. The artist backtracked through side streets and alleyways until he spotted the church of Saint-Sulpice, where he cut across a small park to rue de Furstemberg. Two German soldiers were stationed in front of the building. Crouching, he made his way to the back, and there, with one hand gripping the small wooden crate, he used the other to hoist himself up and over the low stone wall.

The once carefully manicured garden had grown wild and ragged, the pebbled pathways strewn with bottles and cigarette butts. He knew the place well, the former home and studio of the great French painter Eugène Delacroix, now a museum. He'd had a print of the artist's Liberty Leading the People *tacked to his studio wall for years. He put the painting's image of a woman carrying the French flag in his mind and mounted the stairs to the back door, heart beating like a trapped bird.*

The door was unlocked. Inside, a wall-size flag with a black swastika drooped from the ceiling in the same way the Germans had draped a Nazi flag on top of the Eiffel Tower and over the Hotel de Ville, images he would never forget. Beside the flag were a map of Paris dotted with strategic multicolored pins and a long table strewn with papers and telegrams that made it clear the place been used as a Third Reich headquarters, everything looking as if it had been abandoned in a hurry. He took in the naked hooks on the walls, more than half the paintings gone, and not surprising; he had seen several Delacroix paintings stored at the Jeu de Paume.

The sound of footsteps and he turned, tense, but ready.

The woman was small and strong-looking, blouse buttoned to the neck, shoulders padded, eyes peering out from under her beret, face camouflaged with ashes. "Nicole Minet," she whispered, code name of a well-known resistance fighter, and the artist answered with the resistance fighter's given name, "Simone Segouin," as planned.

"Vive la Résistance!" she said and slipped the crate from his hands. She beckoned him to follow, but at the top of the landing they heard footsteps below, and she told him to wait and took the stairs alone.

The artist stood there shivering though the night was hot. They had not been expecting anyone else, and when he heard the sounds of a struggle and a strangled squeal, he took the stairs two at a time. At the bottom, the resistance fighter was gasping for breath, shirtsleeves stained with blood, a knife in her hand. Beneath her, a German soldier, blood covering his uniform black in the moonlight.

No words exchanged, she handed the artist the knife and slipped away.

He knew the rules. If one resistance fighter did the killing, another disposed of the weapon.

Stepping over the body, he buried the knife in the dirt, then tugged off the dead soldier's boots. The soles of his own were practically worn through, and he tossed them behind a bush and slipped on the new ones, a decent fit and still warm.

Over the stone wall, he made his way back along side streets and alleyways. He had no idea where the picture was headed, but he had done his job, an important painting camouflaged and now on its way to safety.

20

The Present
Bowery, New York City

It was just too early in the morning to see Smith on my couch, legs spread, mansplaining to me and Alex how he'd gotten information on Anika Van Straten.

"I got the easy stuff—Motor Vehicles, Social Security, work history. With the right tools, I'll dig deeper."

"And you have those tools?" I asked. He looked way too comfortable in my loft, on my couch, sipping coffee Alex had made, so out of context that it made me itch with discomfort. I had to ask myself what he was doing back in my life, though I knew the answer: I'd invited him.

He dipped a hand into the pocket of his cargo pants, came up with one of the little Rhodia pads he always had on him, flipped a page, and read, "Van Straten worked for the leading auction house in the Netherlands, for almost a decade, something called AAG."

"I've heard of it," Alex said.

"Van Straten appears to have kept her nose clean," he said.

"Appears to?" I asked.

"I'm quoting from the director of AAG, a guy named De Vries. *He* used those words, not me. That okay with you, Perrone?" He peered over his glasses, one of the rare times I got to see his eyes, dark and probing, like they were looking through me. "De Vries said she was a tireless worker—when she was there. Apparently, she took too many days off, sick days, vacation days, other days without giving a reason. He said if she hadn't been so good at her job, he would have fired her. Then out of nowhere, she quit."

"And before that?" Alex asked.

"I found what might have been a family business at one time, Van Straten Fine Arts, in Berlin, but it appears to have closed sometime during or after the war. I couldn't find any other jobs for her. Nothing before AAG, and that's a long span."

"How old is she?" Alex asked.

"Good question," Smith said. "I couldn't find a birthday or birthplace."

"Odd," Alex said.

"Wiped," Smith said. "Erased. Had to be. I used the standard engines: Intelius, CheckPeople, TruthFinder. Nada, but no criminal record either. Then some INTERPOL programs, again nada."

"A woman without a past," Alex said.

"Everyone has a past," Smith said.

"The question is why is she trying to hide it?" I said.

"You can run, but you can't hide, not anymore. It's all out there somewhere," Smith said. "I'm starting a dossier."

Smith's forte, the dossier. I knew he had one on me, my great-grandfather, my parents, even a few of my ex-girlfriends. I wondered if he had one on Alex, but of course he did.

Alex suggested she talk to Van Straten to feel her out. "A friendly chat between two art professionals. I'll apologize in person for not showing up."

"Don't stir the soup," Smith said. "Let me do some more digging first. That's what you're paying me for."

Were we? No money had yet been exchanged, and he hadn't asked so I hadn't offered.

"Any news on the vase, on the fingerprints?" Alex asked.

"The lab should be getting back to me soon."

I asked which lab, and Smith asked why it mattered. It didn't. But I was curious to know his connections. Were they all old INTERPOL contacts?

Smith ignored my question. "If we get readable prints, I'll put them through IAFIS to start."

"The FBI's print system?"

"You become an agent since we last met, Perrone, or just showing off for your girlfriend?"

Maybe I was showing off a little. "I was just curious if you had FBI connections," I said.

"Yeah, but I don't need them. The Bureau's integrated automated fingerprint ID system is accessible if you have permission or a license or the right digital program."

"Which you have?"

"I've retained some of my INTERPOL databases, connections too. That okay with you, Perrone?"

"Okay with me if it's okay with the FBI and INTERPOL."

Smith lifted his shades again to give me an intimidating stare. I gave him one back. We'd fallen into our old sparring ways. Everything he said annoyed me, and I guessed he felt the same way about me.

He exchanged the pad for his cell phone, typed something, then put it away.

"Important note?" I asked.

"Shopping list," he said. "I need milk."

"Yeah, you don't want to run out of milk when you take your coffee black."

That got me another stare from Smith, and one from Alex too. I changed the subject, asked about Amsterdam and what his plans were once we got there.

"I have some appointments, people whose names I can't disclose but they wouldn't mean anything to you. Let's just say they'll know what's currently for sale on all markets, including the black market. If your painting is out there or has been sold or bartered in the past few weeks, these people will know. So far it hasn't been, I know that much, and I'll know more when I meet with them in Amsterdam."

I was impressed and surprised. I hadn't thought he'd been doing much of anything. I asked what we should be doing, and he asked Alex if she'd be meeting with curators at the Van Gogh Museum.

"I'm working on it," she said, then asked about the photos she'd taken of the painting, the ones he'd copied to his phone, and what he was doing with them.

"Right now, they're just for reference. In the future, we'll see. I used them the other day," he said, and explained he'd gone up to the Met to see the Van Gogh self-portrait they had to compare it to the photos. "Tell you the truth, it didn't look much like the one you found."

"That's because it's *earlier*," Alex said.

"Only a year."

His comment set Alex into a scholarly riff about the variety in Van Gogh's paintings, how quickly he made them, and how fast his style evolved.

"I'm just sayin'," he said.

"What? That ours is a fake?"

"I didn't say that, and I have no idea. I just wanted to see the Met's painting for comparison's sake. When was the last time *you* saw it?"

21

Alex had taken Smith's challenge.

I glanced up at the sprawling Beaux Arts building I'd seen so many times, banners flapping from the roof announcing the Metropolitan Museum of Art's current exhibitions, *The Medici: Portraits and Politics, Surrealism Beyond Borders, Cubism and the Trompe L'oeil Tradition*, the first sparking a memory of last year's trip to Florence and all the unexpected tragedy, the trompe l'oeil show bringing me back only a day, to the faux marble pillars at the Eldridge Street Synagogue, both places where I'd felt as if I was being watched, something I should have paid attention to in Florence, but I shook it off again.

"Two million square feet of space able to hold eight full-sized soccer fields or forty White Houses, my high school art teacher told us on our class trip," I said, referring to my first visit to museum twenty-two years ago.

"Really?" Alex said as we headed up the wide stone staircase, then asked me why I'd been so aggressive with Smith. "Is it just the way men communicate? You're like two little boys."

I admitted we had a history of communicating that was more like fighting, a habit that was hard to break. "I don't like the way he dangles bits of information, like he was in touch with people he can't name."

"He said he'd tell us when he knew more," Alex said, which sounded like she was defending him, which annoyed me.

"You don't know him."

"You're the one who suggested him, not me."

She had a point.

Inside, Alex would not let me wander into the Egyptian wing or the Renaissance paintings, leading the way through dimly lit hallways of prints through the sculpture gallery with Rodin's famous *The Thinker*, cutting through school groups and families and tourists. I broke away long enough to look at Edouard Manet's *Lady with a Parakeet*, everything about the painting prim and proper and Victorian, except for a suggestive half-peeled orange at the lady's feet. Alex came back to get me, and I pointed out how the museum had cleverly hung Courbet's version of *Woman with a Parrot* in a sight line from Manet's, both paintings of the same subject but entirely different, Courbet's woman naked and nearly orgasmic as a parrot nips her finger.

"If you've had enough of the male gaze…" Alex said, looped her arm through mine, and we moved through rooms of impressionist paintings without stopping until we reached our destination. The room was crowded but I saw why: an entire wall of Van Gogh. I took a minute to check out a Gauguin self-portrait, then Van Gogh's famous *Sunflowers*, spiky petals and seeds like teeth in a gaping mouth, at once so beautiful and ferocious it was hard to look away, but Alex would not let me linger, leading me toward the plexiglass box in the center of the room.

Our first view was of the painting's *wrong* side, a dark older work of a woman peeling potatoes, but we quickly moved to the other side where Van Gogh had painted his *Self-Portrait with a Straw Hat*, the reason we'd come.

I hadn't seen it in years, and now, with my newfound Van Gogh obsession, I looked at it as if for the first time. A face created from dozens of small brushstrokes, dots and dashes, the gold highlights in

Vincent's blue-green eyes, the yellow brushwork that skittered along his nose and cheeks and neck. "He's set everything in motion," I said, "like the Italian futurist painters."

Alex pointed out the optical mixing he'd borrowed from the impressionists, "two colors side by side to create a third," and the influence of Seurat's pointillism and the fauves' use of pure color to create form, "all that modern art history in one painting."

There was an underlying sadness in the face and the way his eyes met the viewer's that struck me and made me hear his words, *I want to touch people with my art. I want them to say—he feels deeply, he feels tenderly*.

"It's all here," Alex said. "The color, the touch, the same as in our painting. Smith is dead wrong! True, it's sketchier, but Van Gogh painted this one *two* years earlier, not *one*, and he was still experimenting. Our painting has the same elements but it's more mature."

I agreed, pointing out Smith was an art *analyst* and not an art historian. "Why didn't he ask us to come up here with him so we could see the painting together?"

Alex told me to stop creating conspiracies and to stop arguing with him if we were going to work together, but I was wondering about those FBI and INTERPOL connections, and why he hadn't billed us.

"I guess he'll bill us at the end."

At the end of what, finding the painting, or calling it quits?

I was asking myself those questions when I felt it, what I'd been feeling at the synagogue, that I was being watched. I scanned the room crowded with tourists, but it was impossible to pick out one person who was studying me rather than the painting.

22

So much easier watching the two of them together, Cool Guy and Prom Queen, the code names you've given them. You take a photo from across the room, zoom in on the two of them beside the double-sided portrait. Click. Text. Send. Phone slipped into your pocket, you amble closer, but not too close. You're in disguise—an old trench coat you should have thrown away long ago, collar up, knit cap down to your eyebrows—but still you can't take a chance of being seen. Of course, they're not looking at you, only at the painting.

You look at a Gauguin self-portrait, Van Gogh's famous frenemy painting himself against a bright-red background, face all angles and arrogance, self-assured and cocky, but you almost prefer it to Vincent's humility. You look back in time to see Cool Guy scanning the room. Does he feel your presence, your eyes on his back?

You merge into a tour group and out of the room. You've seen enough. Down a hallway into a room of American modernist painters from the early nineteen-hundreds where you take a photo of Marsden Hartley's 1914 *Portrait of a German Officer*, all symbols and codes to hide the artist's homosexual longings. You text the picture to him as a joke, because you know he sold the artwork to one of his collectors a couple of years ago, and that the painting here, in New York's prestigious Metropolitan Museum of Art, is a fake, that he had it copied and exchanged for the original with the help of a greedy security guard who was paid handsomely but did not live long enough to spend it.

23

The text from Smith had come in just as we were leaving the Met:
Fingerprints back.

And more than that, he had matched the prints to a PI in Queens
and tracked him through his phone. Meet me, he'd texted, and we did.

The Court Square Diner in Long Island City was only half-full,
but noisy, customers crammed into booths, waitresses shouting
orders, Lil Nas X on the jukebox.

Smith pointed him out, and we went into action. Alex slipped
into the booth and plunked the McCoy vase onto the table. The guy
froze, a forkful of eggs at his mouth.

From a booth across the aisle, Smith and I observed, just able to
hear above the din.

"You thought I was dead?" Alex said.

"What? No. I hoped—prayed—you were okay."

Alex inched the vase forward and read from her cell phone. "Two
clear prints belonging to James Tully, Private Investigator, 2123
Twenty-Fourth Avenue, Long Island City. That would be you. Plus,
you fit everyone's description—from the owner of the Antique Barn
to Sharon MacIntosh, Interior Design, and *me*." She'd rehearsed the
script and she knew it well. The rest she could improvise. She was a
good actress; I knew that.

"No mustache today?" she asked. "In a hurry?"

Smith leaned into the aisle, tapped my arm, and mouthed *Come
on*, but I stopped him, whispered, "She's got it."

"You hired those kids to mug me. That's not just robbery but aggravated assault," Alex said. "So, where's the painting?"

"I delivered it to the client. What else?" Tully eyed her a moment. "You're not police, so who are you working for?"

Alex ignored the question. "I'm guessing you didn't mean for me to get hurt so I'm giving you a chance to explain. Who's the client? Who hired you to get the painting?"

Tully mumbled something but it was lost under the jukebox and clatter.

"I'm going in," Smith said, already up, waving his INTERPOL ID, me behind him.

And that was it. Tully bolted, knocking me back into the waitress, plates smashing, coffee splashing, people shouting.

Tully made it out the door, Smith on his tail.

"I was getting him to talk," Alex said, the two of us in pursuit. "I didn't need Smith to screw it up!"

Outside, the wind had picked up and it was starting to rain. Smith had already caught Tully at the edge of the diner's parking lot and slammed him against a car, Alex and I sprinting toward them.

"Got him," Smith said, breathing hard, nodding at me, and I looped an arm through Tully's, Alex beside us, stewing.

"Where are you taking me?" Tully whined.

"To your office," Smith said.

"How do you…"

"INTERPOL knows all, my friend."

Tully's office was a basement room with half windows, a wooden desk and chair, a Naugahyde couch, and comic books everywhere.

I asked if his clients were Superman and Batman, while Smith pushed him down on the couch and stood over him like the Incredible Hulk, comic-book ready.

"Who the fuck are you guys?" Tully said.

"INTERPOL," Smith said. "Now tell us about the punks you hired to beat her up."

"I asked them to get her bag, *that's all*. Two guys from the street."

"And your client?"

"We never met. It all came through the web."

"Dark web," Smith said, and Tully nodded. "You ever talk to them?" Smith sat down next to him, leaned in, twice Tully's size.

"Why should I tell you?"

"It's me, here, now, or INTERPOL HQ. Or the feds. You choose."

"Twice. I spoke to them twice. About the setup and first payment. Then the drop."

"You knew it was a painting," Smith said. "Did you look at it?"

"No. Why would I do that? I left it at the prearranged spot. That was it."

"I want the client's contact info, the number, any email."

"It was a burner, man."

"You're going to call again," Smith said. "Tell them there's trouble, that you need to speak. INTERPOL will trace it."

"They'll *kill* me."

"INTERPOL will take care of you."

Seemed to me Smith was playing fast and loose with his threats and his old job.

There was a long pause, quiet, except for rain on those high windows, then Tully said, "They claimed they never got the painting."

"You held it back?" Smith asked.

"*No!* No fucking way. I delivered it to the prearranged drop. Either the client got it and is lying to keep the rest of my money, or someone else got there before them and took it. When you guys came into the diner, I thought you were them. They're accusing me of holding out on them, threatening to kill me. I been laying low, watching my back."

"If they want to find you, they will," Smith said. "Do what I say, contact them. We'll have it traced and get the jump on them before they get to you. INTERPOL will protect you," Smith said again, though I couldn't see how.

24

"I dislike meeting in public," Anika Van Straten said, though no one seemed to notice them, the Midtown Manhattan bar crowded at cocktail hour. She caught small fractions of her reflection in the bar's mirror, most of it collaged with bills—ones, fives, tens—at least fifty of them pasted to the mirror and surrounding wall, crinkled and curling, along with fading photographs of boxers, Tyson and Ali. Above it, three small TV sets all playing ball games, and a printed paper sign that read, LET'S NOT DISCUSS POLITICS HERE.

"Admit it, you love this place," the man beside her said and she took him in: good looks starting to fray, hair thinning, jawline going soft, belly pressed against the bar rail. He pivoted on his barstool, his words just audible above a doo-wop song. "I come here every time I'm in New York."

He was on his third beer. Unprofessional, she thought. She had barely touched her glass of white wine.

"You know, I met Jimmy Glenn, the owner, one night must have been five, six years ago. A legend. Gone now, but this place lives on; gives you hope, doesn't it?"

No, it didn't, but she let him go on, the organization's middleman, a guy she'd met six years ago on another assignment.

A picture tore across her brain, a crate of art in flames, the dealer who'd been selling on the black market destroying the evidence rather than get caught, though he had paid with his life, and Van Straten had almost paid with hers.

Another song played and the man sang along, "'Sittin' on the dock of the bay,'" affecting a bad Southern accent and slapping his palms on the bar shellacked with newspaper clippings and photos of more fighters. He stopped, clinked his beer bottle against her wineglass, and said, "Payday," referring to the assignment, which had gotten the go-ahead.

Finally, she thought.

"The *article*, as you know, has been selected, big enough to attract Trader."

She nodded, knew that his organization and several others had been trying to catch Trader for years, none of them successful.

"He is looking for a new connection," he said. "Here in the States."

"Other bait has been dangled in the past and he did not bite."

"He is biting on this one. Business in Europe is slow. He needs someone here, in the States, where people are brought up to spend money. You follow the art fairs, the auctions... Almost all the buyers are American."

Of course she knew; it was her business to know.

"Can I tell them you are on board, Hunter?" he asked, using her code name.

She made him wait a moment. "There is much to consider," she said, thinking about an upcoming auction at LESAH, one she had put together, but knew she would do it, had agreed to it in her mind as soon as she had been contacted, already considering who she wanted on her team, no way to say no to this, to capturing Trader, a big fish, her white whale. "And I have certain demands."

"Such as?"

"I must be in charge, in full command."

"I do not think that will be possible."

"Then you have my answer," she said, playing the odds. His organization had come to her, an independent operator with no allegiance to any agency, the reason they wanted her.

"I can suggest it, but no promises. I am just the broker."

"Yes, I *know*," she said, and ticked a smile. "I need no title or credit, but in the room, I need to be the leader, or it will not work."

"Like I said, I will suggest it to my people. As for the others, I cannot say."

She knew who he meant by the *others*, the FBI currently overwhelmed with foreign and domestic terrorism, happy to let INTERPOL take the lead, get the credit or the blame. And his organization, INTERPOL, needing to prove they were more than just an expensive name.

"I can wait," she said, knowing they could not, knowing they would give in to her demand or they would lose the lead, lose Trader. "But do not wait too long."

25

AirPods in, Dinah Washington crooning "Cry Me a River," I headed west along Twenty-Third Street toward the Hudson. It was a gray day, clouds like a sheet of lead over the city, but I was in a good mood. I was going to a meeting at my gallery.

My gallery. I loved thinking it, saying it.

Ninth Avenue apartments gave way to the Chelsea art galleries, former province of warehouses, parking lots and prostitutes, and the Mattia Beuhler Gallery just off Eleventh Avenue, a block from the whizzing traffic of the West Side Highway and the calm of the river. More a mini-museum than gallery, four floors linked by a steel-caged elevator and concrete stairwells, a half-dozen showing spaces with white walls and pristine wooden floors, the overall effect templelike, a space designed for the worship of art. And soon people would come to worship mine. Or would they?

The receptionist, an androgynous young person, said Beuhler was waiting for me and sent me up to his private office, plush but spare with pearl-gray walls, a panoramic view of the river, and the softest leather couch I'd ever laid my ass on.

Mattia Beuhler rose from behind his desk, a small dapper man in his sixties, skin tan and glowing, salt-and-pepper hair, eyes like an Alaskan husky, one blue, one brown. He asked how my paintings were going, his accent slight but evident, and I told him they were going well, only half-true.

A striking, almost life-size Max Beckmann self-portrait dominated the office, the artist tuxedo-clad, archly posed with a cigarette in hand, the painting propped against a wall, calculated to look as if someone had left it there by mistake.

"You know, before Hitler came to power, Beckmann was Germany's most famous modern artist," Beuhler said. "This portrait was so well regarded that it had its own room in Berlin's National Gallery. The next year, it was removed by the Nazis for their *Entartete Kunst* exhibition."

"Degenerate art," I said, thinking of my recent conversation with Anika Van Straten.

He nodded. "I am honored to have such a painting here and I will be sad to part with it."

I guessed his commission on the twenty-or-thirty-million-dollar sale would help him get over the loss, the Beckmann just one example of the backroom art he sold so he could take a chance on little-known artists like me.

"The catalog for your show will soon be going to the printer," he said, and talked about the critic he was paying to write about my work. It underscored my pressure to finish the paintings, and I was happy when the subject changed to his upcoming birthday party at the Odeon.

"Of course, you are invited."

I was surprised. Beuhler's annual birthday party was a coveted art-world invitation and sure to be stocked with art dealers, critics, famous artists, and A-list collectors, an event I never imagined I would attend.

"I'll be there. It's right after my trip to Amsterdam," I said, aware of his ability to open doors never before open to me.

He jotted a few names on a piece of paper, dealers for me to see in Amsterdam. "Places that might show your work," he said. "I will send each of them some pictures of your paintings and let them know to expect you."

I thanked him, left the gallery even more excited about the trip to Amsterdam, and feeling lucky.

26

Tully's office was even more of a dump than Smith remembered from the last time, old cups of coffee and chewing gum wrappers on the desk, stacks of comic books everywhere. Smith plucked a few off the couch so he could sit down.

"Careful!" Tully said.

"These really worth anything?" Smith asked.

"You kidding? They're my IRA account."

"Right," Smith said and got down to business, the reason he was there, for Tully to contact the client, something he had been asked to make happen. Anonymously. INTERPOL could not have it on record, not in their offices, their computers or phones, burners or otherwise. And Smith knew Tully wouldn't do it unless he sat on him, no matter how many threats he'd made, and he had made a lot.

"I doubt this email is going anywhere," Tully said, fingers poised above his laptop and shaking slightly.

"Let me worry about that," Smith said, reiterating INTERPOL's ability to trace any email. He stood up and leaned over Tully, dictating the message, "Trouble. Need to speak." He watched as Tully typed the .onion URL and the message, then hit Send. He imagined it spiraling into a black void, bouncing three times to random servers through layers of proxy darknets before reaching its destination website.

"You did good," he said, patting Tully on the back.

"Uh, you remember the client is looking for me, right?"

"Don't worry. The more we get on them, the more I can protect you. The call… Make it now," Smith said.

Tully got the burner to his ear and called. "There's no answer, it just rings and rings."

"Give it a minute," Smith said.

"It's like I told you, like I figured, they dumped the burner."

Smith told him to hang on a while longer, Tully's fingers nervously tapping the side of the cell.

"Okay," Smith said after another minute.

Tully disconnected, folded a stick of Juicy Fruit into his mouth, hands shaking so bad Smith almost felt bad for using the guy, for lying to him.

"Now what?" Tully said.

"We wait," Smith said and hung around a while, even thumbed through an old *Green Lantern* and a second-edition *Swamp Thing*, according to Tully not worth much "or I wouldn't let you touch them."

Tully was jittery, up, down, exchanging old gum for new, getting on Smith's nerves, and when he'd finally had enough, he told Tully to get in touch if he heard back.

"Anything at all, one sentence, one *word*, you get in touch with me day or night," Smith said. "Remember, I'm there for you. INTERPOL is there for you."

Then he left. He'd done what he was told to do, had Tully make the contact so they wouldn't have to.

27

On tiptoes, Tully peered out the half window below the low ceiling of his basement office, watching the lower half of Smith's body walk away, shoes on pavement, pant legs striding, confident. He angled his head to see Smith's face just as he disappeared, then stood back and smiled. He'd pulled it off.

What Smith didn't know was that Tully had another number, a private one that his client had provided "for emergencies only," as opposed to the number he had called, an abandoned burner for sure; he had not lied when he said he'd been listening to dead air. He laughed, having put one over on the INTERPOL man—if Smith really was from INTERPOL; Tully wasn't so sure. He didn't know what Smith's angle was, but right now, he didn't care. He'd played along and Smith had bought it. All he needed was a little time.

As for the email, he'd sent it though imagined his client would have abandoned the address by now. Still, it was possible Smith could get a location from it. Which was why he had to work fast. He needed to make the real call now.

At his desk, he moved comic books aside, found a pad and jotted a few notes, crossed them out and tried again. Not quite right. And it needed to be perfect—his story, his plan, every word. He composed another simple sentence and said it aloud, practicing his tone, his intonation. "I have a deal for you." The words were right, but the tone was off. He needed to sound less aggressive, more sincere. He cleared his throat and tried again. Better. Then he took a moment before he made the call, closed his eyes, and forced himself to breathe. This was it: his big chance and he couldn't blow it.

28

After classes all morning and a long meeting with her thesis advisor, Alex needed air, plus a coffee from her favorite vendor across the street by the park. She took a sip and looked back at the limestone-faced mansion, massive and tomb-like, the Stephen Chan Library of Fine Arts, former home of James Buchanan Duke, one-time president of the American Tobacco Company, now a library devoted to the arts and a research facility, her Upper East Side home away from home for the past two years.

Inside, the library was quiet, the only sounds footsteps and the soft swoosh of pages being turned. Back at her carrel and laptop, Alex went to the Van Gogh Museum's website, scrolled through the artist's self-portraits, and stopped at the last, a thin, haunted-looking Vincent, green shadows in his face playing against the red-orange of his beard and hair, the blue-green swirls of his jacket taking flight to create a spiraling, almost hallucinatory background, not unlike the background in the self-portrait she had found.

She read the museum's notes. The painting made in the small town of Auvers-sur-Oise, where Vincent had spent his final seventy days producing more than a painting a day, and where her painting would have been made too. She was skimming through all the self-portraits when it came to her, what she had been trying to remember—a lecture, here at the Institute, a visiting conservator from the Van Gogh Museum, his talk about a five-year project to authenticate Van Gogh paintings.

Alex scanned her desktop, found her notes from the lecture and the lecturer's name, Finn de Jong, and pictured him: tall, blond, bearded, and handsome. She'd gone up to him after his lecture to thank him and he had surprised her by asking if she was free for a drink, which she turned down; Luke was waiting in a restaurant. But he'd told her to be in touch if she was ever in Amsterdam.

Now she would be. And she needed his expertise, his authentication skills.

Figuring out the museum's email address was easy. Alex started to type, then stopped. Probably not a good idea to write an email that anyone might read. She noted the museum's number and decided it was better to call and let him know she was coming and what she had to show him.

29

You are just starting to lose patience when the library door opens and there she is, jacket unbuttoned, scarf flying, crossing Fifth Avenue, coming right toward you.

But you have anticipated this. A few steps and you are behind a poster in the bus stop shelter, head down until she passes. When you look up, you see she is heading into the park.

You wait a minute, then you follow.

30

Alex dropped the phone into her bag, upset that he'd called again, unplanned, refusing to comply with her one simple rule. Was it too late to stop this, to end it? She didn't owe him anything, not even a reason.

She cut across Fifth Avenue, heading along the wide transverse that led into the park. The sky was deep blue, still a couple of hours till sunset, and the park would be beautiful, a good place to think about what she wanted to do.

At the sloping lawn of Cedar Hill, she stopped to watch children scrambling over large rock outcroppings, then across another of the park's thoroughfares, the call still nagging and what she should do about it: *lay down the law*. If he couldn't respect her limitations, that was it. She was finished.

Feeling better about her decision, she walked on, taking in the beauty of Central Park—the pale-green lawns, the cherry blossoms in bloom—and chose a path that led into the Ramble, a place she'd often walked with her mother as a girl, a magical place, and it was still light, a few other people heading in the same direction.

Only a few yards in and she was surrounded by trees, the narrow path paved with wood chips and bordered by a rustic log railing. Hard to believe she was still in the middle of New York City, that it was all man-made.

She let out a long breath, felt the anxiety she'd been holding in melt away against a soundtrack of birdsongs and frogs croaking in a nearby stream, stopped to watch water rushing over rocks, the thick black trunk of a large tree that blotted out most of the sky, and heard a noise, someone nearby, breathing hard, turned and saw them, two men having sex, the Ramble a known gay hangout.

Time to get going. Down another path, the way out if she remembered correctly, but it ended at the edge of the lake, the city rising beyond it, and the sun just starting to set. A mistake to come into the park, the Ramble of all places, at this hour. She knew better, hadn't been thinking clearly, the call on her mind.

She headed along the path in the other direction, telling herself she was being silly, that she would soon be back on the city streets, across a wooden bridge, walking fast now, pulse quickening, images flicking in the corners of her eyes, something flying overhead and an owl hooting in the distance. *Were there owls in the park?* It didn't sound real, more a person's imitation of an owl. *Woo-woo.*

Alex stopped, rotated slowly.

"Hello?" she said, then louder, "*Hello?*" walking fast again, the path narrowing between rock outcroppings that cast everything in darkness.

When she saw the familiar bridge, she practically ran across, finally out of the Ramble, where she slowed, knowing where she was. A moment to catch her breath and she headed for the arch that would take her out of the park.

The city street, the traffic, the horns, people shouting, all sounded beautiful. She felt ridiculous now for having gone into the park in the first place, then panicking. Her eyes had been playing tricks on her, that's all. Still, she fished out her cell, wanted to hear his voice.

"Hey, you caught me," Luke said. "I was just leaving."

"Oh right," she said. "You're going out."

"Are you okay? You sound funny. Should I stay home?"

"No. I'm fine. I was just calling to say I'd see you later, something I want to talk to you about."

"Am I in trouble?" Luke said, adding a laugh.

"No." Alex laughed too. More like she was in trouble. She needed to tell him the truth. It was time. And she was tired of secrets.

31

I met Jude at our usual spot on Tenth Avenue, a longtime watering hole for the art world, my friend impossible to miss. Gaunt and handsome with a shock of prematurely white hair, he was often mistaken for Jim Jarmusch, though not in the art world where he was a well-known critic and number one expert on art auctions around the globe, often jetting off to London or Paris or Dubai, anywhere people made or sold art. In his usual spot, mid-banquette opposite the bar, bent over a text, a glass of white wine sweating beside him, he looked up and flashed his wolfish smile.

We caught up on his life—he was just back from the Venice Biennale—then mine—about to leave for Amsterdam—two cool guys a bit clueless about our good fortune.

"Someone you must meet in Amsterdam," he said, scrolling through his contacts. Jude knew artists and dealers and collectors everywhere. "Here we go, Carolien Cahill. I met her at an art fair. I'm forwarding her contact info and I'll let her know you're coming. She's a well-known Dutch artist, knows everyone and knows everything about Van Gogh too. Her grandfather or maybe her great-grandfather owned a famous Van Gogh painting. I'm not sure which one but I know she's been in a long, protracted fight to get it back."

"From who?" I asked, and he explained it had been stolen during the war.

"Carolien will tell you about it. And you'll like her." He offered

to put me together with a couple of Dutch art dealers as well, but I
told him I already had three to see in Amsterdam, thanks to Beuhler.

"Recommendations from the mighty Mattia Beuhler," he said.
"You'd better do what he says."

It sounded to me like he didn't like Beuhler, and I asked why, but
he denied it.

"I was the one who put you guys together, remember? Just that
you don't get to his level without crushing a few people along the
way."

"So, you put me together with someone who's going to crush me."

"*You?* Not so easy." He raised his wineglass. "To you and Mattia
Beuhler."

After that, we were interrupted several times, first by a brash
Texas art collector, then a dealer, then an artist, then a curator, all
wanting to talk to Jude. When we were finally left alone, Jude finished his wine, I polished off my Pellegrino, he reminded me to get
in touch with Carolien Cahill, and we said good night.

When I got home, Alex was in bed watching a movie on the Criterion
Channel, an old one I recognized. I tugged off my boots and got in
beside her.

"Does he know she's alive yet?" I asked.

"*What?* She's *alive?*" She swatted me.

"Sorry, I thought you'd seen it before."

"All I know—or *knew*—is that the cop has fallen in love with
Laura's portrait. Now you've ruined it."

I apologized again, gave her a kiss, and she asked about my drink
with Jude.

"It was great," I said and told her about the woman he wanted
me to meet in Amsterdam, and about the Dutch art dealers Mattia

Beuhler was setting up for me. Then she filled me in on an appointment she was planning to make with a painting conservator at the Van Gogh Museum, an expert on authentication.

I wondered what Smith was planning to do and who he was going to see. Alex was sure he'd tell us, though I wasn't.

"So, what was it you wanted to talk about?" I asked.

"Oh." She tapped her lip and shook her head. "I totally forget. I guess it wasn't very important."

"Really?"

"Really." She looked away, then back, flashed a smile and kissed me, her tongue in my mouth, and I didn't care what it was or if she ever told me.

32

You stare up at the building, to the fifth floor, the lights on, and you know she's home, know where she's been, had a little fun with her too, would have done more if you could.

You light a cigarette, suck the smoke into your lungs, tired of watching, bored with this surveillance, wondering for a moment why he is wasting you on this. Is he trying to keep you busy, out of the way? He knows you're better than this, a valued colleague, a lover, and soon-to-be partner. You swallow your annoyance, will do what he asks because you have a goal.

A glance in the other direction and you see him, the Cool Guy, and he sees you, but it doesn't matter. He doesn't know you. You walk toward him, even dare a look as you pass, eyes meeting for a few seconds though he's not really looking, his AirPods in, and he's humming, happy. A feeling you know will not last. You walk on, then turn to see him unlocking his front door and note the time, then report that he is home, that they are both home and in for the night.

You move back to your spot on the sidewalk and look up, imagine them kissing, undressing, and feel a little jealous, a little turned on. But it's enough watching for tonight. Time to go home, an aching of your own that needs taking care of.

33

With no place in the Bowery loft that was specifically hers, Alex settled onto the leather couch in the open-ended living room. It was the reason she kept her Murray Hill apartment despite the financial drain.

At least she was alone this morning, Luke teaching, and would be for several hours. She loved having the place to herself, though she couldn't imagine life without Luke and didn't want to. Why she had to tell him the truth, annoyed at herself for not telling him last night, hadn't been able to find the words, but she would.

She checked the time and did the math, afternoon in Amsterdam, then reread the short speech, crossing out a sentence, changing a couple of words before she called the museum and asked for Finn de Jong's extension. Only a moment before he was on the line.

"Alexis, how wonderful to hear from you!"

"I wasn't sure you'd remember me, Mr. de Jong."

"Not remember you? Impossible! But *Mister*? Finn. Please. Though it is, by the way, *doctor*."

Alex went into her prepared speech, something to discuss in relation to Van Gogh, briefly outlining how she'd found the painting, how it looked like a late self-portrait and to her eye authentic, the whole time talking fast. "I realize this must sound far-fetched. If someone came to me with this story, I'd probably laugh."

"I am not laughing," he said.

Which she appreciated, underscoring how of course it could be a forgery, which was why she was coming to him.

"You want me to authenticate it?" he asked, and she said she did.

"I realize that's a process but…"

"Naturally, I will need to see it," he said, and she told him she was coming to Amsterdam and would show him photos, careful with the phrasing, *photos*, not the painting.

"How marvelous! I will show you the city. It is lovely in spring."

He made it sound as if she'd called for a date. Had he not taken what she'd said seriously? She brought the conversation back to the painting, to its authenticity, and when he asked for a picture, she scrolled through her photos, chose a few, one of the fully revealed painting, and hit Send before she lost her nerve. Then she followed with a couple of details.

He was quiet but she heard him on the other end, an intake of breath. She asked if he'd gotten the photos, and he said yes.

"I know it's impossible to see the actual surface, but look at the details and you can see some of the brushwork. Do you?"

"Yes."

"And?"

"I am not sure what to say."

She told him to say it, whatever it was, whatever he thought.

"My first thought is that it must be a forgery, but of course, I will have to see it in person to be certain," he said, then talked about other late self-portraits, one in a similar jacket and vest, and another of Vincent without his beard, which he had authenticated for a museum in Oslo.

"I know the painting," Alex said. "Vincent gave it to his mother as a gift."

"Yes," he said, sounding impressed, which had been her intention.

"What about Émile Bernard's letter, citing a second *last* self-portrait?"

"A letter written by a bereaved young man just after his friend's funeral cannot be considered proof of a painting's existence."

Maybe not, but Alex knew there were art historians who agreed with her that a second self-portrait had existed and disappeared, but she was not about to argue. She needed Finn's help, his expertise.

"We can discuss it further when you are here, in Amsterdam." He paused. "There is something I want you to see..." He stopped and when Alex asked him what it was, he said he would let her know when he saw her painting.

She was about to tell him the rest of the story, that she didn't have it, when he asked, "How many people have you told about the painting?"

"Other than my boyfriend, no one has seen it," she said, which was true. Only she and Luke had *seen* the painting.

"Your boyfriend. I see. Will he be coming to Amsterdam with you?"

"Yes, but he'll be busy with gallery appointments. He's a painter, about to have an important show and..." She could hear herself talking too much.

"Good. Better we keep this between us, at least for now."

"Yes," she said, thinking that was exactly what she was going to say to him, to keep this news to himself. *But why had he said it?*

34

Van Gogh Museum
Amsterdam

This time, using his fingers to enlarge them, Finn de Jong went through the pictures again. Though it was impossible to be sure from photographs, there was no way to dismiss them, nor Alexis Verde, a candidate at New York's prestigious Institute of Fine Arts, a woman with a trained eye—and a beautiful one. His wife, soon-to-be ex-wife, had accused him of letting sex run his life and ruin their marriage—the fact that he had to bed every pretty woman he met.

He tried to ignore the pornographic images of Alexis Verde flooding his mind, took a breath, and replayed the conversation, heard himself say, *My first thought is that it must be a forgery*. Not true.

Now he entered his password into the museum's website, searched for Émile Bernard, and read the letter Bernard had written to a friend after Vincent's funeral, particularly a description of the artist's last canvases, including two self-portraits, one of which disappeared after the funeral and was never seen again.

He looked at the photos Alexis Verde had sent, comparing them to Bernard's description. A few weeks ago, he might have dismissed them but not now, not after meeting Olivier Toussaint and seeing his sketch.

He thought back to their meeting at a recent art conservation convention in Paris, the usual crowd and papers delivered, including his, the same one he had been giving for well over a year on authenticating Van Gogh paintings. He had been packing up when he'd been approached by Toussaint claiming he had something important to show him. No doubt some junk discovered in an attic or closet. Finn had tried to brush him off, but he'd persisted, explaining he had come all the way from his hometown of Auvers-sur-Oise to find an expert conservator, and he refused to leave until Finn had a look. And so, Finn had followed him to the end of the hallway where Toussaint had untied a portfolio and removed a small sketch on heavy cardboard, a pencil drawing, one that stopped Finn cold.

"You would agree the sketch needs conservation?" Toussaint had said.

It took a moment for Finn to find his voice. "Yes." Trying to sound casual, he pointed out a few cracks and a crumbling edge. "I can help you with that." Then, noting the man's somewhat furtive quality, he asked if it was stolen.

Toussaint reeled back.

"No, monsieur! I simply want to keep it private," he said, explaining how the sketch had been in his family for years, a gift from the artist to his great-grandfather.

A gift from the artist himself! "I see," Finn said, still working to keep his excitement in check, thinking what this could mean, a previously unknown Van Gogh, a major discovery, and a major sale. If it was real, he would have to persuade the man to part with it. "I will need to have it tested for authenticity."

"It *is* real, monsieur, I guarantee it. I have my great-grandfather's diary at home to prove it."

Finn nodded slowly, while Toussaint went on about finding someone to conserve the sketch. "Might that be you?"

"Yes!" Finn said, and though he could not do the work himself, he knew someone who could, a conservator he had been doing business with for years, someone who worked on his own and asked no questions. Another look at the sketch, and Finn raised his phone to photograph it, but Toussaint stopped him.

"No! I do not want the picture to be known, people urging me to sell it, and worse, worrying about thieves coming to my home."

Finn assured him he would tell no one, and that he would do the work himself.

That was less than a week ago.

Since then, Finn had been busy. He had contacted the independent conservator and his business associate, the former ready to do the work, the latter ready to advance money to buy the sketch, once it was authenticated, which was what Finn did professionally and publicly and, on occasion, privately.

He sat back in his chair and pictured Toussaint's sketch and how it was almost identical to the painting in Alexis Verde's photos! Clearly, the drawing had been a preparatory sketch for the painting—again, if they were real. But that was not a problem. Finn could authenticate them both and they would be sold through his associate, a man in the business of selling paintings with dubious provenance.

A moment to scroll through recent auction prices revealed that Van Gogh's *Portrait of Dr. Gachet* had sold at auction in 1990 for $83 million. In 2022, Christie's auctioned a Van Gogh painting that had sold for $117 million. He also noted that almost every high-priced auction sale was for Van Gogh artworks made in the last two years of his life. Like these. He let himself imagine what the artist's last self-portrait and the sketch made for it would fetch at auction. Two hundred million was not out of the question.

He would make Toussaint an offer of a few million, something a middle-class man in a small French town would find impossible to turn down. He only had to call his associate to get the okay.

He checked the time. He was already late for a lecture he was obliged to attend, the team from ASML, the technology company who partnered with the Van Gogh Museum to make sure Vincent's sunflowers retained their rich color and his drawings did not fade. The call would have to wait a few minutes.

Hands through his hair, tie straightened, he made his way through the conservation areas—treatment tables, storage areas for tools and equipment, solvent exhausts snaking down from the ceiling. He stopped for a moment to watch a conservator who was removing yellowed varnish from a still life. A meticulous process and, like everything in conservation, slow and with no margin for error: strip away paint with the varnish and there was no going back.

The man had been at the museum forever, a good technician who would never do anything more. Unlike Finn, who, at thirty-six, was the youngest member of the conservation team and had risen to an administrative position. His colleagues sniped it was because his conservation skills were so poor that they'd had to promote him to keep him from ruining art. That was fine with Finn, who had no interest in wasting his life in a low-paying conservation job and, when this sale went through, no job at all.

He slipped into the lecture room, making sure his appearance was noted, and found a seat in the back where he scrolled through Alexis's photos while the lecturer droned on about new conservation techniques and equipment, nothing of interest to him.

After ten minutes, he slipped out and strode quickly across the Museumplein, the large expanse of lawn shared by the city's three major museums, but it was too crowded with tourists to make a call. He cut between a twin row of blossoming cherry trees, their fuchsia flowers dropping petals that he crushed beneath his shoes without noticing as he headed out to the street where he found an isolated spot to finally make the call, told his associate about Alexis Verde's painting and its uncanny similarity to the Toussaint sketch, then sent him a picture. The man was unexpectedly blasé about the discovery, though prepared to acquire both works.

Now, with the go-ahead, Finn called Toussaint to let him know he would be coming to Auvers-sur-Oise to start the conservation. Then he headed back to his office high on the prospect of two major sales and the idea of Alexis Verde in his bed. Nothing he liked better than mixing business and pleasure.

35

It was happening, whatever *it* was. Smith had been given no facts, just to be here and someone would meet him.

He mounted the concrete stairs at Twenty-Eighth Street and Tenth Avenue. A couple of decades ago, the area was crawling with prostitutes and drug dealers, but now the High Line was a major tourist attraction.

A wide swath of blue sky appeared as he reached the top, the once abandoned elevated rail line transformed into a public park, a floating garden bordered by the river on one side and the city on the other, some of the buildings so close Smith could see people in bed, or in kitchens making coffee, few apartments with shades or blinds, nothing to obstruct the coveted river views.

He joined the steady stream of people heading south as he'd been told to do and tried to relax, impossible despite the cool river breezes and the cruise ships and sailboats on the water, all picture-postcard pretty.

Smith looked downtown, then up at the new skyline of Hudson Yards, the city within the city, a self-sufficient city-state, its inhabitants never needing to venture beyond its borders.

He walked on a bit until he saw it, the mural where he had been told to stop, two over-life-size figures covering an entire building wall, the work of artist Jordan Casteel. He was reading the identifying plaque when a man beside him said, "Impressive painting."

"Uh, yes. Are you…an art lover?" Smith said.

The man said, "Only when it suits me."

The prearranged questions and answers.

"Let's walk," the man said.

Smith eyed him sideways as they moved into the crowd, assessed him as somewhere in his late forties or early fifties. He looked like INTERPOL middle management, with a crew cut starting to gray at the temples. Smith pegged him as most likely former military.

"I've been told you are the right person for this job, but you do not have to agree to it right away. It is a dangerous job."

"The danger has been explained to me."

"One cannot explain *danger*." The man bit off the word. "Have you served in the military?"

"Never had the pleasure," Smith said, immediately sorry for the sarcasm, the agent looking at him, trying to figure out if he'd been kidding.

"I was a marine. Eight years. Still have my full-dress blues."

I'll bet you do, Smith thought, picturing him taking the uniform out and trying it on from time to time, noticed the guy's slight paunch which must make it hard to button.

"I did not join our organization till later," he said. Then, "You know there are more than five hundred varieties of plants and trees up here." He pointed out clusters of small white flowers. "Wild spurge, *Euphorbia corollata*, native to New York and a High Line favorite."

"You don't say."

"I do. The High Line is exactly 1.45 miles long, from Gansevoort and Washington Streets up to Thirty-Fourth. You know what they used to call Tenth Avenue, just below?"

Smith shook his head. Was he supposed to know?

"*Death* Avenue. The freight train that used to travel along Tenth

Avenue killed hundreds of innocent pedestrians. If it wasn't for public outcry, it would still be here, running people down. Public outcry is a powerful tool," he said, then pointed to another plant. "Northern maidenhair fern. You like that name?"

"Uh, sure," Smith said.

The ex-marine leaned closer, lowering his voice, "This particular unsub has evaded arrest for decades, shifting his HQ from one European city to another, always one step ahead of the authorities. According to our intel and the cell tower hit, he's now operating out of Amsterdam, but that's only location. We need proof of his actions. That's where you come in." He let that hang there a minute. "If you're ready to take on the assignment."

Smith nodded. He'd been getting ready for the past year.

"You will be going inside to lure him out."

"What does that mean, like the little drummer girl?"

"Who?"

Smith started to explain it was a John Le Carré novel, also a movie, actually two movies, even a TV series, but the guy talked over him.

"You will be reporting to the national and municipal police, *rijkspolitie* and *gemeentepolitie*, local law enforcement in Amsterdam. There will be another member of our organization involved. It's a small team, some deep state. The team leader is an independent, but seasoned. They will contact you," he said, pointing out another group of flowers and reeling off their names, giving Smith time to consider the assignment, which was finally becoming clear: he would be infiltrating a high-level, high-risk den of art criminals.

"And the painting," he asked. "They have it?"

The ex-marine did not answer the question. "The assignment will be explained to you. But your job is to get the painting and return it to its rightful owners, *publicly*."

So, it's an INTERPOL PR scheme, Smith thought, but only said, "I see."

"You and the team are there to prevent it from being trafficked again."

"It's been trafficked before?"

"In a sense. This is not only a valuable work of art but a symbol, you understand?"

Smith wasn't sure he did; they'd only told him so much.

They walked on a bit, the Circle Line cruising by on the river, the tour guide's monologue through a loudspeaker muffled and droning across the water.

"We will need your answer in twenty-four hours."

"I've already agreed to the job," Smith said.

"That was before you knew all the intel. And now?"

Though he still didn't have all the intel he said, "I'll do it." It was what he'd signed up for, to get him out from behind a desk, to be a player, to become part of INTERPOL's ruling body, the General Assembly.

"Do a good job and it will not go unnoticed."

"You don't have to sell me," Smith said. "I've agreed to do it."

"Does anyone know you're still working for us?"

"No. They think I'm a PI."

The man nodded, then spoke so softly Smith was practically leaning against him to hear. "You understand INTERPOL cannot afford exposure without success. If anything goes wrong, we will need to disavow any connection to this op as it is not how our organization works."

"I understand, Mr. Phelps."

"*Who?*"

"Never mind," Smith said. "What am I supposed to tell Perrone and Verde?"

"They found the painting inadvertently. Their job is done. They're expendable."

"*Expendable?*"

"Bad choice of words. Let's say just they're…redundant."

"But what do I tell them? They're my clients."

The ex-marine lowered his shades and squinted at him. "You have no *clients*, Analyst Smith. You are a *fictional* PI, and they were your fictional clients. *Blow them off.* Or we will."

Smith sucked in a breath. "What about Tully?"

"His client turned out to be our man, that's all. You could say he was at the wrong place at the right time. He'll be lucky to come out of this alive. But that's not our concern, nor yours. He served his purpose. So have your *clients*." The ex-marine raised his shades again and looked out at the river. "Nice view, isn't it?"

36

Yura on Madison was crowded with young Upper East Side mothers, nannies, and yuppies who did not like to cook, all stocking up on expensive premade meals the way Jennifer did, her basket filled with nuts and cheese and turkey roll-ups, German hunter stew, glazed salmon, and kale salad.

Anika leaned across her and plucked a bag of dark-cherry chip cookies—Jennifer's favorites—off the counter and held them up. "These or the marble pound cake?"

Jennifer shrugged and Anika put them both in the cart. They'd been arguing and Anika wanted to keep the peace. She paid the bill before Jennifer could get her card out and didn't fuss about the cost as she normally would.

Outside, the afternoon sky had gone dark with clouds. Anika turned up the collar of her Prada jacket and told Jennifer to do the same.

"I'm not a child," Jennifer said.

Oh no? Anika thought. That was exactly who she was, a *child*, almost twenty years her junior, moody and petulant and right now annoying. She had to stop herself from buttoning Jennifer's jacket for her, a gift she'd bought her in Switzerland, ridiculously overpriced but she'd been high on the success of her last assignment.

They crossed Madison to Park, Anika's mind inside that mountain vault in the Alps, something she would never forget, all of it playing like fragments of a movie, stepping off the private plane, the metal door set into the granite-faced mountain, behind it two more heavy doors, a code, an eye scan, facial recognition, then making her way through a maze of rock-cut tunnels. More codes and scans and heavy metal doors before she saw the booty, canvases stacked against the walls: Picasso, Matisse, Beckmann, Munch, a long-lost Leonardo da Vinci, a Botticelli nude, a Raphael portrait, all of it astonishing.

Only a moment to gape before sorting through it and taking pictures that would later be used to locate the owners of artwork that had been missing for more than eighty years. Then, she and her three-man crew ferrying the art back through the tunnel to the plane, and that last view of the mountain growing smaller as the plane ascended... Then Jennifer called her name and she hurried to catch up with her, surprised to see they had walked a dozen blocks, a wide swath of tulips on Park Avenue about to bloom.

She took hold of Jennifer's arm. "I told you I will only be gone a few days."

"And that I *can't* come."

Did she really have to go through this fiction again, her rich aunt's funeral, reading of the will, twenty-four seven with annoying relatives and lawyers and no time to socialize, no time to show Jennifer the city.

"Next time," she said. "I'll make it up to you," though she wasn't entirely sure she wanted to or if there would be time before this was over.

"You'd better," Jennifer said, lighting up an American Spirit.

"I will," Anika said, not wanting to fight, more important things on her mind, meeting Dispatcher for one. He was on his way to Amsterdam or possibly there, someone she could trust, essential as she did not know the others: the Dutch police merely there to follow orders, the new agent hand-picked by INTERPOL, tough enough she'd seen from their one brief meeting, but green.

Back home, she nibbled cheese and drank wine, Jennifer moody and interrogating her.

"So, this aunt, is she on your mother or father's side?"

"Mother's."

"I didn't know your mother had sisters."

"How would you know? But she doesn't. It is her older brother's wife." Anika washed down the lie with a sip of wine.

"Any children?"

"Why so many questions?"

"*Excuse me* for showing an interest in your life," Jennifer said, and Anika apologized, hoping to end the conversation, though Jennifer wouldn't quit. "It's odd that your flight is in the morning. Aren't all European flights in the evening?"

"Apparently not *all*," Anika said, sorry she had mentioned the flight, one more thing to lie about. She changed the subject with a kiss, and when Jennifer responded, they made love on the sofa, Anika trying to be in the moment, not thinking about what she was doing here or the crew she hadn't met waiting for her in Amsterdam, or the many things that could go wrong. After, she took an Ambien, hoping for at least a few hours of sleep.

Jennifer turned both faucets on, along with the exhaust fan, and closed the door of the bathroom just off the master bedroom firmly, though Anika had taken a pill and would soon be asleep. Cell phone to her ear, Jennifer strained to hear him.

"You realize it is nearly midnight here," he said. "It had better be important."

"She *says* she's going home for a funeral. Of course she's lying."

"You don't think her coming here has anything to do with *me*, do you?"

Jennifer didn't know and said so.

"That is why you are *there*, to *know*!" He had an idea what Anika did outside of the auction house, the reason he'd wanted Jennifer there, though she had not confirmed it. She had failed him.

Jennifer wanted to shout, *Don't I do enough for you?* but controlled herself. "I told you she's leaving for Amsterdam in the morning," she said softly, and he said he was sorry for shouting, but there had been rumors of a crackdown on the kind of work he did, his nerves on edge.

"You'll be fine, darling. You always are," she said, and he agreed he was being foolish, though he was already thinking about a move. "But I like Amsterdam."

"You liked Vienna too," he said.

"True," she said and pictured the office where she'd first interned two summers ago, no idea of what he really did, though she had discovered the truth going through his safe while he was out of town and found evidence of unrecorded business transactions. Then dug some more. She could have blackmailed him—she'd spent hours going through those bills of sale and made copies too—and one day she might. Knowledge was power. Instead, she'd initiated the affair with an eye on the future and did not let on what she'd done; he was a ruthless man and she worried what he might do if he found out. But she had stopped worrying now that they were planning a future, a partnership, perhaps even a wedding, the reason she was willing to do what he asked.

"It's late," he said. "I must get some sleep. I have an important art sale tomorrow, and even more important ones pending."

"Good night," she said and wished him good luck, then turned the faucets and fan off and slipped into bed beside Anika, who was fast asleep, snoring lightly.

Jennifer rolled over, thinking about her flight to Amsterdam, the ticket open-ended. If all went to plan, she would not be coming back.

37

Thanks to Jennifer's annoying phone call he was awake now, anxious, mind cycling, the idea that they were after him *again* infuriating. Those pesky do-good organizations would never let up. Silk robe pulled tight, he moved from bedroom to office, where he lived unimportant, his business conducted in free-trade zones, on burner phones, underground networks, and the dark web, this place, like the others, transitory. A shame, as he had come to like Amsterdam with its murky canals that suggested the underworld.

He sagged into the office chair and switched on a lamp, its Bakelite shade casting a perfect circle onto the Biedermeier desk, polished walnut with brass fittings, a piece that once belonged to the Rothschild family. No matter how many times he moved, he always brought a few favored possessions with him.

He took in the Franz Marc painting, a series of abstract horses painted in lush blues, a picture removed from a German museum in the 1930s and never seen again, on his wall temporarily, in between its route from one collector to the next. The entire room outfitted with transient objets, a small round side table with stepped spandrels and black japanning, a perfect example of German chinoiserie removed from the Hôtel de Tallyrand during the French occupation, a piece he would sell or leave behind when he moved on; one always sacrificed precious objects when survival was at stake, something history bore out, though in his case he was abandoning them by choice.

The burner shivered on his desk—one of his informants, apologizing for the late-night call, but he needed to update him on an important painting, one the art fence had been tracking for some time, the same one various authorities had been tracking as well, and at the same time. He would have had it if not for that inept detective bungling a simple job, arriving too late at the upstate antique store after months of research to find it, something he would pay for.

"You will have it soon," the informant said.

"I had better," the man said, and disconnected, picturing the painting, possibly the most valuable he would ever broker, on his wall for a few days before he resold it and it disappeared again. Everything was replaceable. Like the girl who had awakened him, who believed she had something on him. Did she not realize that he *knew*, that he could get rid of her with a snap of his fingers?

He glanced back at the Franz Marc painting, considered the fact that paintings and drawings were tangible objects, the only worthwhile art, unlike those silly *intangible* arts, music and dance and theater, worthless as there was nothing to trade, other than a ticket!

Still feeling agitated, he found one of the disposable syringes, unhappy his new supplier only stocked the kind with preservative. He disliked the idea of putting the ersatz chemical into his body, though the supplier claimed it was necessary to keep the morphine from degrading. He located a vein on his calf—it was recommended that a new injection site be used each time—and slid the needle under the skin, then sank back into bed, his worry breaking apart like soft clouds. No reason he would not be able to continue his work unchecked, exactly the way his father and his grandfather had done before him.

38

Smith had called the meeting. Alex and I huddled together on his worn leather love seat, Smith behind his desk, shirtsleeves rolled up, ropy muscled arms folded across his chest, a guarded pose.

"Anyone want coffee?" he asked, a first, and unlike him. We both said no, anxious to hear what he had to report. "So, Amsterdam..." he said and stopped, shook a cigarette out of the pack, and lit it despite my look of disapproval.

I asked him to open the window, and he told me it didn't open, then went quiet, but Alex filled the silence with her news.

"I have an appointment with a painting conservator who I think can shed some light on our missing painting."

Smith asked how, and she explained he authenticated Van Gogh paintings.

"From photographs?"

"No," Alex said. "But he might have some thoughts—when it was made, how it compares to other Van Gogh self-portraits."

Smith sighed a long plume of smoke. "Sounds like a waste of time to me."

Alex stiffened. "I don't see it that way."

Smith shrugged and I asked if he was checking into Van Gogh paintings on the market. "You said you were talking to people with connections to art on the black market, unless I heard you wrong."

"Nothing has shown up," he said, terse.

"So, what then?" Alex said. "That's it?"

"Could be. Probably," he said, his face closed, impossible to read. "Maybe it's for the best. Before you waste your money on the trip."

"Wait, *what?*" Alex said. "Are you suggesting we not go?"

"More than suggesting. It's a dead end. It's...over."

"But it was *your* idea," she said.

"Before we investigated. I was hopeful. But now... Look, we followed the route best we could, spoke to the right people, came up with Tully's fingerprints—and Tully—which was something. *You* did that, Alexis, and it was damn good investigating. But Tully's told us all he knows." He pushed his glasses up his nose, looked up, then down, anywhere but at us.

Was he lying? Holding something back?

"I thought you were leaning on Tully, having him email his client to find the location," I said.

"Yeah, I did. But it didn't pan out. The call wasn't traceable. Neither was the email." He crushed his cigarette out hard. "There's nothing more to get from Tully. Forget him."

"Well, I'm still interested in getting the conservator's opinion," Alex said and stood. "If it's okay with you."

"What's that going to get you other than an *opinion?*" Smith said.

"So, you no longer have appointments with any of those *unnamed* people in Amsterdam?" I asked.

"None." He stood too, the Coca-Cola sign shimmering around him, neon red. "Sorry. But none of my contacts have heard anything about your Van Gogh, about *any* Van Gogh."

"So, what are you saying?" I asked. "That you're out?"

Smith sighed. "Look, I did my best. *You* did your best. We always knew it was a crapshoot, a big one, but it's time to give it up. All of us."

"Just because *you've* lost interest doesn't mean *I* have," Alex said.

"It's not about losing *interest*," he said. "Like I said, it's a dead end. There's nowhere to go. It's time to throw in the towel, time to quit."

"I don't care *what* he says, I'm going!" Alex said. "We have our tickets. I'll cancel *his*, the hell with him!" We were outside Smith's office, the perfect place for Alex to vent—Times Square, where no one could hear or care. "He decides to quit, just like that, and we're supposed to be, like, 'Okay, fine, thanks so much.'" Above her, neon signs punctuated her words, the LED news feed wrapping around 10 Times Square as if telegraphing her rant.

I didn't get it either, Smith's sudden change of heart.

Alex wondered if he'd taken on a new client. I didn't know, though maybe that was it. We hadn't paid him anything and maybe he needed money.

"But we *would have* paid him," Alex said. "He never asked."

A lone Minnie Mouse sidled up to Alex, and she handed her a few dollars but avoided the photo op.

"They're mostly illegal aliens trying to make a buck," she said, but it was like waving a red flag in front of a bull. We were suddenly surrounded by Spider-Man, Batman, the naked cowboy strumming his guitar beside us in his tighty-whities. I took Alex by the arm and led her toward the subway.

On the crowded platform, she started up again, this time on the conservator she was going to see in Amsterdam. "He said he has something that relates to the Van Gogh self-portrait that he's going to show me in Amsterdam. So, I'm going, no matter what."

"I never thought for a minute you weren't," I said. As for me, the art dealer appointments Beuhler had set up were more than enough reason to go.

"And why is Smith suddenly so dismissive of Tully, our only

connection to the client and maybe to the painting?" she said. "Do you think Smith scared him off, or what?"

I had no idea and didn't think we'd ever find out.

The subway roared into the station and Alex got on, still in a huff.

"Well, we don't need Smith or Tully," she said. "We can do this ourselves!"

Could we? I wasn't so sure, but I knew better than to argue with Alex when she had her mind set.

"That painting got lost and found once," she said. "No reason it can't be found again."

I wondered about that too, how it had gotten lost in the first place, but there was no way to know, and I wasn't going to bring it up now.

39

August 1944
Paris

Keeping to the shadows, she moved through the backstreets of Paris like a thief. Two more stops, two more artworks retrieved. Neither concealed; there'd been no time.

As a resistance member for the past three years, she had performed many tasks: destroying telephone lines, underground cables, and German munition depots, acts more dangerous than this but with less urgency. It was known the Germans were loading trains with their looted art and antiques, and destroying what they could not take before the Allies reached the city.

The sky was suddenly blue/white, a flare illuminating the streets, darkened buildings, a small group of German soldiers hunched and huddled together like rats. She ducked into an alleyway, waited until the light faded, then headed out again. She knew the city and the Germans did not. It was her city, not theirs.

Across a bridge, crouching and skittering, moonlight on the Seine sparkling like black diamonds, then north toward her destination, where the truck would be waiting. At least she hoped so; she was late, slowed by the German soldier in Delacroix's garden, his face in her mind, young and scared, her hand over his mouth too late to stifle his scream as she drove the knife in, his last breath in her ear before he fell. Not the first time she had killed for her country, and she would do it again. "Vivre vaincu, c'est mourir chaque jour," *she whispered to herself.* "*To live defeated is to die every day," Napoleon's words adopted by the resistance.*

With two of the paintings strapped to her back, the crated one pressed tightly to her chest, digging into her breasts, she heard the trains, then saw them. Saw the soldiers too. Dozens of them. Loading crates onto a train, one in front barking orders.

Squatting behind a van, she watched. When she heard his name, she dared a peek and recognized him, Reichsmarschall Hermann Göring, architect of the Nazi police state, commander of the Luftwaffe. He was set apart from the other soldiers and easy to identify by the pearl-gray uniform studded with pendants, medals, gold eagles, and black swastikas. With iron crosses dangling from his neck, a belt studded with gold straining across his large girth, Reichsmarschall Göring was a flamboyant dandy who had devoted much of the war to amassing property and stealing art from the people he murdered.

There was a rumor that Hitler intended to commit suicide when the Allies invaded and that Göring had sent the Führer a telegram saying he would gladly take over, the message so infuriating Hitler that he was planning to strip Göring of his command and declare him a traitor. But if it was true, the enlisted men hadn't heard or didn't care, continuing to load Göring's private train with crate after crate of looted art.

The truck she was to meet was on the other side of the station, the only way to get there by using the next departing train as cover, and she did, darting across the tracks through clouds of steam, holding her breath and she was almost there, could see the truck when she heard the cries, "Halt! Stop!" but she kept running, the truck only a few yards ahead when she felt it, like a fist slamming into her back, then inflating inside her like a balloon. Then she saw the blood, the gunshot having gone through her shoulder, as the soldiers tackled her and tore the paintings off her back and from her arms and pushed her to the ground. Two pairs of boots, inches from her face, then joined by another set.

"Reichsmarschall," the soldiers said in unison, and clicked their heels.

She dared a look up and it was him, the Nazi monster, arms stretched out holding the two artworks from her back, admiring them, while the soldier removed the rags from the other painting and handed it over to the Reichsmarschall.

"Was ist das?" he asked, looking at the painting, a woman's face in black and white. Then he handed all three paintings to the soldiers and said, "Der zug."

The train. The resistance fighter had learned enough German in the past few years to understand that much. They were putting the art on the train but she had to stop them. It was her job. Her duty. Knife stealthily unsheathed, she sprung, forgetting her fear and the wound in her shoulder, screaming, "Cochon! Meurtrier!" and lunging at the Reichsmarschall.

But the soldiers were too fast, one breaking her fingers to wrest the knife from her hand, the other kicking her so hard she fell back, the wind knocked out of her though she managed to raise herself and charged toward them again, shouting, "Vive la Résistance!" Then the Reichsmarschall turned, aimed his gun, and shot her.

40

Out of the Midtown Tunnel, the traffic was bumper to bumper, not unusual, but why now in the middle of the night when he had to get out? Tully folded a stick of Juicy Fruit into his mouth and chewed so hard his jaw ached.

Why the hell had he made that call? His big plan had backfired.

Oh, Jimmy, the things you get yourself into, what his mom always said. His father's mantra, *Use your brain, if you have one*.

Well, he'd show them, he'd show everyone. If he got out of this alive.

A deep drag on the cigarette, stale but good.

At Forest Hills, the traffic opened for a while and he was hopeful he'd get out of town before they came looking for him, but it didn't last long, more traffic just a few miles on.

Why did he have to make that call?

I have a deal for you?

Who did he think he was, the fucking Godfather? But it had all made sense—let the client know about Smith and his cronies, what they were up to, show he was loyal, and give them information in exchange for getting them off his back.

We…do not make…deals, the words thick, echoing through the burner and a voice changer, every breath amplified like Darth Vader.

He tried to fix it. *Bad choice of words. Not a deal. An exchange. I give you what I find out about them and we're even.*

It made perfect sense when he'd planned it, a way out, a clean break so they'd leave him alone and he could get on with the rest of his plan. And he'd given them good information—that Smith and his cronies knew about the painting, and how they had come to him and asked him to work for them to find out about the client and report back. *Something I'd never do, man.*

So…what have you…told them?

Nothing, nada. What is there to tell? I don't know you and don't want to. Then he'd fed them what he knew about Smith: *He's from INTERPOL. I saw his ID.*

And you called…because he asked you to…so he could locate us.

No, I did it to alert you to Smith, that's all. You can trust me, man.

A kind of barking sound on the other end might have been a laugh, followed by a long pause. Then nervously, stupidly, he'd asked again, *Do we have a deal?*

All they'd said was *We know…where you live*, then the phone went dead.

He had to get away and stay away. He sneaked a look at the back seat, at his suitcase and his best comic books, more of them in the trunk, extra insurance. He could sell a few on eBay if he got desperate.

The traffic stopped short and Tully almost slammed into the car in front of him, brakes screeching, hands shaking on the wheel.

How long ago had he made that call to the client? Was someone already at his Queens apartment?

He tugged the plastic bag out of his pocket, then the reefer, lit it and took a long drag. The weed was hot on his throat but hit him fast. His tension eased, and for a moment he felt almost amused by his situation, then hungry. He called Denise to let her know he was on his way.

"Have you eaten, Jimmy?"

Good ol' Denise, one in the morning and she was worried if he was hungry, and he was. He pictured her standing in her kitchen at the old appliances, pretty face tired from her shift at Agway and raising two toddlers on her own.

"Yeah. I'll eat anything," he said, then laughed. "And you got anything to drink in the house?" Not a house, a shack more like it, an anomaly right there in the middle of East Hampton hidden down a narrow dirt road behind the farmers' market, a throwback to a time when the town belonged to potato farmers, not hedge funders. A temporary hideout. The client didn't know about Denise. Once Tully got the money he'd split, Mexico or South America.

"I have some vodka," Denise said.

"That'll do." He exhaled.

"Are you smoking, Jimmy?"

"No way, babe." And he wasn't, not the way she thought. "I quit years ago. You know that."

"Good," she said. "I'll make you a sandwich when you get here."

Tully thanked her, disconnected, and glanced at the package on the seat beside him, his security blanket, his way out. He would not be hiding out at Deenie's for long.

41

Two Days Later

Alex and I buckled our seat belts, the flight attendant giving her spiel, "In the event of an emergency landing..." never my favorite words, or Alex's. She was a fearful flyer, clutching my hand like her life depended on it. I handed her a copy of *The New Yorker*.

"There's an interesting story on the melting polar ice caps, some global warming to take your mind off flying."

She gave me a look and sighed while I tried to get comfortable, my legs in the aisle, economy made for people under five feet, not over six. I noted again the empty window seat, Smith's, and it got us going, trying to figure out why he had suddenly given up on the job.

"He was so into it at the beginning," Alex said.

It was true, at least I thought so, and not like the John Washington Smith I knew, never one to quit. I pictured him behind his desk delivering blunt responses to our questions without excuses or much explanation.

Alex asked again about Tully, and I suggested we try to talk with him when we got back, though I wasn't sure there was anything to say.

"Smith hasn't billed us for anything, not even lab fees," she said. I wondered if his bill would be waiting for us when we got home, but we gave up on Smith and talked about Van Gogh, how much of his work we'd soon be seeing. The plane cut through clouds and smoothed out, and Alex finally let go of my hand to rifle through her bag to get her Kindle. She began to read, so I put in my earphones and listened to more of Naifeh and Smith's Van Gogh biography and ate dinner, something that might have been chicken, and half of Alex's. She only drank wine, proclaimed it "dreadful" but finished two tiny bottles, then fell asleep. I tuned back into the bio, a chapter about Van Gogh's time in the south of France with Gauguin, their incessant arguing that ended in Vincent's famous ear-slashing.

When the plane's interior lights dimmed, I switched off the book and closed my eyes, still trying to make sense of Smith's sudden defection, then worried about my upcoming show and the paintings I had yet to finish to fill the Beuhler Gallery. I pictured myself scraping and uncovering the Van Gogh self-portrait bit by bit, revealing his jacket and vest, beard and hair, his haunting blue eyes, then Anika Van Straten said, "Entartete Kunst, over two thousand plundered artworks," her lighter flicking on and off and the artworks catching fire, flames burning through canvases and Mattia Beuhler's gallery walls, tall and white, and my paintings on them melting, paint sliding onto the floor while I raced between them trying to catch the paint and put it back, but it was the Van Gogh self-portrait, face coming to life, razor glinting in his hand, slicing his ear, then mine, my hand clasped to my cheek, feeling the blood icy cold, and my name called over and over "Luke, Luke…"

I opened my eyes, felt the blast of cold air from the air ducts above my head, and saw Alex's face blurring in close-up.

"Luke, wake up, we're landing."

"Where?" I asked, my head and mouth filled with cotton.

"Amsterdam," Alex said. "Where else? It's going to be so great!"

"Right," I said, and touched my ear as the dream receded, though Van Gogh's painted face and canvases in flames hovered like ghosts forecasting disaster.

42

Amsterdam

Smith breezed through customs, INTERPOL badge and passport in one hand, carry-on duffel in the other. He made his way into the airport slightly disoriented from the overnight flight, so he did not see the two men until he felt them on either side of him gripping his arms.

"Keep going," they said, the three of them moving as one through the automatic doors, cool indoor light exchanged for a blast of warm sun but only for the briefest moment before he was forced into the back seat of a van with dark windows.

"Who are you?" he asked, not sure if these were his contacts or if he'd been abducted. "Municipal police? National police?"

The men said nothing.

He tried it in Dutch, the way he'd practiced, *"Gemeentepolitie? Rijkspolitie?"*

Still no answer, the landscape blurring past darkened windows, his mind moving just as fast.

They will contact you. So said the man on the High Line.

Smith drew in breath and tried to stay calm, praying it was them, the men he was supposed to meet. Not the ones he was supposed to infiltrate, who would question him, torture him to find out what he knew, and then, no matter what he told them, kill him.

43

Amsterdam

It was in baggage claim, waiting for Alex's suitcase, groggy from the flight, my nightmare hanging on like a nasty aftertaste, that I first saw him standing by himself and texting. A young guy, twentysomething, with neck, arms, and hands completely covered by tattoos—the reason I noticed him at all.

Just outside the airport, waiting for a cab, I saw him again, close enough to make out the tattoos around his neck, which were inked armor with pointy prongs poking the underside of his jaw, his hands iron crosses, skulls, lightning bolts, and when he looked up, there were Roman numerals inked above one eyebrow and a Gen Z tattoo below his ear.

When he went back to texting, I pointed him out to Alex, who said, "Please, don't ever," something she did not have to say. I had enough ink.

We were soon in a taxi, drab suburbs giving way to city streets lined with tan and sienna-colored town houses, every so often a kind of storybook castle, trees in bloom, tulips everywhere, and canals, one after another, our taxi bumping over narrow bridges.

The hotel Alex had booked was on a tree-lined street, our room a walk up three short flights. A king-sized bed occupied most of the space; the padded half-moon headboard and fringed hanging lamps filled the rest.

Alex called it "early Dutch bordello," then checked out the bathroom, clean and neat though the door hit the bed and only opened halfway.

But there were two windows that looked over rooftops and flooded the room with light, and Alex, the picky one, proclaimed it "adorable," so I was happy and suggested we try out the bed.

"I thought you were jet-lagged," she said, and I was, but hotel rooms always made me horny.

"Later," she said, suggesting I take a shower, "a cold one," though she took one first, the bathroom not big enough for both of us. I was almost asleep when she came out, but she got me up and into the shower, anxious to get out and see some of the city.

Outside, it was colder than expected, the sky overcast, neither of us with a coat, but I wrapped my arm around Alex. We took in the neighborhood, which was well tended and upscale, wide tubs of tulips every few yards, designer shops—Dior, Prada, Furla—just opening for the morning. And bicycles everywhere.

Alex wanted to check out a floating flower market, which, according to my GPS, was twenty minutes away, a route that took us down narrow lanes crowded with more bikes and into a wide thoroughfare with tourists, restaurants, shops, cars, buses, and a pink cable car running down the center.

It was there, ironically in front of a tattoo parlor, that I saw him again, the tattooed guy from the airport, and pointed him out.

"Maybe he *lives* inside," Alex said.

He was texting again, leaning against a bike rack, but raised his head, looking up but past me, then back down, and we kept going, across a bridge into an open sprawling square where several streets converged, making it impossible to cross between the cable cars, buses, and bicycles coming in every direction. It struck me that I had imagined Amsterdam small, almost in miniature, but it was a big city, thrumming with life, and crowded.

We dodged the traffic and took a quieter path beside a wide canal, weeping willows dipping into dark waters, and Alex's phone buzzed again. She fished it out of her bag and walked away, phone to her ear, stopped to lean on a bench, then sat, almost in slow motion, as if she'd gotten bad news. But she was up fast, phone dropped back in her bag and heading toward me.

"Everything okay?" I asked.

"Nothing serious," she said. "Just someone from school."

"Isn't it like three in morning back home?"

"Is it?" Alex shrugged, looped her arm through mine, and we kept walking.

I had imagined the market to be floating barges of flowers with walkways or bridges to reach them, but it was a regular city block, one side filled with open flower stalls built over the water with no feeling of them floating, every stall pretty much the same, rows of seed packets and tulip bulbs, the sidewalk filled with crates of hairy-rooted bulbs that gave me the creeps.

"Not as nice as West Twenty-Eighth Street," I said.

Alex told me not to be an ugly American, but I thought Manhattan's flower market felt more authentic, with its retail shops up and down the street, plants and flowers blanketing the sidewalks.

The nonfloating floating flower market ended in a wide circular plaza bordered by stores and castle-like buildings, the way I'd imagined Amsterdam, only bigger. We skirted the edge, then chose a smaller street beside a narrow canal where we stopped at a coffee shop, the Dutch name for a smoke shop, its window crammed with boxes of CBD gummies, bottles of tinctures, and multicolored packets of unspecified drugs with names like Energy Plz and Sleep Plz and Sex Plz. I suggested we buy some for our friends as jokes and was about to go in when I saw him, the tattooed guy, standing beside the canal, head down texting again, the long shadow of his silhouette exaggerated and rippling in the dark water.

I was elbowing Alex when a guy came out of the shop and called, "Gunther!" and the tattooed guy looked up, then turned and quickly walked away.

"Gunther," I repeated under my breath. Then we went into the head shop, where I bought the packets of Sleep Plz and Sex Plz and a box of gummies. When we came out, I looked for Gunther, but he was gone, and we headed back to the hotel, jet lag kicking our ass the whole way.

It was on the block with the designer shops that I saw him again, in front of the Prada store where he looked totally out of place with his torn jeans and tattoos, and this time, I looked right at him and waited until he returned my stare, which he did for a second before he turned and headed off. But had he wanted me to know he was watching? I was suddenly too tired to care.

Back at our hotel I crawled into bed and was out for several hours before Alex's phone woke me. She reached across me, turned it off, and went back to sleep, but I didn't. After a few minutes, I slipped out of bed. The room was dark except for the tiny blinking light on Alex's phone, which I picked up and took into the bathroom, where I closed the door and checked her voicemail, something I had never done before and wasn't proud of doing now, but the calls and Alex's evasiveness had touched some nagging residue of mistrust.

There were no messages, the last call only a number with no name attached. I forwarded the number to my phone, erased the fact that I'd sent it, then got back in bed feeling like the worst kind of creep. When Alex stirred, I put my arms around her and, feeling doubly ashamed, vowed I would delete the number in the morning.

44

Near Centraal Station
Amsterdam

Smith, still recovering from his abduction at the airport, now sat in a conference room in the back of a police station, staring at gray-green walls, a blinking light fixture, and a rotating fan whipping up the air along with his nerves.

Bruno Steiner was the first to introduce himself. "Your INTERPOL liaison," he said. "Art Theft and Cultural Heritage Crime, but of course I will be reporting to the General Assembly."

No doubt, Interpol's snitch. Smith had never met him and didn't like him. Small pointy face, no lips, cheap suit, cheap rug.

Next the Dutch national police, represented by a big guy in a uniform, belted jacket over puffy pants tucked into knee-high boots. "Pieter Koner, Rijkspolitie," he said, with a slight bow.

Then Noah Jaager, one of two municipal cops, blue uniform with a wide green stripe from chest to back spelling out POLITIE. He didn't look old enough to drive. "In-house techie," Jaager said, then gestured toward the other municipal cop, a tall, athletic-looking woman, red hair pulled back from an attractive face, same uniform.

"Tess Vox," she said, offering Smith a Styrofoam cup of coffee and indicating a plate of cookies in the center of the table. "Have a stroopwafel," she said, "but beware, they are very sweet."

Smith took two and put them both in his mouth at the same time. He was starving, and she was right. The gooey caramel center was cloying. He was trying to swallow the cookie when the door opened, and a woman entered.

"*You*," he said.

"Close your mouth," she said without a hint of humor.

"Are you responsible for those goons at the airport?" Smith managed to ask.

"The directive was to bring you here before anyone could see you, for your own safety and the operation's security."

"They could have told me that."

"They were instructed to say nothing." She retrieved a pack of Dunhills and a lighter, lit a cigarette, then handed the pack to Smith. "If I remember correctly, you liked these."

Trying to make sense of it, of *her*, Smith took a cigarette. She flicked her lighter and he leaned in, read the name on the side. "Der Römer," he said. "Yeah, I remember."

"So, we both have good memories," she said. Other than the whir of the overhead fan, the room had gone quiet, everyone watching them. "Analyst Smith and I are old friends," she said.

Smith eyed Anika Van Straten above his tinted glasses, considering the strong, handsome face he remembered from the Lower East Side Auction House.

"Yeah, friends," he said, trying to be cool, taking in the black sleeveless tee that showed off her muscled arms, the same bangle bracelets and silver cuff that circled one bicep. Everything the same but different. "Where am I?"

"A police station in the old center of Amsterdam, De Wallen, near Centraal Station. I take it you have met everyone."

Smith tried to place her accent again, the way she said *gooot* for "good," the hard *d*, the elongated *o*'s.

Van Straten motioned with her hands, and everyone sat. Clearly, she was in charge.

Steiner stage-whispered to Smith. "Municipal and National have to be here. It is, as you know, the way we work, through members of local law enforcement. They are our fallback if anything goes wrong."

National Police Koner glared at him. "So, what you are saying is if the plan fails, we get the blame?"

"I was speaking to my colleague," Steiner said, a hand unconsciously straightening his toupee. "Restating INTERPOL policy. It will be Analyst Smith inside, doing the work."

"What Steiner is trying to say," Smith said, "is that *I'm* the fall guy, not you."

Van Straten stopped them. "We are a team with only *one* goal. If you have a problem with that, Mr. Steiner, I can ask INTERPOL to replace you."

"*Analyst* Steiner, and I am expert in my area," he said, "not easily replaced."

"And I have great respect for the work you have done on INTERPOL's ID-Art app," she said. "It is a great tool in the fight against cultural heritage crime."

Smith knew all about the downloadable app that made it possible to tap into INTERPOL's database of stolen art and identify blood antiquities. He also knew it had taken a large team to develop it because he had been a part of that team, and he'd never met Steiner. "I worked on that too," he said, then regretted saying it; it sounded childish and petty.

"Just one of the reasons you were chosen for this assignment," Van Straten said. She looked around the table at each person. "What goes on in this room stays in this room. Understood?" She focused on the three Dutch police. "You are not to share any of this with your coworkers or your superiors." Then she spoke to Smith, her eyes on his. "As you know, you will be infiltrating the client's team. *Trader* will be his code name from now on. He has been primed for several months. Other possibilities had been dangled in front of him, all of them rejected as we expected. But not this one. He is anxious for a new partner. That will be you. If all goes to plan.

"From now on you are Calvin Lewis, private art dealer. Your birth certificate, as Lewis, is on record at Northwestern Memorial Hospital, Chicago." She handed him a driver's license, a somewhat worn-looking social security card, credit cards, a Triple A membership, all with his new identity. "Your birth date, height, and weight remain the same. Other facts about Lewis's childhood, *your* childhood—your family, education, and employment—are in here." She slid a folder toward him.

"Memorize it," she said, then continued to outline the plan, the paintings that would serve as bait, the services Lewis would be offering—to fence paintings to clients in the United States. "Something our fictitious Mr. Lewis has been doing for years, above but mostly below the law," she said. "His identity and art trading will be verified by several dealers Trader has done business with, recently arrested and cooperating with us, cutting deals for lighter sentences."

"And who exactly is *us*?"

"A group of people representing various agencies. That is enough. Better you do not know everything."

"In case things go south and they try to get those names out of me?"

"You have been watching too much television, Analyst Smith. I was going to say because you have more important things to remember." She slid another, thicker folder toward him. "Some history, things Lewis would know in his line of work. There is a glossary in the back. Learn it."

"How will I find this Trader?"

"He will find *you*," Van Straten said, explaining how the artworks Lewis was selling had already been leaked on the black market and darknet.

"Encoded in a way that the people who deal in such merchandise will understand," techie Jaager said. "It is likely several buyers will make contact."

"But for now, we are focusing on Trader," Van Straten said. "Quite possibly the major dealer of plundered art in Europe."

"If he's so major, he must have existing contacts in the States," Smith said.

"Indeed," Van Straten said. "Many of whom have been recently detained or arrested. Like I said, Trader is looking for someone new, and less known, like Lewis. We believe he has had a longtime silent partner in the United States, someone we do not know, though we have a list of possible suspects and hope to find him. But that is secondary. Right now, our target is Trader." She paused, her eyes on Steiner, who was typing on his iPad. "We do not need a recording secretary, Mr. Steiner."

He looked up. "My personal notes. So I do not forget anything imp…"

Van Straten talked over him, reviewing the cache of newly recovered artworks that Smith, as Lewis, would be offering. "Pictures have been sent to your cell phone."

"Encrypted," Jaager added. "For your access only, and when you need to show them to Trader."

Van Straten handed Smith a burner phone. "Only to be used in the direst circumstance," she said, then recited a similar disavowal to the one made by the agent on the High Line. This time, Smith did not make his *Mission Impossible* crack. "Rijkspolitie Koner will be following you throughout, though he will not interfere unless your life is in danger."

"Hopefully in something less conspicuous than that bloomer outfit," Smith quipped, and Koner sat up. "Sorry, I wasn't making fun of you, just the uniform."

"Uniforms are *symbols*," Van Straten said. "Do you know that your designer, Hugo Boss, manufactured uniforms with Jewish slave labor?"

"He's not *my* designer," Smith said, plucking at his work shirt.

"People no longer know Boss was an active member of the Nazi party, or that Holocaust survivors sued his company, and yet his company continues to thrive," she said, and went on about war criminals and how many continued to do business after the war just as they had before. "Relabeled 'followers,' rather than party 'members' or 'supporters.' Only the biggest war criminals stood trial, but there were so many others that—" She stopped abruptly, as if she'd been talking too much, then asked the team to leave them so she could speak with Smith alone. Only Steiner protested before leaving in a huff.

"I am afraid we are stuck with Mr. Steiner," Van Straten said, then paused. "I am certain you did some checking on me, so let me confirm that I did work for Veilinghuis AAG, the Amsterdam auction house, and my current position is at LESAH. They are both legitimate jobs."

"And now?" Smith asked.

"Now, I am *here*," she said. "That is all you need know."

Smith recalled the guy on the High Line referring to *deep state*, no doubt Van Straten.

"And of course, you did a background check on me," he said. "Find anything interesting?"

"Yes," she said, citing the fact that he'd gone rogue in pursuit of a certain famous diary, how that had almost gotten him fired and killed. "You like taking chances and courting danger, one of the reasons you were selected for this job."

He said he wasn't crazy about the danger part. "How about you?"

"I do not like danger," she said. "But I do not run from it either. And I think the same could be said of you."

"I'm here for self-advancement, not danger."

"Oh? Nothing to do with a boy from the projects trying to prove himself?" she asked but didn't wait for a response. "So, let us talk about the painting your friends, your *clients*, have been chasing." She removed a paper from a folder and handed it to him, a bill of sale dated 1933 from a Parisian art dealer. "Note, the painting is identified only as a self-portrait by Van Gogh, dated 1890. The man who bought it, a wealthy French banker. In less than a decade, the painting disappeared."

"The banker sold it?"

"In a manner of speaking. A forced sale, a gun to his head. Soon after, he and his family were transported to Auschwitz, where they were murdered."

"You say it so matter-of-factly."

"Because it is a fact." Van Straten stopped to light a Dunhill, and Smith noted her hand shook slightly. "The banker's family had converted to Catholicism, a perverse irony that so many wealthy French Jews distanced themselves from their heritage or were only a fourth or an eighth Jewish, and yet they paid for that Jewishness with their lives." She dragged on the cigarette, and when she spoke again her hand was steady, her voice resolute. "In Paris, toward the end of the war, many paintings were hidden to keep them from being destroyed and out of Nazi hands. Resistance fighters sneaked them out of the Jeu de Paume, where the Nazis had stockpiled their stolen art. Some pieces were painted over and smuggled out as unimportant artworks."

Smith stopped her, retrieved his cell phone, scrolled through photos, then handed the phone over. "The painting my clients,

Perrone and Verde, discovered. Like you described, it had been hidden under another painting, painted over."

"The painting everyone had been looking for," she said, as if to herself, then asked him to send the photos to her and delete them from his phone, which he did, explaining that Perrone and Verde only had the painting for a day before it was stolen from them.

She nodded again as if the information was no surprise. Then she spoke of the painting's value. "It is not just the money. The painting is a symbol, a famous blood antiquity, paid for with lives. Many people have been after the Van Gogh, but we are quite sure Trader has it or he will have it soon. It is important, *essential*, that *we* get it. That is the assignment." She sat and faced Smith, her dark eyes on his. "It is what I do, what I have been doing for some time. Now, it is your job too. That painting was stolen once. It cannot be stolen again. You understand?"

"I'll do my best," he said.

"Do not be flip, Analyst Smith. Your best is not enough. There is no room for failure here. None."

"Sorry," he said, then asked how the Van Gogh had survived and made it to this country.

"I cannot say for sure, but many stolen paintings were resold after the war by Hitler's approved art dealers."

"How did they get away with that?"

"The art dealers were not prosecuted for their actions. The smarter ones prepared for any outcome to the war, win or lose, passing artworks on to relatives for hiding and safekeeping. Much of that artwork is still surfacing today, like this one. You will read more about that in here." She tapped the thicker folder. "The Van Gogh might never have gotten here if it had not been hidden. Paintings of this quality were often slated for the museum Hitler was planning to build in his hometown of Linz, the Führermuseum. Others were sold to finance the Third Reich's war effort. Still others were chosen by Hitler's highest-ranking henchmen, Goebbels and Göring, for their private art collections. It is possible this painting was transported along with other artworks to Göring's castle, Carinhall, whether he knew what it was or not, and stored with his other looted art and antiquities. What is important is that it has survived and we get it back. No more stolen artworks will be hidden away in castles!" She stabbed her cigarette out. "They must be returned to their rightful owners, who paid for them with their lives. Do you understand?"

"Yes," Smith said. "I do."

"Good," she said. "Then let us get back to work."

45

April 20, 1945
Carinhall
Schorfheide Forest, Germany

Reichsmarschall Hermann Göring strutted about the room, barking orders at men wrapping artwork, his massive gut barely contained in the pale-blue uniform adorned with gold embroidered eagles, swastikas, medals, and crosses, his fingernails painted bright red.

With his sixth sense for knowing when things were going well or badly, he had advanced from military officer to president of the Reichstag to Reichsmarschall, Marshal of the Empire, in less than six years, at present Hitler's number two man. But right now, he knew things were not going well; it was clear the tide of the war had turned against them. In a few months it would be over.

But he had been making plans.

Here, at Carinhall, the massive manor house he had built in the Schorfheide Forest, an hour's drive from Berlin but secluded and restricted, he had amassed over 4,000 artworks, the spoils of Jewish art collectors from Germany and the countries they had occupied, their owners sent to concentration camps that Göring himself had created, stripped of everything by the Gestapo Göring had established. He had begun moving the artwork as early as two years ago, part of it to a converted salt mine in Austria, and now, with news of the advancing Red Army, he was moving what remained *into bunkers or tunnels or burying it in the garden, while other selected works were being readied to leave the country, his men building crates for art dealers and galleries in America, several large ones destined for the Buchholz Gallery, its director a friend of the Reich, a Jew who had swapped survival for profit. There, the artworks would be sold and dispersed when the war was over for a hefty commission that would go into Göring's pocket once he was safely in South America.*

This was his last day at Carinhall, the estate named for his first wife whose body was interred on the property, and he was filled with a kind of melancholy he rarely felt, the fact that he would never come back to these sumptuously outfitted rooms—the ballroom, the library, the pool, the loft that housed his model trains equipped with model airplanes that dropped miniature bombs—the lavish hunting parties he'd held on the grounds, the lions he had borrowed from the Berlin Zoo. All of it over, but he would take what he could.

Soon he would be leaving to make an appearance at a party for Hitler's birthday, and from there to Berchtesgaden, in southern Germany. He gazed through the panoramic windows as if trying to memorize the sprawling grounds and forest, then looked around the room, a last look; he had already given orders to a small unit of the Luftwaffe, the air force over which he presided, to blow up the estate as soon as the Soviets were in sight. The thought pained him, but it was essential, and he had a temporary remedy—the vial slipped from his pocket, two paracodeine tablets popped into his mouth in plain sight of his men, his morphine addiction no secret.

The men packing the art were working fast, two sweating uniformed soldiers filling the crates with artwork for the Buchholz Gallery in New York, a city they dreamed of seeing and never would. The paintings, chosen by the gallery's director, Curt Valentin, were stacked along one wall: important work by Picasso, Braque, Cézanne, Gauguin, Van Gogh, Beckmann, all degenerate work that would fetch handsome fees in the United States. The men packing the work knew nothing about the art or why anyone would want it, but they were good soldiers who followed orders, even now, with defeat staring them in the face, and they hoped the Reichsmarschall would remember their hard work and loyalty when the time came.

One of them, a young man from a modest Bavarian town, plucked a small painting off the floor where it had fallen facedown, a mostly black-and-white portrait of a woman with a realistically painted tear in her eye. It was one of the few artworks he understood or liked.

"This one too?" he asked the other soldier and held it up for inspection.

The other soldier shrugged. "Ask der Eiserne," he said, using Göring's nickname, the iron man.

The young Bavarian soldier glanced across the room to where the Reichsmarschall was berating a soldier for his clumsy work, snapping his riding crop inches from the man's face. No, he would not ask the Reichsmarschall anything at all. Instead, he wrapped the small portrait of the woman with the realistic tear in her eye and wedged it into the crate with other paintings bound for the New York gallery. He thought the painting had a better chance of survival than he did.

46

Museumplein was only a few blocks from our hotel, open and airy with paths and lawns, people milling about or lined up in front of one of the three museums that shared the sprawling campus-like space. It was a beautiful day, full-on spring, the blue sky with cotton-ball clouds reflected in the curving glass of the Van Gogh Museum.

A few minutes early for our 9:00 a.m. slot, Alex and I joined the line. The guard was just beginning to let people in when a woman came striding across the lawn.

"Luke Perrone?" she asked, a bit breathless, drawing out my name, *Loook*. "Jude's friend, Carolien Cahill. Car-o-leen," she repeated for emphasis.

Jude hadn't described her, and she wasn't at all what I'd expected. I guessed she was in her sixties though her skin was smooth, eyes clear and blue with appealing laugh lines, her hair bright white, a strikingly beautiful woman almost my height and slender in tight black jeans and a blazer that looked like iridescent snakeskin.

She admired Alex's gold locket. "My mother's," Alex said, then admired her jacket. "Imitation python," Carolien said, and told Alex where to buy one and offered to take her, and Alex agreed. I had to interrupt to let them know the guard was asking for our tickets, and they laughed as if they were old friends.

Inside, light streamed through the glass ceiling and glinted off the chrome escalator that took us down to the recessed lobby and bookstore, behind it a wide, dimly lit room, its entire back wall covered with a mural of Van Gogh's painted eyes.

Carolien pointed out that all Van Gogh's self-portraits were in here. "Except his last, the one that disappeared from his funeral." Alex and I exchanged a look. Maybe Jude had told Carolien about the painting we'd found, but before I could ask, she added, "I too lost a painting, my grandfather's. Not a portrait, but a very well-known painting, a version of which you will see upstairs."

I remembered Jude having said something about her grandfather or great-grandfather owning a famous Van Gogh, but I was already walking past her into the room of self-portraits, some sketchy, others more finished, some in his famous straw hat, others with a pipe, several of a young, boyish Vincent, others of an older Van Gogh, though he had never gotten very old.

Carolien directed us to one of the two paintings in plexi boxes on stands in the center of the room, Vincent in his straw hat, like the one in New York's Met, a pipe dangling from his mouth, lower lip a slash of hot pink, brows highlighted in a way that gave him a brooding look. "You feel like you know him in this one, don't you?" Carolien said, and she was right. There was something alive in the painting.

"I feel things, sense things in paintings," she said. "In people too, always have. I am sort of an empath. Perhaps it is from my upbringing…the tragedy my family suffered, something I did not witness, but was passed down to me in…feeling."

Alex asked her about her tragedy, but she waved a hand. "Not now. Later," she said, and directed us back to the painting, noting the date, 1887. "Vincent at thirty-four."

Three years younger than me, though I thought he looked older, a little worn down by life.

"He made it during the two years he lived with his brother Theo in Paris," Alex added, while I moved from portrait to portrait, noting several had been painted in the same year, but all different, as if there was more than one Vincent, and I supposed there was, depending on his mood and mental state. I stopped at another plexiglass box, this one with a small rectangular palette and a few partially squeezed tubes of paint, and for a moment I could see Vincent, thumb looped through the palette mixing colors. I could have stood there for hours had Alex not urged me on.

Upstairs, we went through painted scenes of peasant life, and Van Gogh's famous *The Potato Eaters*, dark and moody. Alex remarked it was like Cézanne's *Card Players*, which was true, though I thought Cézanne was all about structure, and Van Gogh all about emotion, perhaps why he appealed to so many.

Carolien and Alex were swapping tales of Vincent's thwarted love life, the unrequited love for his cousin, when we came upon a group of skull paintings I'd never seen before.

"Memento mori," Carolien said. "Latin for 'Remember you must die.'" She crossed herself, then laughed. "An odd habit for a Jewish girl, but I was brought up Catholic." She explained she hadn't known about her Jewish roots until her father died and she'd found letters and a journal he'd written about his parents' lives.

Alex told her that her grandmother was Jewish, her mother's mother, someone she had adored who had died when she was a young girl, and how she too had been brought up a Christian, her grandmother's religion never discussed. "I didn't find out about my grandmother until I was in college."

"Family secrets," Carolien whispered.

I noted the way Van Gogh had outlined one of the skulls, and how it reminded me of Jean-Michel Basquiat, the famous New York artist whose brilliant career was even shorter than Vincent's, and how he too had painted skulls. Carolien asked if I was an art historian.

"No, but I teach it. Alex is the art historian. I'm just a painter."

"Me too," Carolien said. "Though I haven't painted much in the last few years because my search has consumed my life."

Alex asked how, but again Carolien put her off, commenting instead on a group of landscapes, how they depicted the harvest, "the cycle of life and death," she said, and Alex concurred, the two women in sync.

Carolien stopped us in the next room. "This is it," she said indicating a painting of Van Gogh's famous bedroom in Arles. "His first version. There are two others, one in the Musée d'Orsay in Paris, the other in the Art Institute of Chicago. But this one belonged to my grandfather." She elbowed her way through the crowd surrounding the painting, taking us with her. "A great painting, so witty, so ugly."

And it was true, the painting was exaggerated and awkward, the bed, the floor atilt, the color harsh but striking, though over time we had come to see it as beautiful.

"It belonged to your *grandfather*?" Alex asked, incredulous.

"He owned many impressionist and post-impressionist works. He was one of the great art collectors of his time, of any time," she said, and I expected her to say more about her grandfather, but she talked instead about Vincent's time in Arles in the yellow house and of his stormy relationship with Gauguin, who had come to live but left after only six weeks. "He was unable to bear the constant arguments with Vincent," she said. "It was after he left that Vincent cut off his ear."

"And he wrapped it up and delivered it to a prostitute," I said.

"Yes," she said. "Though in fact, he was bringing it to Gauguin to show him what his desertion had caused. He expected to find his friend at the brothel. Alas, some poor girl got the ear! Can you imagine?"

"Talk about bad boyfriends and bad gifts," Alex said, and they laughed.

We went through the rest of the museum, all three floors, my eyes and mind on overload, feet starting to ache. Then, we sat in the lobby where Carolien told us she was a widow with a grown daughter who lived in Germany.

"Where my people are originally from," she said, and Alex asked if her daughter was visiting family. "No, there is no family left," Carolien said, then painted on a smile and asked how we liked Amsterdam.

"I wish we were staying longer," I said, listing all the places I still wanted to see, and Alex said she'd been dying to see the Anne Frank House, but there were no tickets.

"My friend is a curator there," Carolien said and was immediately on her cell, speaking in Dutch, then off quickly. "You can go in an hour."

We were tired but no way we'd have said no, Alex clearly thrilled.

I suggested we all get coffee, but Carolien had to run an errand, so we swapped cell numbers and planned to meet at the Anne Frank House in an hour.

47

Carolien kept Alex company in the lobby while Luke hit the restroom, the two of them still gossiping like old friends. Above them, a band of digital images was constantly changing, a Van Gogh self-portrait in triplicate, details of his painted eyes, then his bedroom in Arles, the painting, then a photo.

Alex pointed out it was the bedroom in her grandfather's painting, but Carolien corrected her.

"No. The bedroom in my grandfather's painting is in Arles. That one is Vincent's bedroom in Auvers-sur-Oise, his last bedroom, where he died." She was explaining how her quest had taken her to that town several times when Alex glanced past her and thought she saw her schoolmate.

"Jennifer? Is that you?" Alex wasn't entirely sure it was her NYU friend behind the Jackie O sunglasses and scarf.

"My God! Alex!" she said, tugging off her scarf and patting her hair into place. "What are you doing here?"

"Looking at Van Gogh, what else?" Alex said and laughed, noting that the usually perfect Jennifer looked a bit disheveled. She introduced Carolien. "I told you I was going to Amsterdam, didn't I?"

"Oh. Yes. Of course," Jennifer said, a digital Van Gogh self-portrait reflecting in her sunglasses. "So, what happened with your visit to LESAH? Did they ever authenticate that mysterious painting of yours?"

Alex realized she hadn't seen or spoken to Jennifer since the day of the mugging. She touched her eye reflexively, said she'd never made it to the auction house but waved it away like it wasn't important. "If I'd known you'd be here, we could have had drinks or dinner."

"I'm only here a few days," Jennifer said. "Let's have dinner when we get back." She replaced her scarf and tied it under her neck. "Sorry, I've got to run. Nice to meet you," she said to Carolien, then flashed a smile and stepped onto the escalator.

Alex watched her ascend. "What a coincidence! She's a classmate of mine, a friend."

"She is not your friend," Carolien said, a hand to her lips. "Forgive me, I did not mean to say that. I must go. I will see you at the Frank House." She started to leave, but Alex stopped her.

"What did you mean by that?"

The digital pictures had switched to anime versions of Van Gogh, casting the room in garish colors. "Sorry, I just sensed something," Carolien said. "As I told you, I get these…feelings, these sensations. But it is nothing, I am not a fortune teller. Please, forget I said it. I am sure she is perfectly lovely." She smiled. "So, what is this mysterious painting of yours she referred to?"

"Oh. That," Alex said, debating whether she was ready or willing to discuss it. "I'll tell you later."

Carolien raised an eyebrow. "We have so much to discuss *later*."

"You won't believe who I bumped into," Alex said, sunlight streaming in as we headed up the escalator. "Jennifer."

"Who's that?" I asked, my mind still preoccupied with all the Van Gogh paintings.

"You know, from school. The friend who got me to the Lower East Side Auction House," she said, then frowned and I asked what was wrong. "Something Carolien said about Jennifer, that she wasn't my friend."

"How could Carolien know that?"

"Just something she felt, all very woo-woo, witchy woman."

"Old world," I suggested, something I'd felt about Carolien, an air of history and the past about her.

"And a little mysterious about that past," Alex said. "But I'll find out."

"Now, who's being a witch?" I put my arm around her, and we stepped outside into the sunlight.

Alex suggested we get something to eat to fortify ourselves for the Anne Frank House, so we each got coffee and a snack at an outdoor kiosk, then found a bench where I ate a sandwich, a *broodje* as the Dutch called them, mine grilled ham and cheese with mustard, specifically a *tosti*, while Alex settled for a slice of buttered bread with crispy sugar-coated anise seeds that looked like bugs. The sky was clear and bright, the temperature perfect, and I felt happy in a way I hadn't felt for a long time, away from home and teaching and the responsibilities of daily life.

"Let's stay here forever," I said.

Alex reminded me I had a show coming up, and my classes wouldn't wait, and she needed to finish her thesis, and that was it: real life came charging back.

"I still can't get over running into Jennifer," she said. "What a coincidence."

I reminded her what my uncle Tommy, the retired cop always said. "No such thing as coincidence."

"That's funny," Alex said. "Because my mother always said the exact opposite, that *everything* is coincidence."

48

Alone with the folders, his mind in overdrive, Smith tried to take it in, the assignment in front of him: to find a black-market art dealer who had eluded arrest for years.

But not this time, not if Van Straten had her way. He pictured the woman he'd met at the auction house and hadn't liked, reassessing her now, the way she commanded the room.

From his years at INTERPOL, he knew the dangers of the underground art world and the risks he was taking but he could not entertain them now. He had made a decision, he was here, and he would do it.

He opened the first folder.

Two cups of coffee and several stroopwafels later, he had memorized most of his new identity as Calvin Lewis, private art dealer, and the recent sales he had supposedly made—a Beckmann group portrait, an Emil Nolde nude, a Picasso cubist painting, an etching of a rotting skull by the German artist Otto Dix, all the work "degenerate," all of it looted.

He made a note to ask Van Straten if the sales, like Lewis, were fictional, at least the part about Lewis being the person who'd sold them.

Then he sat up, stretched, did a few squats before he sagged back into his chair and opened the second folder, the history. He started at the beginning, reviewing Alfred Rosenberg's ERR, "the most effective art-looting organization of the Third Reich." Then, the Dienststelle Mühlmann, an organization that operated like the ERR in the Netherlands. That was followed by a list of prominent French Jews whose art collections had been sold in "paradigmatic forced transfer," in other words sales made under duress, under the gun, their homes and apartments plundered once they had fled or were sent to camps, all their possessions up for grabs because they had been declared "ownerless."

The word stopped him, images developing like old photographs in his mind: an evening alone in the projects while his mother worked, his one-bedroom apartment in Lyon after his divorce, two places without character, and ones he had not owned. But had he felt *ownerless?*

Municipal Cop Vox interrupted with a plate of cheese and fruit.

"I thought you might be hungry," she said. He thanked her, even managed a smile.

When she left, he went back to the folder, memorizing the names of Hitler's approved art dealers, Hildebrand Gurlitt, Karl Buchholz, Ferdinand Möller, Bernhard Böhmer. These were most infamous Nazi art advisors in charge of procuring art for the Führermuseum, Hitler's proposed museum for his hometown of Linz, Austria, to be stocked entirely with stolen art. There were subheadings and paragraphs on each of the dealers and one on Gurlitt's son, Cornelius, which included a police report of a search made on his Munich apartment in 2012 that had uncovered more than 1,200 pieces of Nazi-looted art. More in his home in Salzburg, Austria.

Only a decade ago, Smith thought, recognizing that the men who dealt in looted art had continued to do so.

He kept reading—of Nazi confiscation committees, of anti-Jewish laws that had banned Jews from parks, museums, cafés, movies, prohibited them from using trams or buses, or driving their own cars, even owning a car, everything closed to them, signs in shop windows declaring, Voor Joden Verboden. He checked the glossary: *Forbidden for Jews.*

It brought to mind what Van Straten had said about Jews who had distanced themselves from their religion or were only a fraction Jewish, but who had paid for their Jewishness with their lives, and it struck a chord about his own racial mix, what it would have meant then and still meant.

Several pages detailed the 1939 Fischer auction at the Grand Hotel National at Lake Lucerne, along with a faded photo that showed a beautiful Alpine setting where 350 invited guests had come to bid on stolen art. Smith noted how some, like Alfred Barr, then director of New York's Museum of Modern Art, had publicly boycotted the event but purchased artwork indirectly, a way to hide the fact that he was buying art from murdered Jews.

Someone had written in the margin, *Stolen art = stolen lives.*

One of the auction's lots was circled in red: Lot 45, Vincent van Gogh, *Self-Portrait.*

Was this the painting Perrone and Verde had hired him to find? He wondered where they were now and what they were doing. He was thinking he had to find them and tell them to quit, to warn them, when the door opened.

It was Steiner. "I just wanted to remind you that you are working for INTERPOL."

"Noted," Smith said, just as Van Straten appeared in the doorway, with Jaager behind her.

"What are you doing here?" she asked Steiner.

"I wanted to see how my colleague was faring."

"Well, you have seen him," she said, holding the door open and waiting until he left, then asked, "What did he say to you?"

"Nothing," Smith said.

She made a face, then gave him the news they had already gotten several hits, responses to the art they had put on the dark web. "We are sure one of them is our target, Trader."

"That was fast."

"Things move swiftly when there are no rules or regulations," she said, then nodded at Jaager, who took over.

"The art went out on a site like Silk Road 2.0, now defunct thanks to the FBI, but there are others cropping up all the time. The dark web is like a garden of weeds: kill a patch here and another patch sprouts up there." Jaager went on about *dot.onion* sites, "part of the onion router. You know what that is?"

"The Tor network," Smith said. "I know a little from investigating stolen artwork being sold on the network at INTERPOL."

Jaager nodded, describing how Tor inhabited the fringes of the internet and served as the underlying technology of the dark web, a collection of hidden sites inaccessible by regular browsers or a search engine like Google.

"You can skip the Dark Web 101," Smith said.

Jaager frowned but got the point and cut to the chase. "We followed a format used by the FBI, establishing nodes in an existing network that we know sells stolen art, arms, and other illegal contraband. Then we assumed one of their identities, anonymously of course, and offered our wares—that is, Lewis's wares. Being inside the network allowed us to see the identities and locations of the buyers who responded to the art being offered. You follow?"

Smith nodded. "How many buyers were there?"

"Several dozen. But we narrowed it down, first by location, then other intel we have on Trader. Emails, phone log, not as hidden as he thinks."

Smith was impressed. "So, what do you do with the other buyers?"

"They are now on a list," Van Straten said. "In time they will be pursued. For now, we are concentrating on our target, on Trader." She thanked Jaager, who left the room.

"He is very good at what he does, if a little overzealous," she said, then took a seat across from Smith and quizzed him on his new identity. He thought he did well, stumbling on only one or two answers. "Those mistakes could jeopardize this project and cost you your life."

Smith noted the order of her priorities but didn't say so, only that he would study harder.

"Good," she said. "I have rarely lost an agent and I do not want to lose one now. You understand?"

Smith nodded, the word *rarely* echoing in his mind.

49

Except for a modest white plaque, there was little to distinguish Prinsengracht 263 from others on the street. It was an Amsterdam canal house, with an attached modern wing and open courtyard, which was where we waited for Carolien, Alex reflecting on the first time she'd read Anne Frank's diary. "I was her age, twelve, and felt such a kinship with her, both of us girls on the cusp of becoming young women." Then she talked about Anne's father, Otto, the only survivor of the eight residents who'd been in hiding. "Anne adored him," she said, and stopped, her cell phone ringing. She gave it a quick, almost furtive look, then turned it off. But I had to ask.

"Who was it?"

"No one."

"No one has been calling a lot," I said.

Alex said nothing for a minute, then looked at me, her eyes so skittish I got scared.

"What is it?" I asked.

She took a deep breath. "It's my father. He's been in touch and…"

"Your *father*?"

"I've been meaning to tell you, but things kept getting in the way. And I knew what you'd say, what you'd think."

Did she really know all the things that were firing in my brain— what had gone down a year ago, the lies and deceitfulness, her father's arrest and disappearance? "I can't believe it," I said. "That you'd let him back in your life."

"He's my father, all I've got. My mother is fading. You know that. He got in touch. He begged my forgiveness. At first, I wouldn't speak to him, wanted nothing to do with him, but he kept calling and…"

I was trying to control my anger and judgment, the idea that she'd kept this from me, while she repeated how she'd wanted to tell me but knew I wouldn't understand. And she was right, I didn't.

"Have you seen him?" I asked.

"No. He just wants me in his life in some small way, that's all. He isn't well."

"What does that mean?" I asked, and she said she wasn't sure, but he'd implied it was serious, life-threatening, and she'd found it impossible to deny him these small communications.

"Are you going to see him?"

"Maybe," she said. "I haven't decided but—"

I didn't let her finish; I exploded. "Jesus! I can't believe it! Bringing a criminal back into your life, into *our* life, *my* life, without asking, without consulting with me."

"It's not up to you," she said. "I knew you wouldn't understand. It's exactly why I didn't tell you."

"Why you lied."

"I didn't *lie*."

"Just forgot to tell me. Like the last time."

Alex faced me with a look of hurt and anger. "You won't ever give that up, will you? It's always there in your back pocket to use against me!"

She was right about that too. I held on to it even though I didn't want to, my secret weapon against her. But I didn't say any more, and she didn't either, both of us quietly seething, looking past each other. And that's when I saw Carolien coming toward us.

"Sorry," she said, a bit breathless. "The errands took longer than expected and the bus was slow."

"It's *fine*," I said, biting off the word.

"Oh." Carolien apologized and I did too. She looked from me to Alex. "Everything okay?"

"*Fine*," we said simultaneously.

Carolien nodded slowly, told us her friend would be here in a minute to bring us into the museum, the three of us standing there, no one speaking, the air around us thick. Then Carolien cut through it. "You know what I miss most about marriage? The small things, the things that seem to mean nothing, even the arguing because it means what we had was real. Sometimes, I am in a shop or on the street and I see a young couple fighting, and I want to go up to them and say, "There is so little time, less than you imagine, and in the end, it will not matter, this thing you are fighting about." She gave us each a sharp, sweet look.

"Wow, you *are* an empath," Alex said, and managed a laugh, and for one terrible moment, I thought about life without Alex and put my arm around her. Then Carolien's friend was there, ushering us into the Anne Frank House where we put on headphones, the audio guide describing what had gone on in each room.

The first, an introduction with photos and text; the next, more pictures and a yellow Star of David that Jews had been forced to wear, framed under glass like a piece of art.

I had imagined the hiding place as an attic, but it was the back half of the house, the front Otto Frank's business, where a few of his loyal employees had risked their lives to protect his family until they could no longer.

A light box mounted on the wall had photos of the people who'd been in hiding, presenting them like the cast of a play, before we headed up a narrow staircase, the steps worn over time.

The line stopped at the top. Carolien, just ahead of me, looked over her shoulder and whispered, "I have been here many times and each time, just here, I want to turn back, the memories…" Then the line moved and she turned away and continued up the stairs, and I wondered what she had been about to say.

We were on a small landing with faded wallpaper and an old bookcase that had been built to hide the annex, a secret entranceway that swiveled open and closed. We stepped through it into a dimly lit hallway, into the past.

Carolien saw me looking at pencil marks on the wall.

"It is where Otto Frank measured his children's growth during their two years in hiding," she said at the same time I heard it on audio in unsettling stereo.

Anne's bedroom, the focal point, was narrow and dimly lit, almost claustrophobic, no furniture, only Anne's photographs and clippings pasted to both walls and preserved under glass.

We moved from one picture to the next, bygone movie stars like Greta Garbo and Ginger Rogers, the Dutch and English royal families, a large color photo that Alex pointed out was Norma Shearer, "a thirties movie star, and Anne's favorite." She stood back to take in the wall of photos and clippings. "It's a scrapbook of dreams she created to escape reality, a portal into Anne's imagination and fantasies."

I was drawn to a reproduction of Michelangelo's *Pietà* and a Leonardo self-portrait that took me back to Florence a year ago, my own ghosts competing with the ones here.

On the far wall, a large photo of Anne, laughing, its silence filling the room. Alex was staring at it too, tears in her eyes. I touched her arm and thought, *I will not be mad at her; life is too short.*

"Anne's father moved the family from Germany to Amsterdam to save them," Carolien said so quietly I removed my headset to hear her. "A tragic mistake made by so many…" She drew in a breath and her words drifted off.

Just beyond Anne's bedroom, the one spartan bathroom shared by eight people. I thought about my childhood home with its two bathrooms, one full upstairs, a half downstairs, and how much I'd resented sharing them with my parents.

Another narrow staircase led us to where the other family, the van Pels, had lived, and where everyone ate, photos on the wall that showed what it had looked like at the time, with a dining table and chairs and a rug. Now, only a granite sink remained, and on one wall, a framed shopping list found in the pocket of a coat left behind, its poignant banality bringing everything to life.

A cordoned-off staircase led to the attic which had served as a room for the van Pelses' teenage son, Peter.

"Anne's first kiss," Alex said, and touched my hand.

Then a room of videos, Otto Frank speaking of their capture—"a man came to the attic, and that was the end"—a shock as the Allies had already landed at Normandy and he'd expected they would be saved any day. Instead, they'd been arrested, sent to Westerbork transit camp, then to Auschwitz. "That terrible journey," he said. "Three days in a closed cattle truck…" His words in my head as I watched a grainy black-and-white film that filled a wall, of Jews being herded onto trains, Gestapo soldiers slamming doors and strutting beside them, the audio supplying details, "September 3, 1944, the last transport to Auschwitz… Overall, nearly 107,000 Dutch Jews were transported to Nazi extermination camps."

On a separate wall, two pages, typed and faded. "Transport lists of the people sent to Auschwitz-Birkenau, all of it documented, the orderliness of killing," Carolien said, her finger tracing a column. "Here, Cohen, Hans. And here, Cohen, Gertrud. It is hard to believe. I know because I could not believe it until it became personal." She seemed to be talking to herself, and though I wanted to ask questions, it didn't feel right to intrude.

In the next room, there were more videos, survivors bearing witness, describing the camps, "the filth and dirt, the starving children...unorganized hell... Anne had no chance to survive with the typhoid... I don't know how I survived," and I wondered how anyone survived, if *I* would have survived.

"Anne and her sister went to Bergen-Belsen," Carolien said, "where they both contracted typhus and died. Only two months before the camp was liberated."

I didn't want to imagine it, these two young women guilty of nothing but their faith, condemned to die.

At the end of the room a map pinpointed the locations of every Nazi concentration camp. Alex grasped my arm, and we headed downstairs past a wall-sized black-and-white photo of the entrance to Auschwitz. It was as if we were entering, not leaving, and we moved quickly under it and into the Diary Room, where we paused in front of Anne's red plaid diary and a photograph of the hopeful teenager at her desk. On it, a page with her small, precise handwriting.

In the museum shop, Alex bought a new copy of the diary, and then we were outside, walking along a canal, people strolling past and laughing, boats gliding on the water, the midday sun bright, the sky blue, flower stalls and tulips everywhere, a world seemingly untroubled, as if someone had plucked us out of a black-and-white horror film and dropped us into a candy-colored musical.

Carolien suggested a drink and we stopped at an outdoor café where she ordered a beer, Alex a white wine, and though I wanted a scotch, I knew better and settled for coffee. Conversation was difficult at first, the ghosts of Prinsengracht 263 still with us, then Carolien started telling us her story.

50

"Those names on the transport list," Carolien said. "They were my grandparents, Hans and Gertrud Cohen. My grandfather's family changed their name to Cahill in the early 1900s and converted to Catholicism." She explained how both her grandparents were raised as Christians, "so far removed from their Jewish heritage they did not know it," then paused to take a breath. "They were first taken to Theresienstadt, the *model* camp. *Only* thirty-five thousand Jews died within its walls. I did a lot of research on them, and the camp," she said. "Sometimes I wish I had not, that I could *un*know it, *un*see it."

She stopped, downed half her beer, then spoke fast, almost without taking a breath. "My grandfather arrived at the camp in his best suit, my grandmother in a fancy dress and fur coat. They had no idea what lay in store for them, the two of them immediately separated, put in isolation cells, my grandfather interned in the Little Fortress, a hell within hell, run by sadistic guards. There are eyewitness accounts to his death, savagely beaten to death by guards, while my grandmother was sent to Auschwitz and gassed almost immediately, one might say mercifully. She was spared years of suffering." Carolien finally took that breath, and sighed deeply. "The only reason I am here is that their son, my father, was in boarding school in England. He never saw his parents again. After the war, he came back to Holland, where he met my mother."

A group of people at a nearby table were talking and laughing loudly, and an upbeat Taylor Swift tune emanated from inside the café. Alex reached for my hand.

After a minute, I asked Carolien why her grandparents had not fled.

She gave me a sad, ironic smile. "Because they believed they were *safe*. They were full-fledged Dutch citizens who moved in the highest strata of society, the most refined, cultured people one could imagine, art lovers, music lovers, one of the most respected banking families in Germany, then Holland, assured by their gentile friends they had nothing to fear. An all-too-common story, a tragic one, and a cautionary tale." She leaned forward, her look sad but fierce. "Do not think you are safe, that something like this could not happen to you. When the wolves are at your neighbor's door, they will soon be at yours. And they were at my grandparents' door, forcing them to sell their art, their jewelry, their antiques and furniture, everything they owned. With bills of sale and guarantees of money they never saw."

"What happened to their art collection after that?" Alex asked.

"It was dispersed, some pieces likely fought over by Hitler and his cronies, who competed for the best work. Some pieces were possibly destroyed out of ignorance, but most were resold by opportunistic art dealers, art *thieves*, many who continue to thrive off such sales today." She took a sip of beer, her hand shaking slightly. "My grandfather had a coveted collection. It is why the Nazis targeted him. Old masters, impressionism, that Van Gogh you saw earlier today."

It seemed like days ago we'd seen Van Gogh's *Bedroom in Arles*, like something I had dreamed. I asked if her grandfather had other Van Gogh works.

"Ink and pencil drawings, two landscape paintings, a well-known portrait of Madame Ginoux. It has taken me years to reconstruct the collection." She described going through auction records and bills of sales, hundreds of pieces, then trying to prove her grandfather had owned them to get them back. "The people in charge of restitution do not always make it easy. But my search continues, and I will not stop. Many pieces are still missing, and when the legal ways to find them dry up, there are other ways."

"How?" Alex asked.

Carolien paused a moment. "There are ways, people who deal in 'black money,' off-the-books transactions, who trade on the dark web. But they do not scare me. One cannot allow the thieves and thugs to win!"

"So, you've done this before, dealt with such people?" I asked.

Carolien fixed me with her cool blue eyes. "If you want something bad enough—and I am determined to locate *all* of my grandfather's collection—you must be willing to take risks."

We were quiet a moment. Then I looked at Alex and nodded, and she understood what I was thinking and we told Carolien about the painting we had found and lost and were trying to find again.

Carolien listened until we had finished, then she said, "If there is one thing I know, it is how to find a lost painting, where to look and who to ask. If you like, I will help you."

"Yes!" Alex said, excited, but I held back. I had been down this road before and knew the danger. "Don't you agree?" Alex asked me.

I took a moment, thought about an innocent monk in Florence who had tried to help me and lost his life in the process. "Maybe," I said. "I'm not sure."

"Well, *I* am," Alex said.

And because I could not let her do it alone, I said, "Okay, I'm with you."

51

You watch them, wondering who the older woman is. You had no idea they knew anyone in Amsterdam. Could she be a competitor, someone interested in the painting? You must report this right away. Unless he already knows. Lately, he seems to know things before you tell him. But you know something else: that you are no longer the only one watching.

A look one way, then the other, checking the boats on the canal, the dark alley behind you, and sure enough, you spot the guy amid a small crowd of Japanese tourists. He stands out so easily with that tattooed neck of his. This is the second time you've seen Gunther since you arrived, no coincidence. So, he is watching them too. Or is he watching *you*?

Cigarette lit with a shaking hand, you ask yourself what has changed, replaying your conversations while you watch the three of them, the older woman doing most of the talking, the old fool.

Or are you the fool?

After all you have done, the chances you've taken, he wouldn't dare cut you out, not with everything you know about him. You send a text, ask who you should follow, casually mention if he knows about Gunther. But of course he knows; he knows everything.

The trio is finishing a second round of drinks, but you still don't know which of them to follow when they leave, waiting for his reply to your text with an eye on Gunther, loitering under a tree beside the canal. Gunther, of all people.

You watch the trio pay the bill and check your phone; still no answer to your text. You are debating who to follow when you see Gunther move out of the shadows and follow the guy, and you feel better. He is not watching you after all. But still, you wonder: Why bring in a second watchdog? Aren't you enough? Are you no longer trusted? Something to find out. Though right now, you have to decide which of the women to follow.

52

Carolien took off with a promise to meet us again, leaving Alex and me alone after a temporary if not quite agreed-upon truce, but Alex did not waste time getting back to our earlier discussion.

"What upsets me is that you don't understand that it's not about you or our relationship," she said, admitting she should have told me but hadn't because she didn't want to defend herself and hadn't yet figured out if she really wanted her father back in her life. "But it's *my* decision," she said. "Do you see that?"

I said I did, even if I didn't think it was a good idea for her to reconnect with her father, even if it still annoyed me that she'd kept it from me. I apologized for the things I'd said. "What Carolien said is true, life's too short."

"So, we're okay?" she asked, and I said we were because I intended to make sure of it. Then we talked about Carolien and the possibility of her helping us find the painting, something I was a lot less sure of, but Alex was excited.

We paid the bill, exchanged a kiss, and despite being tired, we were energized. Alex dashed off to see the conservator while I headed to my gallery meetings.

According to Google Maps, the Visscher Gallery was ten minutes away and I had twenty-five till my two thirty appointment, so I took it slow, ambling along a canal and looking in store windows. I rehashed a bit of the fight, though I didn't want to, still surprised Alex could forgive her father after all he'd done; I'd barely forgiven mine for a lot less. But I pushed it out of my mind, not wanting to think about her father, or mine.

I crossed a bridge, stopping a moment to look into the canal, the dark water reflecting a string of red and gray peak-roofed houses, then a wide street where I waited for a cable car to pass and followed my GPS, which took me down a small cobblestone street lined with pots of tulips and bicycles, past lots of stores including a coffee shop, the window advertising every kind of weed, CBG, and CBD, something I'd quit along with alcohol a decade ago. Just in front, a group of young people were huddled in a cloud of smoke, among them the tattooed guy. I moved fast, ready to confront him, to find out why he was following me. But when I got closer, I saw I was wrong. It was just another kid with a tattooed neck he would regret one day.

Inside the coffee shop was marijuana in all its forms: loose, bagged, rolled joints, with names like Haze, Stoney, White Widow, one called Amnesia, a name that brought back a memory of blackouts.

The young guy behind the counter, long hair, a droopy mustache, asked if I was looking for anything special, and before I could say "just looking," laid a reefer on the counter.

"Try this," he said. "Best hashish we have. A few tokes and your heart rate will drop, the world slows, and you will be worry free."

Worry free sounded good but I said, "No thanks," started out of the store, then turned back and bought it. It's only weed, I told myself, not booze. How can it hurt?

Outside, with the joint between my lips, I heard my sponsor's words, *For you, it's a gateway back to drinking*, and saw myself waking up in a dumpster or falling off the wagon a year ago in Paris, and dropped the reefer in a trash can. Then, feeling righteous, I rechecked my GPS and walked a few blocks until I found the Visscher Gallery.

A moment to think up a few good things to say about my work, then I pushed through the gallery doors.

53

The Visscher Gallery, a converted industrial space, was cool and minimal with whitewashed walls and a concrete floor, the current exhibition by an artist best known for a piece that had caused a stir at a U.S. art fair, now here, a banana duct-taped to the wall. An affluent-looking couple, furs on her, a gold Rolex on him, were debating whether to buy the piece with a gallery representative.

"Is it a special banana?" the wife asked.

"No," the rep said. "That is the point. It is very Warholian."

I leaned in, couldn't help it. "More Duchampian than Warholian," I said, though they ignored me as they were joined by a stocky middle-aged man in a bold striped suit, Vigo Visscher, who informed them there were two holds on the piece, but it could be theirs for $120K less a 10 percent "collector's discount."

The man said, "Sold," and Visscher promised to get them the piece once the show came down in three weeks.

That's going to be one rotten banana, I thought, and waited for them to leave, then introduced myself to Visscher and mentioned Mattia Beuhler's name, which got me an invitation to the back room, where he proudly pointed out a small tin on a pedestal, *"Merde d'artiste."*

I knew from teaching that it was the work of Italian artist Piero Manzoni who had vacuum-packed ninety tins of his own shit, all numbered and dated.

"The artist's body, its fluids and excrement, as art and commodity," I said in my most professorial tone.

"Very good, I will use that," Visscher said, then indicated several other well-known pieces of conceptual art, Bruce Nauman's *Self-Portrait as a Fountain*, a photo of the artist spewing a thin stream of water out of his mouth, next to color photographs of Robert Smithson's *Spiral Jetty*, an earthwork in Utah's Great Salt Lake.

I was surprised to see an actual painting leaning against the back wall, all black, though after a minute I began to see the squares within the square, all in subtle shades of black, and recognized the artist too, "Ad Reinhardt."

Visscher nodded, then directed my attention to a sculpture, about three feet high, of what appeared to be a child on his knees, facing in the opposite direction. "It is called *Him*," he said, leading me to the other side where I saw it was a miniature, perfectly rendered sculptural portrait of Adolf Hitler, so realistic it gave me a chill.

"Wax and polyester resin with applied pigment. So lifelike, isn't it? Of course, the suit and hair are real."

Too real, I thought.

"Hitler was a great art lover," Visscher said.

"A wannabe artist, rejected from art school."

"History might have gone differently had he been accepted."

"Some people take rejection worse than others," I said, immediately regretting the quip but Visscher laughed, which made it worse. "I am selling the piece for your dealer."

"Mattia Beuhler is buying it?"

"No. He is *selling* it. Rather, I am, for him. Like most Americans, Mattia likes to appear pure and innocent."

I didn't bother to argue that Beuhler wasn't American or that few Americans I knew cared about looking pure or innocent, especially when he dangled the possibility of an exhibition at his gallery.

"Of course, Mattia will get you into U.S. shows—the Whitney Biennial, the Carnegie International—but I can guarantee your work is in Documenta and the Venice Biennale and the Berlin Biennale and the Italian Biennale Gherdëina."

Wow. I never thought anyone could guarantee that, though I could see he was serious. Still, I wasn't sure I liked the idea of my paintings sharing a room with a mini-Hitler, but I thanked him and told him I'd consider it, which seemed to annoy him *and* whet his appetite. He offered to buy a couple of my paintings outright. I didn't say yes or no—the only time in my art life I'd ever played it cool—told him I was running late, and took off. It seemed to be my day for being self-righteous.

My second appointment was at the Wil Kuhr Gallery, a town house, two stories and brightly lit, a dream space for someone who made big paintings, like me.

The young man at the front desk, dressed in white tee, white jeans, red lipstick, and matching nails, fetched Wil Kuhr while I circled the gallery, taking in its eclectic mix of sculpture, pottery, and paintings.

I was bent over a large ceramic bowl when I smelled perfume and stood to face a woman with dark-red lipstick, hennaed hair, and Elton John glasses. All in white, obviously the gallery costume, hers a starched white shirt and skinny white jeans. I guessed she was sixtysomething, though her face was practically unlined.

"I am Wil Kuhr," she said, quickly adding, "You were expecting a man?"

"Only from your name," I said.

"Wil, as in Wilhelmina. But no one calls me that. They wouldn't *dare.*" She trilled a laugh, then stopped, tilted her head, and studied me. "Mattia did not tell me you were so *gorgeous*." She put her hand under my chin to raise it. "Such dark, mysterious eyes and that black, black hair, like a gypsy. But this"—she tugged on my beard—"must go! Why hide such a beautiful face?"

"It's new," I said.

"The face or the beard?" She trilled another laugh, raised her specs, and came in closer. "Broken nose?"

"Many times," I said, a few incidents sparking in my mind: fist-fights, breaking and entering.

"It is good. It keeps you from being too pretty," she said, linked her arm through mine, and led me across the gallery and into the back room. The space was packed, sculpture on the floor, on stands, triple-hung paintings on the walls. She gestured for me to sit on a small love seat and sat beside me summarizing her history and the gallery's. "A family business, my father and his father before him. All men until *me*. They taught me to be *ruthless*," she said, no sign of that girlish trill now, and it made sense. Her gallery was one of the best in Europe. She stood and, going from one artwork to another, supplied artist names and titles and dates.

She stopped at a striking Gauguin painting of naked island girls. "A shame I have to sell it, but backroom sales help the gallery survive, a fact of life." She went into a riff about Gauguin's obsession with primitivism and prostitutes, and how the painting had come to her "by way of your dealer, Mattia Beuhler. We do business from time to time. He always comes up with the highest-quality work. It is on consignment, of course, so I won't have it for long, a shame. You are a lucky young man." She sat down beside me again. "Mattia Beuhler is going to make you a *very* successful artist."

I said I wasn't sure, my relationship with Beuhler still new, but she waved my words away, told me not to be modest, and that Beuhler had sent her images of my work, which she liked and wondered if I would have an exhibition with her. "After your show with Mattia. But I do not want *leftovers*! I insist you make new paintings!"

I didn't know what to say. I was amazed at the way Beuhler's name opened doors that had always been closed to me.

"You do not have to tell me now," she said. "Think it over for a minute before you say *yes*!" She walked me to the door, kissed my cheeks, tugged my beard, and one more time said, "You will shave this off *before* your show in my gallery!" Then trilled another laugh and that was it, I was out on the street.

I headed to my last appointment, no more than ten minutes away if Google Maps was to be trusted. The sky threatened rain but I felt good, elated by Wil Kuhr's offer, and nothing was going to ruin my mood.

54

Alex got off the bus a few blocks from the Museumplein. She needed to walk, so many things on her mind—the Anne Frank visit, Caroliens offer, her father.

Luke was probably right; it was a mistake to let her father back into her life, something she should cut off now. She checked the time, almost 4:00 p.m., did the math, almost 10:00 p.m. in New York. But was her father in New York? She had no idea where he was.

The first thing she asked him was, "Where are you?"

"Home."

"Which is where?"

"I'll tell you when I see you."

As manipulative as ever, Alex thought, and that's when she told him she wouldn't be speaking to him *for a while*, letting him down gently.

"How long is 'a while'?" he asked, reminding her he didn't have much time.

Alex didn't ask him to explain, didn't want to be manipulated, and changed the subject, telling him she was in Amsterdam for her thesis.

"Not to look for Van Gogh?"

She said she was seeing lots of Van Gogh, chatted about the weather in Amsterdam, and got off the phone feeling guilty though she hadn't wanted to, but looked forward to telling Luke she had broken it off.

At the museum's entrance, the conversation played back, particularly his question, "Not to look for Van Gogh?" Not *at* Van Gogh. *For* Van Gogh. Had she heard him correctly? Was it possible he knew about the painting? No. She'd never mentioned it. Was she was being paranoid, making a case out of one word. *For. At.* Ridiculous, she thought, ran her fingers through her hair and headed into the museum.

Just off the elevator Finn de Jong was waiting, leaning in a doorway, tall and blond and even better looking than she remembered.

"Alexis!" He reached out with both arms. "Is it all right to hug these days?" he asked, then wrapped his arms around her before she answered yes or no, his beard against her cheek, woodsy cologne in her nose, the hug going on too long.

His office was small and cramped, permeated by his woodsy smell, one window looking out to the paths and lawn of the Museumplein, the Rijksmuseum's towers in the distance.

Alex commented on the view, a little nervous with this man she didn't know and what she was about to tell him, now sitting in a chair opposite his, their knees practically touching.

He asked to see the painting, and she finally had to say she didn't have it. She told him the story about buying the painting in the antique store, and discovering the painting underneath the painting, and her plan to have it appraised but how she'd been mugged and the picture stolen. Then she handed him her cell phone and told him to scroll through the pictures, which he did, slowly, Alex watching him.

"Its authenticity is a long shot," he said after a minute. "Though I believe such a painting exists, or existed, that it is not just a myth. But I need to ask you something first." He rubbed his hands together nervously, and Alex noticed his wedding ring. "I looked you up and I discovered something, something about…your father. Does he have anything to do with this?"

"My *father*? No, not at all!" Alex stood up, trying to stay calm. A month ago, she would have been able to say she didn't even speak to her father. "Everything I've told you about the painting is true, and my father has absolutely nothing to do with it!"

"Okay. Fine," Finn said, his hands reaching for her arms, telling her to sit, that he was sorry if he had upset her. And she sat, heart thudding, the two of them face-to-face, too close, not speaking. "Your father is well-known," he said. "I just needed to know he was not part of this, that the painting is not…"

"Stolen?" Alex said, finishing his sentence. "It *isn't*. I told you how I found it, and that's the truth."

Finn regarded her a moment, his blue eyes searching her face till she looked away. Then he told her about a man he wanted her to meet in a small town not far from Paris, Auvers-sur-Oise.

"Where Van Gogh spent the last months of his life."

"Yes," he said, pausing as if making a decision. "He has a sketch you need to see. I will explain everything on the way."

"On the way?" Alex asked.

"Yes," he said, Finn leaning in again, too close. "To Auvers-sur-Oise."

55

They had been at it for hours, Van Straten and the team firing questions at Smith about his new identity, his birthplace, his schools, his parents' jobs, facts about Lewis's last art sales, the names and dates of when and where and to whom, more questions about historic art auctions, who bought what, until finally he couldn't think anymore, his mind a porridge of names and dates, and he sagged back, exhausted, and said, "Uncle!" and Van Straten gave the signal for them to stop.

"I understand this is not easy," she said. "But Trader's people are willing to meet, soon. It is an opportunity we cannot afford to lose." She lit a cigarette and handed it to Smith. "Trader knows he has been located, that the organizations will be closing in on him and he will have to move again soon."

"Who leaked the information?" Steiner said. "Not *me*."

"No," Van Straten said. "*I* did. *We* did. Through Jaager." She nodded at the young tech cop, and he nodded back. "We *want* Trader to feel the pressure, to feel threatened, to feel us closing in, so he will have to act fast. He knows we are ready to meet, and we must be." She signaled Jaager again, and he displayed a neck chain for Smith and how it worked, with a mini-microphone and a tracking device.

Smith put the neck chain on, and said, "Thanks, Q."

Jaager said, "Bond, James Bond," and Smith laughed for the first time in a long time, and he was grateful.

Van Straten looked him over.

"What is it?" Smith asked.

"You don't look like an art dealer," she said and signaled to Municipal Police Vox. "You will take Agent Smith shopping," she said, and explained what they needed to buy: "black pants, high-quality shirts, white and black, a couple of designer sports jackets too, nothing flashy. And most important, good shoes."

"What's wrong with these?" Smith asked and raised a foot to show off his worn New Balance sneaks.

Van Straten spoke to Vox as if Smith were not there, describing the kind of shoes and jackets to buy, where to go, then handed Vox a credit card. "You have an hour. Just let me finish up with Agent Smith here, then he is all yours."

Vox smiled at Smith, and he couldn't help but smile back.

Jaager took the neck chain back to refine it, Steiner excused himself, no doubt to report everything to INTERPOL, and Van Straten asked the Dutch police to leave her alone with Smith.

When they were gone, she said, "There are some loose ends to attend to."

"Such as?"

"James Tully."

"What about him?"

"Do you know where he is?"

Smith shook his head; he had no idea. "Is it important we know?"

"He was initially involved. I would like to know where he is now. I would not want him to show up at an inopportune moment."

That seemed unlikely to Smith. He imagined Tully was off somewhere, up to his old tricks. "You want me to look into it?"

"Yes. And let me know what you find."

"Anything else? I should get back to the folders, review everything again."

"You should," she said. "After the shopping. But there is something else. I understand that Perrone and Verde are here, in Amsterdam, and are looking for the painting."

Smith said he wasn't sure; he hadn't spoken to them.

"They cannot be anywhere near this operation," Van Straten said. "You must stop them. If you don't, I will."

"I tried to talk them out of coming."

"Unsuccessfully. I *know* they are here." She came around the table and sat beside him. "I speak not only for the good of the operation, but for your safety. Perrone and Verde could accidentally put you, and themselves, in danger. Do you understand?" she said, and Smith nodded. "Then take care of it *now*. I will not have this operation jeopardized by them or by Tully or by anyone else!"

56

Tully was halfway down the dirt road, two bags of groceries in the trunk and feeling good having grabbed a couple of pints at that dive bar out on Montauk Highway. But he stopped short when he saw the cop car idling in front of Denise's house and did an about-face so fast his tires burned rubber, not the coolest move.

Was this something to do with the email he'd gotten from Smith, totally out of blue, asking where he was and how he was doing, snooping around, but why? He'd changed his email address so how did Smith get it? Had to be through INTERPOL, fucking INTERPOL.

He cruised down Main Street, conscious of the speed limit—he didn't need a ticket—passed the familiar high-end shops he'd never gone into, Ralph Lauren, Manolo Blahnik, Gucci, then headed out of East Hampton, stopping again at the bar on Montauk Highway, and downed another beer before he called Denise.

"Where *are* you?" she asked, her voice strained.

"The grocery store was crowded, lots of traffic too. Why? Anything wrong?" he asked, all innocence.

"There's been a break-in, here, at my house!"

"You're kidding?" *A break-in? Shit. Were they looking for him?* "You and the boys okay, Deenie?"

"Yes. I was at work, the boys at day care. Thank God."

"Good, good," he said, mind spinning, then asked if she'd called the cops and she said yes, but they'd gone. "Be right there."

The place looked like it had been ransacked by a bomb squad—rugs rolled back, sofa cushions slashed, kitchen cabinets and drawers open, pots and pans on the floor along with broken dishes.

"What could they possibly be after, Jimmy?"

Tully sucked his lip and shook his head. "Damned if I know."

"It doesn't make sense. I mean, I have nothing, and this house, it's a shack among mansions." She kneeled to pick up a broken teacup. "My mom's porcelain, one of the few nice things I had," she said, choking back tears.

Tully said he'd get her a new set. "What matters is you and the boys are safe." He hugged her, and she asked if he'd been drinking, and he backed away. "Jesus, Deenie, I stopped for a beer. Is that a crime?"

"In the middle of the day, Jimmy?"

Tully shook his head, Deenie the Narc was almost enough reason to leave, and now this. He looked past the trashed kitchen into the trashed living room. "Damn," he said.

"What is it, Jimmy?"

"The break-in, that's all," he said, knowing he had to get out of there, his perfect hideout not so perfect after all. But how'd they find him? Because you could find anyone nowadays. He thought about Smith again, and INTERPOL, actually hoped it was him and not the client. But would INTERPOL trash a house like this? "I've got to go."

"Now? Where?"

"Just…away. For…a while." He didn't explain, just handed her a wad of cash, money he'd earned on eBay selling a first-edition Lois

Lane. He told her he'd send her more. "I'll be back soon," he said, a lie.

Denise trailed him outside, hanging on to him. "Tell the truth, Jimmy. What's going on?"

Tully thought a minute, came up with a reasonable story, a version of the truth. She'd known when he'd arrived that he was getting away from a client. "Maybe it's that weirdo client I told you about."

"But why? What were they looking for?"

"I got no idea, Deenie. They're wackos," he said, thinking where he might go next, to his sister's place in Tucson? "I'll just stay away till this cools down."

"Till *what* cools down?"

"Damn it, Deenie. *This*, when *this* calms down. What does it matter?" He drew a breath, felt a little bad, Deenie caught in the middle. "I just want you and the boys to be safe. A couple of weeks at most, then I'll come back." He kissed her cheek, then got into his car thinking about the client. Maybe Smith tipped them off. Or had they found him on their own?

Either way, it didn't matter. He had to go.

57

Raamstraat was a narrow lane off a side street, practically deserted, no room for cars, a couple of parked bicycles, the houses reminiscent of Greenwich Village brownstones, some with short staircases leading up to the front door, others with doors right on the street, but almost all the buildings identical. My last gallery destination was one of them, a brass plaque beside the front door, S. ALBRECHT, so small I would have missed it had I not been looking. I gave my name into the intercom, and when the door clicked open, I entered a small vestibule with one elevator, antique and creaky. It delivered me to the top floor, where an older, starchily dressed woman let me in.

"Mr. Albrecht will be with you shortly," she said, then led me into a large old-fashioned-looking living room with an Empire sofa, an Oriental rug on the floor, a couple of paintings hung on the walls, a few propped against it. She planted herself behind a desk while I looked at the art: an old master *Madonna and Child*, an impressionist landscape by Sisley, a bold Kandinsky abstraction among them.

I was studying Sisley's brushwork when a man entered, casually but expensively dressed in an open-necked polo and soft-looking wool pants.

"Stefan Albrecht," he said, and extended a hand. Tall and striking with cropped white hair and white eyebrows, stubbled cheeks as if sprinkled with snow, the thought in my mind: *Mr. Freeze.* "Mattia has conveyed such nice things about you," he said, his accent crisp and hard to place.

His matronly assistant stood, buttoned her jacket, and told him she would be back in twenty minutes, which I guessed was my allotted time.

Albrecht apologized for the mess, but other than the few wrapped paintings, there was no mess that I could see.

"Artwork is always coming in and going out of here," he said. "As a private dealer I do not have exhibitions. My job is to match the right art to the right person." He patted the edge of a canvas as if petting a child. "These will not be here long. A shame, but then I will have others to replace them." He said he'd seen images of my work, thanks again to Mattia Beuhler, and had a couple of collectors in mind who might be interested.

I was flattered as he reeled off a succession of collectors' names that meant nothing to me and said he would discuss it with Beuhler, then said exactly what the other gallerists had said: "Mattia Beuhler is one of the best art dealers in the world and you are lucky to have him."

"I agree, Mr. Albrecht."

He insisted I call him Stefan, asked about my life in New York, where I'd grown up, and about my artwork, and listened attentively as if he was really interested while I explained what I was trying to do in my new paintings. When I got sick of hearing myself talk, I asked about him.

"Art is in my blood," he said, "a family tradition, my father and grandfather," his story very much like Wil Kuhr's. Then, as if reciting, he said, "'I have nature and art and poetry, and if that is not enough, what is?'"

My reading had paid off. I recognized the quote. "Van Gogh!"

"Yes!" he said. "Here is another: 'The heart of man is very much like the sea. It has its storms, it has its tides and...'"

I finished the sentence, "'and in its depths, it has its pearls too.'"

"Bravo!" he said. After that, we talked of Van Gogh's evolving style, from the dark peasant paintings to the bright impressionist work, to his personal brand of expressionism, and we named our favorites. When we talked about the self-portraits, I asked if he believed the stories about the lost one, and he thought a moment, ran a hand over his cropped white hair, and said, "Who knows? But if you find it, you must promise to tell me, and we will sell it together and become very rich!" and we both laughed.

Then his starchy assistant returned and eyed me with a look that said, *Are you still here?*

I took the hint and said it was time I left.

Albrecht stood and we shook hands, both of his wrapped around mine, and he said it had been a pleasure to meet another Van Gogh fan, and that he would speak to Beuhler about my paintings and find a few appropriate clients. "I promise," he said, and I believed him.

Then I was outside, my dinner plan with Alex still an hour away, so I decided to walk, the sky going cobalt, streetlights winking on, all of it beautiful.

I'd only gone a block when my phone rang. Carolien, asking if Alex and I were free tomorrow, that she was setting up a meeting with one of the people who had helped her locate some of her grandfather's artwork, that he might be able to give us some information on our painting. "If it is out there, he will know," she said.

A part of me had been hoping she would not come through, but I knew Alex would be excited.

Carolien was still waiting for an exact time and place but said she would get back to me, and I was about to ask a lot of questions, like who this person was, how she'd met him, and if he was reputable, but she had already hung up.

58

I met Alex at a place called The Seafood Bar, not far from our hotel, bright and cheerful with white tiled walls and an open bar where good-looking waiters and waitresses shucked oysters and cut lemon wedges while we caught up on the events of our day.

"You first," Alex said, and I told her about my gallery visits, Visscher's Hitler sculpture, Wil Kuhr insisting I shave my beard. "Good idea," she said. "I want that handsome face back."

"Exactly what Wil Kuhr said."

"*Oh?* Should I be jealous?"

"Never. And not just because Wil Kuhr is probably in her sixties."

"Tell that to Emmanuel Macron!" she said.

I laughed, then told her about Stefan Albrecht and how he looked like Mr. Freeze, but she had no idea who that was. "A Batman villain."

"Seriously? How old are you?"

I reminded her that comic books were collectibles, which reminded us both of Tully, and for a moment I wondered what had happened to him, and that brought us back to Smith and how annoyed we were about his bailing on the trip and our search.

"Let's not talk about him. I don't want to ruin the night," Alex said, and I agreed, still trying to figure out what made him change his mind so suddenly.

I went back to the art dealers, how Albrecht and I had bonded over Van Gogh, and that I liked him and how he'd offered to sell a few of my paintings. Alex was impressed, and even more so when I mentioned that Visscher and Wil Kuhr had both offered me shows. "The power of Mattia Beuhler," I said.

"Wow, a show with a Hitler lover or a woman who liked your face. That's a tough call," she said.

I told her I would not be showing with Visscher, who gave me the creeps though he was probably the most powerful of the three dealers, then asked about her meeting with the curator.

"*Conservator*," she corrected me. "It was good." She paused a moment, swirling her wine in the glass, then told me she was going with him to Auvers-sur-Oise, to see a drawing, something that supposedly related to our Van Gogh self-portrait.

"In *France*?"

"Yes. But it's close. Only an hour-and-twenty-minute flight from Amsterdam to Paris, then a forty-or-so-minute car ride. Do you want to come along?"

I was dying to see Van Gogh's resting place, but I declined. Alex and I tried not to interfere in each other's professional lives. She said they would go in the morning and be back by night.

"You won't even have time to miss me."

"I always miss you," I said, and it was true, the anger I'd felt earlier gone, and when she told me she'd broken it off with her father, I was surprised but even happier.

"I thought about it," she said, "and I'm not sure I'm ready to have him back in my life."

I was thrilled but kept my cool. And when Alex asked again if I wanted to go to Auvers-sur-Oise, I remembered Carolien's call and told her.

"Oh no," she said. "I want to go with you but I'll be in Auvers-sur-Oise."

I wasn't sure I wanted to go at all and, without Alex, even less so. "We'll see," I said.

"You *must* go," she said. "We might learn something about the painting."

I still had my doubts but I agreed to go.

Back at our hotel, I was tired, but one kiss and we tumbled into bed and made love as if we'd never had a fight that morning and never would again.

I didn't know what time it was when my phone buzzed, jolting me awake.

It was Smith, here in Amsterdam, wanting to see me.

Alex sat up, half-asleep, and I told her.

"You're kidding? When?"

"Now."

"*Now?* You're not going, are you?"

"He said it's important."

Alex yawned and said he had a lot of nerve, which was true, but she was curious and so was I.

"Want to come?" I asked.

"No way," she said, and rolled over and pulled the covers with her. "You can tell me about it in the morning."

59

According to the Uber driver, my destination was in the Wallen quarter, the oldest part of Amsterdam, "and not always safe," he said, launching into a monologue about which neighborhoods were the best, the worst, and which cites in Europe had the most crime, but I wasn't listening, anxious to get where I was going.

We crossed several bridges and headed along wide roads, then narrower ones for fifteen or twenty minutes until we came to a stop in front of a building that filled a corner, modern in an institutional sort of way and out of sync with the rest of the neighborhood, which looked old, medieval, and Gothic. It wasn't until I was out of the Uber that I saw it was a police station, police cars and motorcycles lining the sidewalk. Then I saw Smith, the tip of his cigarette flickering like a firefly.

"You have to give up the painting," he said.

"Hello to you too," I said. Under the streetlamp and without his shades, his eyes were puffy, as if he hadn't slept. "I don't have the painting, so there's nothing to give up."

"I mean stop *looking* for it."

I had planned on telling him to go to hell, but I wanted to hear what this was about. "Why?" I asked.

"Come," he said, and took hold of my arm roughly, and we walked four or five blocks without speaking, Smith's shoulders hunched, tension coming off him like radiant heat. We crossed a small bridge, the water below rippling red and pink. On the other side, the neon of porn shops and peep shows tinted the sky and reflected in the canal like someone was scribbling on the water with a red fluorescent marker.

The next street was all doorways lit up red—two, then four in a row, girls behind them in fishnets and heels and white lace panties, some pressed up against the glass, leering come-ons. I didn't have to be told it was Amsterdam's red-light district, but it was kind of shocking, practically naked girls behind doors like specimens in glass cages.

It was the middle of the night, but the street was crowded, some couples, but mostly young men in packs like wolves on the prowl, laughing and guzzling beer, shouting at the girls behind glass, showing off for their friends.

Smith finally spoke, oblivious to the surroundings. "Talk to Alex. And back off. It's that simple."

"No, *you* back off! You bail on us, then show up here telling us what to do. Forget it."

"It's for your own good," he said, still moving as if propelled into a narrow alley, wall-to-wall girls behind glass on either side, Smith's face splashed red like the devil.

If I'd been ambivalent about looking for the painting before, his incessant demand only spurred me on. I told him it was too late, that Alex was already seeing a curator about the painting. And I was about to tell him about my meeting with Carolien, but stopped; it was no longer his business.

"You could get hurt," he said, heading along a street lined with bars and strip joints, barkers out front promising girls and nudity and sex and dreams.

I asked if that was a threat, and he said I could take it however I liked and started to leave, but I got my hands on his shoulders and stopped him.

"If you want me and Alex to back off, tell me *why*."

He shrugged out of my grip and walked away, but I stayed with him, asking *why* over and over, following him through a labyrinth of narrow streets that opened into an irregular square where he finally stopped and leaned against the wall of an old church. He lit another cigarette, the nearby doorways casting everything—the church, Smith—in red light.

"Explain it to me," I said. "What's going on?"

Smith sighed. "You've got to *trust* me."

"Tell me what's going on, and maybe I will. For starters, who are you working for? And don't tell me it's for me and Alex."

He hesitated a moment, then said, "INTERPOL. It's a job. Something I signed on for before yours. I just didn't expect it to be happening now." He paused, then met my eyes. "Look, it's important you stop looking. It's dangerous."

"What's the job? What are you doing?"

A pack of guys entered the square, whistling and jeering at the girls in windows, and we waited till they'd gone.

"It concerns the painting, the Van Gogh," he said. "That's enough, better you don't know any more. Just that there are other people looking for it."

I considered that a moment and something came to me and I told him, "Alex's father might know about the painting."

"*Baine? The art thief? How?*"

I tried to calm him down, told him I wasn't sure. "All I know is Alex spoke to him and got a feeling."

"A *feeling*? Jesus. What's that supposed to mean, Perrone? I thought Baine was in jail."

"No one knows where he is."

"Not even Alex?"

I wasn't sure but I said she didn't know.

"You have to talk to Alex about this, right now," he said. "No, Alex has to talk to Van Straten."

It took me a moment to process the name, though it made no sense. "Van Straten? From the Lower East Side Auction House?"

"She's a lot more than that, and this is something she has to know." He told me to sit tight and do nothing until he got back to me. Then he took off, leaving me on a street with semi-naked women in windows undulating and beckoning me, like I'd been dumped into *Dante's Inferno* by way of *Fifty Shades of Grey*, but the only woman on my mind was Alex, and how I was going to tell her she had to back off from the painting and that I'd told Smith about her father.

60

I hadn't gotten back until three in morning, had slipped into bed beside a sound-asleep Alex, who was up now, bright and early and buzzing around the room getting ready for her trip, changing her clothes and asking my opinion.

Still in bed, I roused myself enough to tell her about Smith, how he'd said we needed to stop looking for the painting and that he was still working for INTERPOL.

That stopped her.

"Are you kidding?"

I tried to explain but didn't have the details.

Alex sagged onto the edge of the bed. "So, he expects us to pack up and go home?"

"He just said to stop looking for the painting, that other people were looking for it and it was dangerous."

"Dangerous *how*?"

I didn't know, but Alex had made her plans with Finn and said she had no intention of changing them.

"He's showing me a sketch or something, and I intend to see it. I mean, how could it matter to Smith or whatever he's doing? And it's *not* the painting."

"So, what do we do about Smith?"

"Fuck him," she said, a surprise, Alex rarely cursed. "He doesn't work for us anymore—if he ever did. We don't owe him anything."

She took a breath. "Look, if I learn anything about the painting, I'll let Smith know. How's that?"

It sounded like a decent compromise, I said, then reminded her I was meeting Carolien and said the same thing. "If I learn anything about the painting, I'll let Smith know too."

Then Alex told me she wouldn't see me until tomorrow, that Finn could not get away till midday and there wouldn't be time to see everything in Auvers-sur-Oise and catch the afternoon flight back to Amsterdam. The news did not thrill me, though she made a point of saying they would be staying at an inn in separate rooms, of course, and I didn't make a wisecrack or act like the jealous boyfriend I was. I sucked it up and wished her good luck in Auvers-sur-Oise, "with What's-His-Name," and Alex said she'd call me when she got there, and that she loved me.

"I love you too," I said, and I kissed her and hugged her, fighting my feelings of jealousy.

Then she said goodbye, and I somehow forgot to tell her that I had told Smith about her father.

61

Smith thought it would be days but suddenly, after stalling, Trader's people had insisted it was now or never. There was no time to think about anything but his new identity before Jaager slipped the neck chain over his head.

Now, as instructed, he was sitting at a table in front of Café de Spuyt, on Korte Leidsedwarsstraat, a quiet, shady lane, one over from a busy street beside a wide canal, but an entirely different, almost secluded world. He was trying hard to appear nonchalant in his new cashmere sports jacket, arm draped around the back of his chair, a guidebook—*Fodor's Essential Croatia*—prominently displayed on the small round table.

"Will someone be joining you?" the waiter asked as he delivered Smith's beer.

Smith said yes, trying to keep his hand steady as he lifted the beer to his lips.

He checked the time. They were ten minutes late. Were they going to show, or was this just a test to see if he could follow orders? He scanned the street, a falafel shop beside a tabac, a few passersby, two on bicycles, a couple walking arm in arm. Was someone watching him? Further down the street, Rijkspolitie Koner, out of uniform, in jeans and a tee, sat at an outdoor café pretending to read the newspaper.

Smith was close to giving up when a woman slipped into the chair opposite and tapped the guidebook.

"Planning a trip?" she asked.

"To Croatia," he said.

"It will be very cold this time of year."

"So I've been told. I will pack a heavy coat and hat."

"And gloves," she said, as preplanned, Smith trying to see beyond her Jackie O sunglasses and the scarf tied over her perfectly bobbed blond hair. All he could make out was that she was young, her accent American. She shook an American Spirit out of a pack, offered him one.

"No thanks," he said. "Organic or not, they're going to kill you." He struck a match and leaned forward to give her a light.

She blew it out and used her own. Then angled a look down the street. "Your bodyguard has been reading the same page of the newspaper for the past half hour."

Smith answered by asking if the big guy in reflector shades who'd just taken a seat on the bench across the street was *her* bodyguard. Neither answered the other's question.

"So, who are you?" Smith asked. "Not Trader."

"I'm a representative. Same as you."

"No," he said. "I'm here representing myself."

"Mr. Lewis?" she said, and Smith nodded. "You must know Miles Waring, senior curator at Chicago's Museum of Modern Art."

"Nope," he said. "No such museum in Chicago. Unless you mean the Museum of *Contemporary* Art, but I know no one there by that name."

She stretched out her hand, palm up. "I need to see your inventory."

Smith retrieved the disposable cell and handed it to her, gave her the code, and watched her scroll through the images.

"How do we know you have the actual artworks in your possession?" she asked.

"You don't," he said. "But I have a couple of samples with me, the Matisse and the Monet. Not on me, but I can produce them."

"All right," she said. "Meanwhile, I will keep this." She gripped the phone.

"I don't think so," Smith said and reached for it.

A split-second move, her hand to the back of her head, then arcing up and down, a steel hat pin lodged beside Smith's fingers in the wooden table, quivering.

"Next time, say *please*," she said, though she let him take the phone. The waiter stopped by to take her order, but she waved him off, waited for him to go. "Bring one of your samples and we will make the first exchange."

"Which one?" Smith asked, watching her, the way she drew the cigarette to her lips, her red lipstick and perfectly manicured nails.

"You choose, Mr. Lewis."

"Another test?"

"If you like." She stabbed her cigarette out, then wrapped it in a napkin, slid it into her pocket, and stood up. "And regarding the other sale, the main sale, we will need the name of your client, your buyer. My employer insists upon keeping track of all inventory."

Smith had not anticipated the question or rehearsed an answer. "We'll see," he said.

"I'm afraid it is essential, a deal breaker," she said, then leaned across the table and whispered in his ear, "There can be no secrets, Mr. Lewis," her breath so hot on his neck he shivered.

"I'll give you the name the next time we meet."

She stood up and Smith watched her head down the street, the tight fit of her jeans, the ends of her headscarf trailing. She stopped beside Koner, plucked the newspaper out of his hand, dropped it to the ground, then turned the corner and disappeared.

Smith raised the neck chain to his lips, said, "You get all that?"

A few minutes later he was in the back seat of a car, Van Straten beside him, Koner driving.

"You did well," she said. "Handling that question about the Chicago museum was good." She offered him a bottle of water, and though he needed something stronger, he took a long slug, his mouth dry.

"Where are we going?"

"You and Koner, back to the station," she said, quiet a moment, a bit distracted. She looked different too, her hair loose around her shoulders. "Now we wait to hear about the exchange of paintings."

"Will it be another test?"

"The exchange of the first set of paintings is the next test. They need to trust us before they deliver the prize."

Smith nodded, suddenly light-headed and dizzy, hands shaking, a feeling like he could jump out of his skin, an adrenaline dump. He knew the symptoms. He focused on his breathing, would need to get out of the fancy clothes and take a run when he got back, maybe lift some weights. "You heard what she said about the buyer?"

"They want to see if Lewis has connections to high-profile customers. We will get to work on it."

The car stopped at a light and Smith opened his window, took several deep breaths. "Oh, I saw Perrone, told him to back off."

"And?"

"Maybe he will. I don't know." He sat back, closed his eyes, still trying to breathe evenly. "Something else. Perrone thinks Verde's father may know something about the Van Gogh painting."

"*What?* How would he know *that*? His daughter told him?"

"Perrone didn't say. He didn't know for sure."

Van Straten was quiet, obviously thinking while she slowly unscrewed the lid off a tiny pot of clear gloss and applied some to her lips with her pinky, an unusually feminine move for her, Smith thought. "But Richard Baine is in prison, is he not?"

"I'm not sure. Perrone didn't know where he was."

It took another five or six minutes to get back to De Wallen, no one talking until Koner stopped the car in front of the station.

"The client, the buyer," Van Straten said as if to herself.

"What do you mean? Who?" Smith asked.

"*Baine*," she said. "Richard Baine! He is the perfect client. A high-profile art criminal, someone Trader will surely know." She tapped her glossed lips several times. "You say Perrone does not know where he is."

"No."

"But his daughter will." She stepped out of the car and took Koner's place behind the wheel. "Speak to Perrone and Verde and get her father's contact info right away," she said, then she pulled her car door shut and drove off.

62

It was like entering a play, from the brightest splashes of light to the darkest recesses, a crowd of soldiers, arms reaching for weapons, everyone poised as if waiting to be called into action. A tap on the shoulder and I started, turned to see Carolien and the swarm of tourists I had been able to block out until now, all of them angling for a better view of the famous painting.

"Sorry, I was lost in Rembrandt's world," I said.

"*The Night Watch* can do that," she said.

"Is your friend, your contact here?"

"Not yet," Carolien said, "but he is not my friend."

"Who is he?"

Carolien shrugged. "An art dealer or fence, likely one who works on the black market. I don't know, not exactly. We have done business before, that is all. He helped me locate a painting." She surveyed the crowd. "He asked to meet here in the Rijksmuseum, in front of this painting, but I do not see him."

We were in the Gallery of Honor, a long corridor, slightly Moorish in style with a domed ceiling and striped columns flanking alcoves filled with the greatest hits of Dutch painting, Johannes Vermeer and Frans Hals.

"Will he want money?" I asked, the idea just coming to me, and I hadn't brought any.

Carolien wasn't sure what he would want, only that she'd told him about the painting I was looking for and he said he would come. She checked her watch. "We are early," she said.

I glanced back at the Rembrandt, trying to take in its enormity: twelve or fourteen feet wide, an assembly of soldiers, civic guards, ready to protect the city of Amsterdam. "Is he honest?" I asked. "Can I trust him?"

"What choice do you have?" Carolien said and told me to be patient.

Not my strong suit, but I moved closer to the painting, my nose practically against the glass, more like a room for the painting, like the one for Hannibal Lecter in *Silence of the Lambs*. "Why the glass house?"

"They are doing restoration," Carolien said. "You know the painting was cut down when it was moved from its original place to Amsterdam's town hall. They needed it to fit it through doors or between pillars, and they just cut several feet off the sides!" She shook her head. "The painting has survived a lot, taken off its stretchers and rolled up when the Nazis invaded, along with other precious artworks." She checked her watch again, noting we were still early, both of us impatient. "The painting was hidden several times, even attacked with knives, people are so crazy. The painting only survived because of its heavy layer of varnish, which is what gave it its name, the varnish so darkened viewers thought it was a nighttime scene rather than a dark room," Carolien was telling me when her phone buzzed. "He is here, but in another room."

I followed her out of the gallery, through hallways, wondering why he had changed the location. Had he seen us in front of *The Night Watch* and checked us out?

Then we arrived in a room with a Van Gogh self-portrait, a large group gathered in front of it. Carolien elbowed her way through and stopped beside a man with coal-black hair, dressed in a tweed jacket buttoned up to a high-collar and tie. He continued looking at the painting while we were introduced.

"Here we have Vincent discovering impressionism," he said. "Is it anything like your painting?"

"Yes and no," I said, adding that in ours Van Gogh wore no hat.

He turned toward me, and I'm pretty sure I flinched, taking in the thick pink scar that zigzagged through a drooping eyelid and over his cheekbone before disappearing into his neat beard.

"I do wish your girlfriend was here," he said.

"She's away," I said, focusing on his eyes, not the scar, and trying not to think of Alex off with the curator.

"Yes, I know," he said. "I understand she was the one who found it, *discovered* it, under another painting, yes?"

I gave Carolien a look, not happy she had told him so much.

He backed up, moving away from the crowd until we were in a corner, just the three of us. "There are several Van Gogh works in circulation, for sale or trade."

"How do you know?"

"Let me just say, it behooves me to know such things." He looked from me to Carolien. "I am only telling you this as a personal favor to Ms. Cahill, who can vouch for my knowledge of such things."

"So, it's out there, the painting we found?"

"Perhaps."

I was intrigued but not in the mood to play games. "You want money for the information?"

He sputtered a laugh, the scar tugging at the corner of his mouth. "You surely do not have enough. But no, I do not want your money." He asked me to tell him more about the painting, and I did, somewhat reluctantly, describing Van Gogh's jacket and vest, the white shirt, the overall blue coloration.

"Nothing else? No small depiction of cows near the bottom?"

I almost flinched again. Unless someone had described the painting to him, he'd seen it. "Yes," I said.

"Well then, you are too late. That painting is already in… negotiation."

"What do you mean, with who?"

"Why? You want in on it?" He scoffed. "Trust me, you want no part of these negotiations, or the people involved in them."

"But *you* can negotiate with them, is that what you're saying?"

He scoffed again. "At one point. But no longer. These negotiations are…how you say…too rich for my blood. I have learned my place." He ran a finger up his cheek, lifting his drooping eyelid which only drooped again. "A memento of aiming too high." He turned to Carolien and said he had a lead on a Raphael painting that once belonged to her grandfather. "I will be in touch," he said, then turned back to me. "I would recommend that you and your girlfriend, Alexis Verde, stay as far away from the Van Gogh self-portrait as possible. Be happy you had the painting for a few hours. It is more time than most people will ever have with anything so precious. Do not be greedy. Greed can be a dangerous thing." He drew a finger over his scar again. "So far you have been lucky." He started away, then turned back again. "And tell Ms. Verde to forget about traveling."

"What do you mean?" I asked, but he was already out of the room, and when I went after him, he was gone. I went back to Carolien and asked if she had given him Alex's name.

"No," she said. "Nor yours."

"But he knew it," I said, realizing there must be other people who knew who we were and what we were looking for. I told Carolien I had to go and thanked her.

Then I was outside, heading through the Rijksmuseum's dark Gothic passageway, looking over my shoulder as I called Smith. I had to tell him about this meeting, that he was not the only one who had warned me to stay away from the painting.

63

After dropping Smith at the station, Van Straten drove on. She did not have much time, but she felt good. Smith had pulled it off. This was the closest they, or anyone, had gotten to Trader so far. They would proceed as planned, but carefully. Trader would be skittish, on alert.

And now, the idea of Baine as the client.

She pulled off the road to scroll through her phone, found her State Department contact, someone who could make the necessary arrangements. He promised he would try, best he could do on such short notice, but it was enough.

Back on the highway, she followed Dispatcher's directions, better to stay offline once she took the exit to Zaanstad-Centrum. She was almost there, butterflies in her stomach. A few more turns and she was in the town. Driving along the river she could see colorful houses, windmills in the distance, symbols of a long-gone era. She thought of her father and grandfather, men who once ran one of the finest art galleries in the Netherlands, aryanized in the nineteen-forties, then closed for good.

She passed a gray stone factory, then a string of attached houses with bright-green facades, and finally a zany-looking building made of multiply stacked homes that looked like it was out of a life-size Lego set: the landmarks Dispatcher had told her to look for. She was close. Heart fluttering like a nervous schoolgirl, she drove slowly, checking the numbers of modest-looking homes with brick fronts and aluminum siding, until she found it and parked beside the narrow canal, noted the ducks floating in the water, a few waddling across the cobblestone path as she got out. A moment to run a hand through her hair as she checked the number again. All the houses were identical with small, gated yards and picture windows. The home she was approaching the only one with its shades drawn.

Their greeting was a little awkward, neither one of them good at small talk. It had been four years since they had spoken, four years since they'd worked together, this their third deep-state assignment.

"Why here?" Van Straten asked, taking in the bourgeois home and its trappings—leather couch, dining room set, framed photos of a family on the wall (and not Dispatcher's family).

"Anonymous and comfortable enough," he said, his deep voice familiar, his accent heavier than hers. "It gives me a little distance too, though my motorcycle will get me to town faster than your car. It belongs to a buddy, former *chayal*, out of town. No longer Sayeret. He has opted for a quieter life."

"But not you," she said.

"Me, a quieter life?" He laughed. "Like you, only when I am dead." He frowned, not a clever thing to say, death always a close companion to the kind of work they did. "Sorry."

"No reason to be," Van Straten said. She knew his history—former IDF, retired after the second intifada in 2005, now part of a special elite unit within the Caesarea department, though he took other *tafkid*, other jobs, some for pay, others like this one because he believed in her cause, which she appreciated.

"I needed an experienced operative," she said. "Just in case."

"You knew I would come," he said and smiled, the lines around his mouth deeper than she remembered, the crow's-feet more pronounced though his eyes were still as blue as turquoise, startling against his tan skin, pockmarked cheeks mostly hidden by stubble, which was going gray like the hair at his temples, the rest of his close-cropped hair still dark, almost black. "I have been ready since you contacted me, but only here since yesterday."

"*Toda raba*," she said. "Thank you, Dispatcher."

"Some coffee, Hunter?"

"No thanks," she said, having smelled the liquor on his breath. "But I will have whatever you are drinking."

He laughed again and poured her a glass of Macallan, the single-malt scotch she remembered he always drank, and which they both liked, warm and smooth on her throat as she filled him in on the assignment and on Trader. "One of the major brokers of looted art. His grandfather one of Hitler's approved art dealers, a mantle his father assumed and now him, a family practice you might say, and one he has no intention of giving up, but we will stop him."

"I know you will," Dispatcher said, and she went on.

"I hope the assignment will go smoothly and without violence so you will not need any of this." She downed her scotch, then crouched on the floor beside his open kit bag, half its contents arranged around it. She picked up his KA-BAR Commando knife and ran her finger over the Star of David etched at the base of the hilt.

"There are Band-Aids and sutures in there if you cut yourself," he said, teasing.

"And these," she said, lifting vials of OxyContin and Vicodin, then a lollipop which she knew was laced with morphine. "Still addicted to candy?"

"Not addicted and not before dinner. They spoil the appetite." He laughed loudly, the Macallan having loosened him up.

Van Straten noted the M84 stun grenade and the military-grade gas mask. She carefully lifted his semiautomatic, a Jericho 941, and peered through the sight. "I thought this old Uzi had been discontinued."

"It has. But I like the way it fits my grip." He took it from her, wrapped his hand around it, and asked about the assignment's timeline, if she wanted him on-site for the exchange of paintings.

"Yes," she said, and gave him a burner phone and told him she would be in touch with the details.

"Will you need Pilot?"

"I don't know yet. But can you contact him, have him standing by, just in case?"

"*Just in case*," he said. "The story of our lives."

"Yes," she said, and they were quiet a moment, drinking the Macallan. After a minute she asked, "How are Shira and the boys?"

"Ariel is six. Levi almost eight, *baruch Hashem*. Both little animals," he said, beaming. "And my wife... She is fine."

"Good," she said.

"You never wanted a family, Hunter?"

"At one time. But it is different for a woman. You have a wife that stays home and raises your children and cooks your meals, so you are free to play the hero—and to cheat on her," the words tumbling out of her mouth. "I am sorry, I did not mean that."

"Yes, you did," he said, his turquoise eyes on hers, making it difficult for her to play this game any longer. She kissed him, and his calloused hands were on her cheeks and in her hair, her hand between his legs feeling him already hard.

After they had finished, Dispatcher poured them more scotch and smoked a Time cigarette, watched her dress and told her she was beautiful, which she waved away, embarrassed, both laughing when she picked up her jeans and his Uzi fell out.

"I will be in touch about the painting exchange," she said, raising the drink to her lips, then putting it down. "I had better not. I have had enough, and I am driving." She kissed his cheek and whispered his name, "Daniel."

"Anni," he said. "*Tihyeh batuach.*"

"You too," she said, and repeated what he'd said in English, "Be safe."

64

I'd finally heard from Smith, a response to the text I'd sent after meeting with Carolien and her scar-faced friend.

meet me in vondelpark under statue of vondel

Vondelpark? I had no idea what he was talking about.

I asked the hotel concierge, who said, "It is like your Central Park," and gave me directions. In less than fifteen minutes I was walking through a wrought-iron gate with VONDELPARK spelled out in brass, which opened onto lawns and paths where I soon found the large statue of a seated man on a rounded knoll covered with tulips. And Smith, standing beside it, polluting the air with cigarette smoke.

I started to tell him about the meeting with Carolien, but he stopped me and led me to a large pond where a woman was feeding bread crumbs to a mama duck and her baby ducklings. When she turned, I was shocked to see it was Anika Van Straten.

She slapped her hands, scattering bread crumbs into the water, the ducklings darting and diving. "Sweet, aren't they?" she said. "And so innocent. All they care about is food, their survival." A group of tourists descended on the scene, cameras snapping pictures of the ducklings, and Van Straten motioned us away, across the lawn until we were alone. "I was going to *demand* that you and Ms. Verde stop looking for the painting, but apparently it is too late for that."

I ignored her statement, telling her instead about my meeting with Carolien and the man who knew about the painting.

"With a scar?" she said, drawing a finger over her cheek. "Ms. Cahill associates with some very questionable characters in pursuit of her family's art. Not that I blame her, but she is reckless. Amateurs tend to get hurt."

"So, you know her and this man."

"I know there are many people looking for the Van Gogh, but we have it, or we will. Has Analyst Smith filled you in?"

I told her he hadn't, and she said she needed to contact Alex's father, and I asked why.

"Because he is the perfect buyer for a particular artwork as he has a well-known history of buying stolen art."

She was speaking in riddles I didn't understand, and I asked her to explain.

It was a moment before she did.

"I keep stolen art from being stolen again. That is enough for you to know." Then she asked again about how to reach Baine.

I told her I didn't know how to find him.

"But his daughter knows."

"From what I gather, *no one* knows where he is."

"Look, Perrone," Smith cut in. "I've had a rough morning, so cut the shit. You told me Alex had been in touch with her father, so she *knows*."

It was true she knew how to reach him, but did she know where he was? I had no idea. And if she did, it was her business, and I said so.

"Not just *her* business anymore," Van Straten said. "I have a deal for Mr. Baine. One he will not refuse. I need to meet with his daughter and get that information, whether she wants to relinquish it or not."

"She's away," I said. "Traveling."

"Where?"

"In France, in Auvers-sur-Oise."

"Why?" she asked but didn't wait for an answer, repeating that she needed to speak with Alex. If she didn't return, Van Straten said she would have her arrested and brought back to Amsterdam.

I doubted she would do that, but said I'd get in touch with her.

"Right now," she said.

I tried Alex's phone, but it went straight to voicemail. "She's not answering."

"I will give you one hour," Van Straten said. "Then I will have her arrested and the French police will get the information."

"Arrested on what grounds?"

"It does not matter. I can make it happen. I need the information. Your friend Analyst Smith's life may depend on it."

I didn't bother to say that Smith was not exactly my friend, as he was right there looking tired and strung out. That's when I remembered that no one had to arrest Alex to get the information.

I got my cell phone out and scrolled until I found the number I had forwarded from Alex's phone the night her father had called. I knew Alex wouldn't be happy that I was making the decision without her, but it was better than her being arrested.

I handed my phone to Van Straten. "I'm pretty sure that's his number."

"How did you get this?"

"Does it matter?"

"Not really," she said. "More important, how did you and Ms. Verde get the painting? Analyst Smith tells me she found it in an in upstate New York antique shop. Is that true?"

I told her it was, then asked a question I thought she could answer. "But how did it end up there?"

"In the upstate antique shop?" Van Straten said. "I have no idea."

65

May 1945
New York City

The large shipment of artwork arrived on a warm, wet afternoon, the Manhattan dock crawling with activity, several boats arriving at once with only a third of the dockworkers on hand, the regular workers absent the past four, five years, the lucky ones on their way back home to the States, the not so lucky missing or dead. The longshoremen working today were older men or young ones with flat feet or conditions that made them unfit for military duty, all of them sweating and cursing as they unloaded cargo in the rain.

Aidan O'Connor, pale, fat, and with a rheumatic heart, had been making money while other men fought and died. An agent for the Hudson Shipping Company, he inspected cargo, checking for companies that paid him to look the other way, which he did now with the crates for the Buchholz Gallery, signing off on the consignment sheet promptly as he had spied government officials at a neighboring dock and knew they were headed his way, eager to seize any unlawful merchandise under the Trading with the Enemy Act.

He pulled men off other jobs to load the crates onto a truck that left the dock just as the government inspectors came on.

Crates dismantled, paintings propped against walls, the two gallery interns—both young men and recent art history graduates hired to deal

with the ever-increasing postwar inventory—checked the artworks off
the consignment sheet, then cataloged them by artist, title, and size, the
information carefully printed on cards the way Mr. Valentin demanded.
"Use the heavy stock cards," he said, his English heavily accented. He
was a German, possibly a Jew, though the interns were not sure. All they
knew was he had worked for an art dealer in Berlin rumored to have
dealt in looted Nazi art, but they didn't believe it: a Jew working for one of
Hitler's art dealers was preposterous.

With white-gloved hands they separated the art, more than half the
work easily recognizable, artists the young men had recently studied in
school: cubist works by Picasso and Braque, landscapes by Cézanne, poin-
tillist paintings by Seurat, portraits by Gauguin and Van Gogh, abstrac-
tions by Paul Klee and Kandinsky. They could not believe their eyes. There
were more works by German artists Max Beckmann, Emil Nolde, and
Otto Dix.

For several hours the young men filled out cards, only a dozen or so of
the artworks unidentifiable or without signatures. These, they set aside.
Then they brought the cards to Mr. Valentin, who thanked them for their
work and dismissed them so he could view the work alone, as he always did.

Though the back room was hot, Curt Valentin did not remove his three-
button, peak-lapeled jacket, nor loosen his tie. He was not a handsome man,
balding, with a broad face, prominent nose, and widely set eyes, but he was
suave and debonair and personable, qualities that had worked well for him
in Germany and again in New York.

He moved between the artwork, stopping to admire a piece here and
there, all Entartete Kunst, degenerate art, a Nazi euphemism for not only
Jewish or Bolshevik art but any form of abstraction, distortion, or experi-
mentation, any work that made the viewer think and question attributes
firmly discouraged by the Third Reich.

A German Jew, Valentin had left Germany in 1937 with the Nazis'
blessing and a job—to sell degenerate art in the United States, the profits to

be used in support of the German war effort. He was, in Nazi vernacular, a Devisenjude, *a Jew who brought in foreign currency.*

For a moment, he wondered what he was now that the war was over. Just a Jew, he supposed, and one who still did business with Hitler's approved art dealers and the larger network of German art agents, all of whom had resumed business as usual, most specializing in Fluchtgut, *art sold by Jews fleeing the Nazis, works acquired under extreme duress.*

Valentin ran his hand over a plaster sculpture by Otto Freundlich, an abstract head reminiscent of the sculptures on Easter Island, a work many believed had been destroyed, but which had been saved by Valentin. It had become his duty, his calling, not only to artists like Freundlich, whom the Nazis had murdered in a Polish extermination camp, but to experimental and degenerate artists everywhere. His mission, to bring modern art to America. And if it meant trading with former Nazi art dealers and selling works with dubious provenance, so be it. One had to make choices to survive, a Faustian bargain to which he had agreed.

Thinking of each piece as an orphaned child in need of a home, Valentin went through the artwork, making notes on the cards of potential buyers. Then he set the cards aside. He didn't need them to identify the art; he knew all of the art and artists with the exception of the small group his young interns had set aside, these unsigned and unidentified. One, he recognized right away as the work of artist Käthe Kollwitz, easily missed by the interns as she was a woman and not well-known in the States. He recognized others in the stack as work by unimportant artists. There was only one he could not identify at all, which he assumed had been included by mistake, a portrait in mostly black and white of a woman looking as if she were about to cry, maudlin and not to his taste. He set it aside and turned off the light.

He was surprised to see his assistant still at her desk, a graduate of a secretarial school that had omitted the liberal arts, an excellent typist and stenographer. Otherwise she was dull and unsophisticated.

He told her to go home, then asked her to wait, went into the back room, and reappeared with the small sentimental portrait of the woman.

"Something for your wall," he said.

The secretary protested, but when he insisted, she thanked him and commented on the woman's sad look, then turned the painting around and noted the date, 1944. "Practically brand new," she said, then asked if it was all right if she gave it to her mother. "I just know she'll love it."

Valentin nodded, thinking of his own mother who had disappeared the year after he'd left Germany.

"My mother has a big old house with lots of empty walls, and this will look great," the assistant said. "It's upstate, in a really small town I'm sure you've never heard of, Stanfordville," she said. But by then, Valentin had stopped listening.

66

First thing I did after Smith and Van Straten left Vondelpark was to call Alex again. When I got her voicemail, I walked through the park, along paths and across wide lawns, and around the pond, which was more like a lake. I found a roll I'd stuffed in my pocket from breakfast and fed it to the ducklings. I tried calling Smith, wanted to know if they'd contacted Baine, but got his voicemail too. Then I walked some more, checking my phone every few minutes.

There were people everywhere—couples strolling hand in hand, young moms pushing strollers, kids playing. It was a beautiful day, and I should have felt good, but I felt lonely and anxious and jealous, picturing Alex with a curator I'd never met. I wondered what I was doing here when I should be home making new work for my show, and I cursed the day Alex had brought that painting home.

I was walking around the pond again when Alex called back.

"Where've you been?"

"Well, that's a nice greeting," she said. "You know where I am. I got your message, but my cell isn't working here. I'm at the airport in Paris, in an actual pay phone—remember them?—waiting for our rental car, which is taking forever." She sounded cheerful, which made it worse.

I told her about the meeting with Carolien and her scar-faced friend, and how he'd warned us to stay away from the painting.

"But we don't have the painting," she said, the phone staticky.

"That's exactly what I told him," I said, then tried to describe my encounter with Smith and Van Straten, but Alex stopped me, confused, no surprise as I was doing a poor job of recounting what had gone down, and because I was avoiding what *I* had said, the information I had given them. I stalled some more, asked how she was doing, and she said fine.

"Or I was," she said. "Before hearing all of this. Though I'm still confused, and this connection is terrible." She said she was with the curator, and they had to get going soon, and I could explain it all tomorrow, and that's when I blurted it out.

"They know about your father and they're going to contact him."

"*What?* Who knows?"

"Van Straten and Smith," I said, and tried to make sense of it though I didn't really understand it myself, just that Van Straten had said she needed a client to buy a painting. "And they're going to call your father."

"I still don't understand," Alex said. "No one knows where my father is. How would they be able to call him?"

"Because I gave them his number."

"How do *you* have the number?"

I didn't want to tell her, but I had to.

There was a pause, then she said, "So you went through my phone, through my calls?"

"Yes," I said and made a mess of an apology by blaming her for her secretive calls, then apologized again and said it was before she told me, and said I'd had no choice. "They were going to arrest you."

"What?" she said again, this time incredulous, and I didn't blame her. I tried to explain it again, then heard a man in the background, the curator I presumed, telling her the car was ready. "I have to go," Alex said.

"I'll explain it all tomorrow," I said. "And you'll understand."

"Will I?" she said.

"Please trust me," I said. "I love you."

Alex said, "Okay," and hung up.

I stood there a minute, watching the ducklings, the phone in my hand, thinking how badly I'd explained it or hadn't explained it, and how I had to make sense of it so Alex would understand. I went over it in my mind, my meetings with Smith and Van Straten and Carolien and her scar-faced friend, and his words came back to me.

I would recommend that you and your girlfriend, Ms. Verde, stay as far away from the Van Gogh self-portrait as possible…and tell Ms. Verde to forget about traveling.

What traveling had he been referring to? Our trip here to Amsterdam? Or her trip to France? But how could he know that?

Because he knew how we'd found the painting under another painting, knew our names when Carolien hadn't told him, knew that people were looking for us.

I called Alex back, but her phone rang and rang, and I remembered she said it wasn't working. I hung up and made another call.

When Carolien answered, I didn't say hello, just that I needed to see that guy again.

"Which guy?" she said.

"Your friend," I said. "The one with the scar."

67

Fluorescent light blinking, smoke clouding the conference room air, everyone on edge. It had been twenty-four hours and not a word from Trader's people.

But there'd been some good news. Baine was in. He had accepted the deal to pose as Lewis's high-profile client in exchange for a get-out-of-jail-free card, thanks to Van Straten and the State Department.

"Does he know how they found him?" Smith asked.

"He believes through a mole in the State Department," she said. "Someone who has been following his case and looking for him."

"Right," Smith said, still hoping to keep Perrone and Verde out of the deal and out of trouble. "You realize that giving Baine access to a great painting is like dangling a mouse in front of a cat."

"Yes," Van Straten said. "But according to the State Department, Mr. Baine is one very happy cat. He will behave."

Smith wasn't so sure. He looked over at the small Matisse painting, one of the artist's early fauve nudes, delivered yesterday, sitting in the corner like a discarded Christmas gift, the first artwork to be exchanged. A Nazi-looted painting not seen for eighty years, recently though not publicly recovered, and part of the highly coveted collection Calvin Lewis had offered Trader.

"Suppose they keep the first painting, the Matisse, and don't come back for the second?" he asked.

"That will not happen," Van Straten said. "It is not about the

Matisse, but about having you sell the Van Gogh, the most high-profile painting to surface in decades. Trader wants to control the sale from a distance, to keep his hands clean if anything goes wrong."

For a while they talked about this possibility or that one, fallbacks and alternatives, Jaager reviewing his tracking system for the team, Steiner posing negative scenarios as usual. Smith felt his anxiety rising like bread in an oven, a low-level buzz moving up and through his body, worrying he'd been found out and Trader had bailed, that they would be forced to scrap the assignment and begin again without him. He was trying to breathe, to be mindful when his burner lit up. He signaled the room to be quiet, phone to his ear. He was off in less than a minute.

"They're ready to meet," he said.

"When?" Van Straten asked.

"Now," he said.

68

Bruno Steiner was not happy, had not been happy since the beginning of this assignment, Van Straten treating him like an underling, not the expert in cultural crime that he was. True, it was his first time physically on an assignment and not behind a desk; and true, he had been instructed to listen, take notes, and report back to INTERPOL. But still, was it asking too much to be treated with respect?

He emailed his daily report, everything that had just gone down in the meeting, then took another step, making formal requests for local law enforcement to be standing by, which he did by the book. A green notice to warn about persons of interest in the criminal investigation, in this case, Trader. Then an orange notice to warn of an event that might represent an imminent threat and danger to persons or property. Again, Trader, as well as Trader's representatives and associates.

Steiner spent a moment describing how he had insisted on being part of the convoy that would follow Analyst Smith on the mission, and how Van Straten had agreed, but only because she had no choice. Otherwise INTERPOL would withdraw their support of the assignment as well as any future assignments in which she was involved. Something he suggested INTERPOL do no matter what the outcome of this operation, referring to her as "incompetent," her leadership abilities "weak."

Then, he filled out the purple notice, the modi operandi, that being the procedures, objects, devices, or hiding places used by the criminals. Here, he listed the Van Gogh and Matisse paintings (the objects) and noted that the exchange (modi operandi) was imminent, the location or hiding places forthcoming.

He knew INTERPOL would review his request immediately as this was a class A-1 assignment with international ramifications, that they would follow through by contacting local law enforcement, which included police and militia that could be mobilized quickly.

A moment to review his requests, then he hit Send.

Within minutes, even quicker than he'd imagined, he received his answer: LSB, Locals Standing By.

Steiner sat back. He was satisfied. If the assignment went well, and he was fairly certain it would, despite his misgivings about Van Straten, he would be moving up the INTERPOL ladder all the way to the General Assembly, its governing body, where he deserved to be and should have been a long time ago.

69

Forty-million-dollar painting tucked into the metal basket of a rented bike, Smith pedaled the one-point-three miles to the city's main train station, Amsterdam Centraal, locked the bike outside, and headed in. Enormous, sprawling, an anthill of activity, hundreds of people coming and going, Smith followed the directions exactly as they had been given, sweating, clock ticking, newspaper-and-Bubble-Wrapped painting under his arm. He paid the six and a half euros for a ticket to the nearby city of Haarlem, a ticket he would never use, then made his way to the station's east wing to the baggage locker room. Number one-three-six was one of the smaller lockers, its door open. He slid the painting in, closed the locker door, and received a small cardboard stub in return.

Down the row to the ticket machine, the number of the locker he had just used displayed on its small screen warning him he had two minutes to pay. Hand shaking, he managed to get the stub into the slot, and seconds later a printed receipt rolled out. He slipped the receipt into his pocket, then found the nearest escalator, which took him down to a long corridor of cafés, food shops, and souvenir stores, among them the store he was looking for, Smoke City, the window with display boxes of cigars, lighters, ads for e-cigarettes, and vapes, hookahs, and glass pipes.

Inside, a young woman with a Dutch boy haircut was waiting on a man in a leather jacket with tanned skin and pockmarked cheeks.

Smith waited until the man paid for his pack of Time brand cigarettes and left.

"Pack of Prince," he said.

The young woman hesitated a moment, looking him over, then said, "'When Doves Cry' is my favorite Prince song."

"Mine's 'Raspberry Beret,'" he said.

She reached behind her for a pack of Prince cigarettes and slid them across the counter.

Smith handed her eight euros, the locker receipt hidden in between the bills. Then he left the store, took the escalator back up, and headed out of the station, where he unlocked the bicycle, hands trembling so bad he had to stop to take a breath. He noticed the same man, the one in the leather jacket with pockmarked cheeks, getting onto a nearby motorcycle and driving away, but thought nothing of it.

By the time he had biked back to the police station and sat down with Van Straten and the team, word had come back that the painting had been retrieved and was on its way to the buyer. When they checked, the newly created Swiss account in the name of Calvin Lewis was $40,000 richer, all according to plan. Apparently Trader had been satisfied.

Van Straten said Trader had been impressed with their buyer for the Van Gogh.

"Almost too impressed," Smith said, relating the initial unease from Trader's people that Baine might be *too* high-profile, something they had obviously come to terms with, having agreed to the exchange. Smith wondered aloud why the Matisse transaction was not enough proof of Trader's illegal activity.

"Because it is only one sale," Van Straten said. "We need to show it is an ongoing operation. And we want the Van Gogh back."

Smith nodded. Though he did not relish the idea of going through another exchange so soon. His pulse and heartbeat had not yet returned to normal and the second painting exchange was pending. They were simply waiting to get the word from Trader's people.

Municipal Cop Vox offered Smith coffee and a sandwich, but he settled for the coffee. No way he could eat anything, his stomach doing flip-flops.

"How are the shoes?" she asked, referring to the black leather monk-straps they'd bought together.

"Tight," Smith said, but smiled. He lit a Prince cigarette, took a puff, then stubbed it out.

Van Straten offered him a Dunhill, which she lit for him, and he was glad; he did not want the team to see his hands were shaking.

The Monet *Haystack*, an incandescent and valuable impressionist oil, had been delivered, wrapped and ready for the next exchange, Van Straten going over particulars again—one painting as the other's collateral, the pieces presold, prices and percentages already agreed upon. After that, the Van Gogh would be going to their client, Baine. At least Trader thought so, half of the prearranged price of $80 million already in Lewis's Swiss account.

"Its market value is double that," Steiner said.

"But it will never come on the market. That is the point," Van Straten said.

Once this second exchange was made and Trader was satisfied, Lewis would presumably go home to resume his art business in Chicago, his new partnership with Trader in effect: Trader locating European and Asian buyers for the rest of Lewis's inventory and Lewis fencing Trader's more high-profile artworks to clients in the United States.

"Of course, none of this will happen," Van Straten said. "Once we have the Van Gogh in our possession, Trader will be arrested."

Smith was wondering where he would be once this was over— back at his old INTERPOL desk, part of the General Assembly, or on another assignment? Then Van Straten disappeared and came back in the room, the man in the leather jacket with tan skin and pockmarked cheeks beside her.

"This is Dispatcher," she said. "He oversaw the last exchange from a distance."

"From a distance?" Smith said. "We practically fell over each other at the smoke shop."

"Not quite," Dispatcher said. He shook Smith's hand in a firm grip.

"Is this man a previously authorized member of this team?" Steiner said. "Is INTERPOL aware of his participation? Who does he represent?"

Neither Dispatcher nor Van Straten answered Steiner's questions. "Dispatcher will be with us for the remainder of the operation" was all Van Straten said.

"I will need your name and who you work for," Steiner said to Dispatcher, who laughed, then patted Steiner on the head, upsetting his toupee.

"That will be all," Van Straten said, then got up and signaled for Smith to follow.

Outside, Smith followed Van Straten and Dispatcher away from the station into the old square, then along a canal, late-day sun skittering along the dark water like quicksilver.

"Dispatcher is here to make sure nothing happens to you," Van Straten said.

"I thought that was *your* job," Smith said.

"My job is the general success of the assignment," she said.

"You will be fine," Dispatcher said, clamping a heavy hand on Smith's shoulder.

"Good to know," Smith said. His adrenaline had drained away and he wanted to curl up on the sidewalk.

"What you are doing is very important," Van Straten said. "More important than you can imagine, Analyst Smith."

"And above my pay grade," he couldn't help but say.

"We will see about that once this is over," she said. Then she and Dispatcher walked ahead, Smith following, listening to them discussing old assignments in Vienna and Moscow, names of artists—Raphael, da Vinci, El Greco, and Picasso—along with inside jokes he didn't understand though he appreciated their easygoing collegial banter, which felt reassuring, like they could handle anything, the two of them laughing and confident. The laughter stopped abruptly when Van Straten checked her burner.

"The time and place," she said and showed the phone to Dispatcher, who read it, then gave Smith's shoulder another squeeze.

"I will see you there," Dispatcher said. "But this time, you will not see me." Then he said, "'*Be-tachbūlōt ta`aseh lekhā milchāmāh*,'" and translated for Smith. "'For by wise guidance you can wage your war.' A former motto of my organization, one they have abandoned, but I still like it."

"Is Pilot ready?" Van Straten asked.

"Yes," Dispatcher said, then he nodded at each of them and headed off.

"Come," Van Straten said. "We need to prepare, and we haven't much time."

70

I met Carolien on a narrow street beside a busy canal, houseboats moored, motorboats cruising, the sun playing peekaboo in between dark clouds.

"He said to meet him here," she said. "He thinks you have information about the painting."

A lie I'd told her to whet his appetite.

Carolien asked what the information was, and I was telling her it was better she didn't know when a small boat pulled up so quietly, I would have missed it if I hadn't been looking.

Scarface was standing on deck, still dressed as he had been when I'd met him at the museum, in a three-piece suit that seemed out of place in a boat on the canal. Beside him was a rough-looking guy in sunglasses and a cap. He offered Carolien a hand, but Scarface shook his head. "There is not enough room for Ms. Cahill," he said, clearly untrue, the boat looked to me to hold six more people easily and it was empty. "Just you," he said to me.

Carolien protested but I told her it was okay. I figured I could take Scarface down—he was half my size and double my age—if there was any trouble, though I wasn't expecting any.

"I will wait here until you come back," she said.

The guy in the cap and shades helped me in, then took up a spot behind the wheel in the back of the boat. There was a small cabin separating the front from the back, and I joined Scarface up front.

"The captain will not bother us. I often rent his boat, and he knows not to speak—or to listen." He folded himself into one of the two seats up front and gestured for me to sit beside him. "I thought you would enjoy a little ride," he said, wrapping a scarf around his neck, deep mauve, almost the color of his scar. In the daylight, I could see his black hair was dyed, with a quarter inch of gray roots, his scar ineptly dabbed with pancake. "This is the best way to see the city. You know, Amsterdam is often referred to as the Venice of the North."

The boat headed down the narrow canal, then turned onto a wider one with even larger houseboats moored on either side, a few speed-boats, engines roaring, and a gondola-type boat that cut across our path too close, the people onboard drinking and laughing.

"Drunken fools," Scarface said, then went on about his boat being electric and quiet and emission free. "The least one can do for the canals and the planet and..." he said, going on about global warming until I interrupted.

"The other day you mentioned my girlfriend's name."

"Did I? Well, Carolien must have told me."

I didn't challenge him, though Carolien had denied it.

"So what is this information you have about the painting?" he asked.

I skirted the question by saying he'd warned me to stay away from it, then asked how he knew Alex was going away, and I quoted him, "You said she should 'forget about traveling.'"

"Did I?" he said. "Why all these questions about your girlfriend?"

"What do you know about her travels?"

"Me? *I* know nothing about her travels. How would I?"

The boat slipped under a bridge, and we were plunged into darkness though I could still see his face in shadow, the scar deep purple. When we emerged, I asked again how he'd known Alex was traveling.

"You seemed to know a lot, that Alex was going away, that the Van Gogh painting had cows in it, and that it was in negotiation."

"I hear things. It is my business," he said, waving a dismissive hand that got on my nerves. "Now, about that information of yours. I am a busy man."

I told him I didn't care about his business. "I want to know what you heard about Alex," I said, leaning toward him. "*Now.*"

"My dear young man, I do not have to tell you *anything*. If this is why you have asked to meet me, I am very disappointed. You have sorely wasted your time, and *mine*."

I took a breath, could feel my anger rising.

The canal widened, boats crisscrossing in front of us, the shore far away.

"You *wanted* me to know, to be scared," I said. "Telling me those things, almost teasing me. Who told you Alex was traveling? How did you know that?"

"I was not trying to scare you. I was *warning* you, doing you a favor. I have no time to tease you about your silly girlfriend." He sighed as if I were an annoying child, and that was it—heat flooded my chest and something like a flashbulb popped behind my eyes, and I grabbed hold of him.

He pulled away and stood up, cursing at me and calling for the captain to turn the boat around, but I had a grip on him, and when he said, "It could already be too late for your girlfriend," I pushed him down hard and leaned his head over the edge of the boat. He was bellowing, his mouth distorted, but his shouts were lost under the sound of motorboats and a tour guide on a loudspeaker pointing out the "dancing houses of Damrak," and me snarling, "*Tell me!*" and pushing him further back, seeing the veins in his neck straining, his scarf and dyed hair dipping into the murky water. And if the captain hadn't pulled me off, I might have drowned him.

He helped Scarface back into his seat and growled something in Dutch at me, Scarface gasping and holding his throat, his mauve-colored scarf floating on the water before I saw it go under.

I sat back, sucking in air and trying to calm down. Scarface was doing the same, but when the captain grabbed me again, Scarface shooed him away.

"All I know is…what I heard," he gasped. "That Ms. Verde was… pursuing the painting elsewhere…and she should not and…that was it." He sat back, pale and spent.

"Nothing else?"

"No. I told you. I was trying to…warn you…as a favor to Ms. Cahill."

The anger drained out of me, not proud of how I'd behaved, a lot closer to my teenage self than I liked to admit. I apologized.

"What I heard," he said, "was secondhand, through…the underground."

"Do you think Alex is in real danger?"

He said he had no idea, just that someone knew that she was traveling and what she was up to. "And I imagine they know what *you* are up to as well. It is why I brought you out here. I could not chance being seen with you."

We were back on the narrow canal. From a distance I spotted Carolien on shore where I'd left her, waving.

This time when I got off the boat, the captain did not offer me a hand.

"I owe you a scarf," I said to Scarface, apologizing again and promised to let him know if I heard anything about the painting. I owed him that.

"Do not bother. I told you I am finished with that painting. But I *will* take a new scarf!"

Carolien was eyeing us as I climbed ashore, Scarface behind me, wet hair, clothes disheveled. I watched his boat take off, didn't tell her what had happened, only that I was worried about Alex and what Scarface had said about other people knowing she was traveling.

She thought I was overreacting, and maybe I was but I didn't like the idea of nefarious people knowing where Alex was. "I'm going," I said.

"Going where?"

"To Auvers-sur-Oise."

Carolien looked surprised, asked if that was a good idea and maybe it wasn't, but if there was any chance that Alex was in danger, I was going. She was already mad at me, so what the hell. I found a bench and googled the various ways to travel, Carolien beside me.

"Flying to Paris is the fastest route, an hour and twenty minutes," she said so I booked a flight, then a car from the Paris airport. According to Google Maps, it was about an hour's drive to Auvers-sur-Oise. In total, a two-and-a-half-hour trip, no faster way unless I charted a helicopter.

Carolien asked to go along to keep me company.

"No thanks," I said, then called a taxi and headed for the airport.

71

Alex was now in a rental car, Finn de Jong beside her, gripping the wheel and speeding along country roads.

She asked him to slow down. "I'd like to live to see where Van Gogh *died*."

Finn laughed. Keeping one hand on the wheel, he reached over and patted her knee for the third or fourth time. "Don't worry, I am a very good driver."

Alex lifted his hand and stared out the window at trees and houses blurring past the windows. Had it been a mistake to come here with this man she hardly knew? But with the soft wind on her face, rustling her hair, she reminded herself that she had come for a reason—to meet someone who had something to show her, something, according to Finn, that might prove her painting's existence.

Past a small village with neat stone houses, Finn made a show of checking his watch, then dropped his hand to her thigh as if by accident. One more time Alex lifted it off.

"I so hope to meet your wife," she said.

"We have recently separated," he said, though Alex noted he still wore his wedding ring and wasn't sure she believed him.

She wished Luke was here—not to protect her, she could handle Finn—then thought about Luke giving Smith and Van Straten her father's telephone number. *They were going to arrest you.* But how, and why? And what did Anika Van Straten have to do with it? Alex was still confused, and annoyed.

The car bumped over a small bridge, sun reflecting off a lake as flat and shiny as glass. She stole a look at Finn, his mouth set tight with determination, his hands on the wheel where she wanted them. They passed through another town, more stone houses, a painted sign, CHAPONVAL.

"What we call a capon. You know, a castrated duck?" She laughed, but Finn didn't.

Then, a few miles on, there was a sign for Auvers-sur-Oise, and Finn took the turnoff, which brought them into the town's main square, quiet and lovely, only a few people milling around.

Out of the car, a relief, until Finn slid his arm over her shoulder. Alex shook him off and walked into the square she had seen in photos, larger than she'd imagined, like a little park, trees dotting the perimeter, its focal point the town hall, the Hôtel de Ville, square and white with French flags flapping from the second-story balcony. She turned to take in the famous Auberge Ravoux just across the road, Van Gogh's last home, its wheat-colored upper floor above a restaurant painted pale rose with lace curtains in the windows.

Finn was in the center of the square on his cell phone, pacing impatiently, and she crossed the road. She looked up at a granite plaque. "*Le peintre* Vincent Van Gogh *vecut dans cette maison et y mourut, le 29 Juillet 1890*—the painter Vincent Van Gogh lived in this house and died here."

Finn joined her, and when she said she was going in, he said there wasn't time, that the man he wanted her to meet would be here soon.

"I'll be quick," she said, following arrows along the side of the house, past a stone wall that led to a little office where the ticket seller, a young Frenchwoman with perfect English, offered to be their guide.

She led them down another path, bordered by an ivy-covered

fence with signs in multiple languages that summarized the phases of Van Gogh's life: The Pastor's Son, A Young Art Dealer, Becoming an Artist—his birth in 1853, his father a Protestant pastor, early drawing lessons in Brussels, and his move to the Hague, where he lived with the prostitute known as Sien.

"Clasina Maria Hoornik," Alex said, who she knew had also been Vincent's model and muse, that they had lived together two years during which Vincent had made many drawings and paintings of her. "Do you know what happened to her?" she asked the guide.

"Vincent's brother Theo forced him to give her up or he would no longer support him. She lived for fourteen years after Vincent's death, then committed suicide by throwing herself into a river."

"Oh, I remember," Alex said. "How awful."

"Theo was right," Finn said. "She was a common whore," and urged them forward, repeating they were short on time.

Alex wished she were here alone, taking her time with each plaque: Continuing to Paint, about Van Gogh's time in Paris, and The High Yellow Note, referring to the yellow house in Arles that Vincent had shared with Gauguin. A plaque titled Continue to Paint noted it was the artist Pissarro who had recommended Auvers-sur-Oise to Vincent, and Dr. Gachet, who resided in the town, to care for him after his year-long stay at the asylum in Saint Rémy, details of which were on the next plaque: Fear of Madness, describing Vincent's breakdown and cutting off his ear.

"The doctor at San Rémy wrote 'cured' on Vincent's papers when he left the asylum. Ten weeks later he was dead," the guide said, leading them up a back stairwell, Finn trying to hold Alex's hand, which she pulled away.

Inside, they mounted another staircase, this one a ziggurat of thick dark wood, a light fixture hanging above illuminating plaster walls veined with cracks.

"He lived here, on the top floor," the guide said.

Alex peered through the open doorway, a small, slanted skylight illuminating the spare attic room, the dark wooden floor and plaster walls, a single chair.

"Vincent's room for the last seventy days of his life," the guide said.

Alex lingered in the doorway trying to imagine the most famous artist in the world living in this tiny Spartan room. She wanted to stay, but Finn was anxious, and the guide led them downstairs and unlocked the restaurant's doors. Alex stepped into a rose-colored room with dark wooden moldings, everything bathed in the soft glow of light through lace-curtained windows, hardwood tables and caned chairs, a large, faded mural.

"All of it has been restored to how it was in Vincent's time," the guide said, pointing out a small wooden table in the corner where Vincent had taken his meals, the only table set with a tablecloth, a wineglass and carafe, an empty wicker basket. A still life without the man, Alex thought, though his presence was so palpable she shivered.

"The table is always set," the guide said. "But no one is allowed to eat there."

There was no billiard table, but Alex tried to imagine it from Van Gogh's paintings of the auberge. It was where he had been laid out, his funeral in this room. She recalled the description in Emile Bernard's letter of the artist surrounded by yellow flowers and his paintings, like a halo.

Had the self-portrait been among them?

Finn broke the moment by answering a phone call, then sidled up beside Alex, his beard brushing up against her cheek as he whispered in her ear. "Monsieur Toussaint is here but wants us to meet him at the cemetery," he said, his hand on her arm, the other wrapping around her waist. "Come. We must go."

72

The tension in the conference room was so palpable Smith thought he could taste it.

Trader had the Van Gogh and was ready for the exchange, same place, Café de Spuyt, so far the only direction they had.

Van Straten reiterated that she would be monitoring him from the van. Dispatcher, with Pilot, from another undisclosed location. Then she turned the briefing over to Jaager, who handed Smith a new pair of glasses.

"Almost identical to your old ones," Jaager said, explaining how the frames were just a hair thicker to support the new carbon fiber and micro video recorder that could film for four hours, plus a mini-audio bug with a 720-meter range. "That is six times the length of an American football field," he said, then exchanged Smith's neck chain for another, the links a tad thicker. "New and improved," he said. "With a mini-GPS tracker in three of the links." He pointed them out to Smith. "But you see, undetectable. And you do not need to shout. Just speak naturally. The recorder will pick up your voice as well as others around you, along with ambient noise."

Steiner looked up from his tablet. "All very nice," he said. "But INTERPOL wants personnel on the scene."

"That personnel being you?" Smith said. "You trying to get me killed? They see an INTERPOL agent, it's not just the deal that's terminated, it's *me*."

"How would they know I am an agent?" Steiner said.

"Because you *reek* of it!" Smith said.

"No one is going to be terminated," Van Straten said, trying to keep Smith calm. She introduced a young cop from Firearms who had been sitting quietly, who opened a small black box and removed an odd-looking but recognizable gun, placed it on the table, then slid it toward Smith. "A ghost gun," she said. "Unregistered and untraceable, one-hundred-percent plastic, 3D-printed thanks to a Texas-based company that supplies downloadable instructions free on their website."

Smith tried it in his hand. It was lightweight and felt like a toy. "Is it any good?" he asked.

"It fires a single shot," she said. "Use it. Then lose it."

"Trader's men will likely pat you down and find it," Van Straten said. "No reason to hide it. It makes sense you would carry a weapon in your line of work but try not to give it up."

"Let them know it is not easy to make," the firearms cop said. "It takes approximately forty hours to print one pistol."

"If they find it," Van Straten went on, "and they will, show them it is not loaded and turn it into a *friendly* conversation. Tell them you will have guns made for them as gifts."

The cop handed him a cartridge, explained how to load it and shoot.

"The cartridge will be sewn into a belt I have for you to wear, easily accessible and, again, undetectable," Jaager said.

Steiner interrupted. "How do we know for sure Trader has the Van Gogh in his possession? It is only his word."

"We do not," Van Straten said. "But you heard Analyst Smith ask for proof, and they said he would get it."

"But they did not say *what* sort of proof or *when* he would get it," Steiner said, unconsciously adjusting his toupee.

"They have nothing to gain by lying," Van Straten said.

"Just two multimillion-dollar paintings, the Monet and the Matisse," Steiner said.

Van Straten turned away. She had considered these questions but could not deal with the negativity, not now when they were so close, when it was all about to happen. She recapped that she would be there, in a van with Jaager listening and watching through the tracking devices in Smith's glasses and neck chain.

"If the devices are detected, they'll kill me," Smith said.

"No one is going to be killed," she said.

"Can you guarantee that?"

Van Straten fixed her eyes on him, the most intimate look he had ever gotten from her. "There are no guarantees in life," she said. "But I have never lost a man, and I will not lose you."

73

The flight from Amsterdam to Paris had been nonstop turbulence, like my mood. I had downed so many peanuts and drunk so much Coke that my brain was now moving at about the same speed as my rented Opel Corsa on a three-lane highway heading out of Paris, commuter cars and trucks cutting across lanes without signaling, horns beeping, and me trying to drive one-handed—next to impossible with a stick shift but the car had no GPS, so I had my cell phone in my other hand, one eye on the road, the other on Google Maps.

It was a while before the traffic eased and I watched for my first landmark, Saint-Denis. After that, I was on the lookout for a stadium, which I found, then merged onto another highway, then onto the Viaduct d'Argenteuil, an elevated road that passed over a river two times in succession.

I tried calling Alex again to let her know I was coming, but this time I didn't even get her voicemail. The phone just rang. She'd said her phone was not working but it still worried me, and when I disconnected, I accidentally lost my Google Maps and had to pull onto the highway's narrow shoulder, where it took me a couple of minutes to reset the map and get back on the road and another ten before I spied the next landmark, a large glitzy casino that looked as if it were floating on a river. If the map was right, I was about forty minutes from my destination.

But then what? If Alex's phone wasn't working, how would I find her?

Traffic was moving at a clip now. I passed signs for towns on my map, Sannois, Franconville, the sides of the highway becoming more suburban—houses and trees, ads for a vocational school, and gas, which I needed.

The pumps were like gas stations everywhere, just the brand name, TotalEnergies, was unfamiliar, and all the signs in French. I'd barely had time to process being in Amsterdam, let alone France.

A few minutes later I was back on the road, in a hurry to get to a place I'd read about and fantasized visiting, but not like this.

I thought about Smith lying about being at INTERPOL, now working with Van Straten, another person who had been lying about who she was and what she did—*I keep stolen art from being stolen again*, if she was telling me the truth now—and about the scar-faced art fence, and faceless people who were following me and Alex, and a tattooed guy named Gunther, my mind spinning when I saw the sign for Val-d'Oise, then one for the town of Ermont. I checked the map to make sure I was still heading in the right direction, and thankfully, I was. Another thirty minutes and I would be in Auvers-sur-Oise. I'd find Alex, and everything would be okay.

74

Smith had been standing in front of the Café de Spuyt for about twenty minutes when a black SUV with tinted windows pulled up, the door opened, and he was ushered in without a word. After that, a pat-down, two thugs opening his shirt, unzipping his pants, a hand inside his underpants, socks pushed down, everything but a cavity search, then the car took off, making its way along the city streets. Smith tried to remain calm, hoped the tracking devices were working as the SUV headed onto a highway.

He was in the back seat, beside him, the same rep as last time, the blond woman in sunglasses and headscarf. Between them, the Bubble-Wrapped Monet painting. On facing seats, the two strip-search thugs in dark glasses and dark suits, *Men in Black*, he thought. One of them, the bigger guy with a halting way of speaking, had found the gun in the search and given it to the woman, who was rotating it in her hand.

"Does this actually shoot?" she asked.

"When it's loaded," Smith said and gave the speech about the 3D printing process and how he'd get them each a copy.

"Nice toy," she said. "Trader will like it."

He promised to have one made for him as the woman looked down the barrel, saw it was empty, and handed it back. The men in black had not found the bullet stitched into the inside of his belt.

"Where are we going?" he asked.

She told him to relax, fumbled a pack of American Spirit out of her bag, asked the driver to crack her window, and offered one to Smith, who took it.

He lit up and took a drag. "Not bad," he said. "If you're going to die, better to die organically."

"Very funny, Mr. Lewis."

"I try," he said, sweat beading under his arms and on his forehead. He pushed the glasses up his nose, more carefully than usual.

"I'm going to have a look at this," the woman said, removing the Bubble Wrap, though she left the translucent glassine intact, the painting beneath clear enough, a Monet *Haystack* in lavender. She snapped a cell phone picture. "For proof," she said. "No one wants to waste their time."

"What about *my* proof?" Smith asked.

"Soon," she said.

Smith squinted through the tinted windows, could make out factories and an industrial complex, the air in the car close despite the cracked window, one of the goons opposite also smoking a cigarette. He made a vow to quit when this was over, stole a look at his watch, noted they'd been driving exactly twenty-three minutes when the car took an exit and he saw the sign and tried to say the name for his team's benefit, one of those difficult Dutch names with lots of vowels, "Ui—th—oorn?"

The woman gave him a look like maybe she understood what he was doing. She slapped his chest, then opened a few of his shirt buttons. "I know you were searched but just in case."

"We searched…him…good," said the slow-talking man in black. He reminded Smith of Lennie in *Of Mice and Men*.

"How long before we get there?" Smith asked, the woman's hand inside his shirt, brushing against his neck chain.

"You're sweating," she said, and removed her hand, making a face and wiping her palm on the car seat. "I told you to relax."

"Sorry, I've got a perspiration problem," Smith said, buttoning his shirt. He glanced through the window. They were still on a highway, electric power lines lining the road. "When do I get my proof?" he asked again.

"Patience," the woman said.

The car took an exit onto a narrower road, and from what Smith could see, they were in the suburbs, cookie-cutter houses for a few miles, then a heavily wooded area.

The driver said, "*Vijftien* minutes."

"*How* many minutes?" Smith asked, again for the benefit of his team.

No one answered.

The woods ended and they were in a field, the car bumping along a gravel road, then it stopped.

"We *zijn hier*," the driver said.

The locks clicked. Smith tried his door and stepped out, the men in black immediately on either side of him.

"This way," the woman said.

Smith followed her through scrub grass that opened onto a pasture, then a long sandy strip. At the end of it was a small plane, its motor idling, propellers spinning.

75

"You see it?" Jaager pointed to the image on the screen, grainy but clear enough.

"A plane, yes," Van Straten said. Then into the mic. "Dispatcher, are you getting this?"

"Roger that," Dispatcher said.

Van Straten asked Jaager to rewind and she watched again, her eyes on the woman in the scarf and sunglasses. "Can you enlarge the woman?" she asked, and he did. The woman's face filled most of the small screen, but it was pixilated and grainy. Van Straten shook her head and told him to back off, the screen resuming its normal view of the woman with Smith beside her, the two of them heading toward the plane.

Steiner was sputtering, "It's a plane, a plane! Where are they taking him?"

Van Straten told him to be quiet, directed Koner to pull the van to the side of the road. They were at the end of the same wooded area they had just seen on their tracking screen, the expanse of field just visible through the trees. She rolled down a window and could hear the plane's engine.

"How long until you can get us?" she asked Dispatcher.

"I am with Pilot now," he said, his voice staticky through the mic. "He is plotting your coordinates."

Jaager asked about his navigation system.

Pilot answered, "BAE, high-speed. Will the copter's cabling be affected by your tracking system?"

"No," Jaager said. "And no modifications needed for the GPS to work with your Doppler system. What are you flying?"

"Eurocopter X3 hybrid," Pilot said.

Jaager let out a loud whistle. "With a five-bladed rotor system?"

"You got it," Pilot said, "with two Rolls-Royce turboshaft engines."

Jaager whistled again.

Van Straten, head out the van window, was watching the small plane through binoculars. "It is still on the ground."

"Let me know when it takes off," Pilot said. "We will be landing near the same area."

Steiner, leaning over the back seat, crowding Van Straten and Jaager, said, "We are going to lose him!"

"We will not," Jaager said calmly, explaining that the trackers would continue to hold for several miles and by then the helicopter's systems would take over.

"What if it *doesn't*?" Steiner said.

"Hey"—Pilot's voice crackled through the speaker—"you, in the background, shut the fuck up!" Then he asked Jaager, "What's the probability of intercept?"

Jaager said, "LPIA," then translated for Van Straten, "Low probability of intercept altimeters, which means it is highly unlikely anyone other than those on the helicopter will be able to hear our communications or break into it."

"What if the plane doesn't get here in time?" Steiner said, wringing his hands.

"Will someone stick a turd in that *tzair's* mouth!" Dispatcher said. "We have already taken off and will be there in a few *minutes*."

"Roger that," Pilot said. "The Eurocopter has an extra engine, which doubles the top speed."

"Wow!" Jaager said. "That is like 430 kilometers per hour, yes?"

"Right," Pilot said. "And kid, whoever you are, I like you. Get your equipment ready to go. Stat."

"Hunter and co, stand by," Dispatcher said.

Jaager disconnected the tracking devices, rolling wires and removing the two small screens. Van Straten told Koner to stay with the van, the rest of them out now, heading onto the field, the plane in the distance and the chopping sound of the helicopter's blades growing louder.

76

Smith followed the woman down the field, the men in black flanking him, the woman clutching the Monet to her chest. It felt like they were walking into a sandstorm, wind from the plane's engines kicking up dirt and pebbles. "Where are we going?" he shouted over the racket, hoping his team could hear him, trying to remember how long before the trackers would quit working.

"You'll see," she shouted back, a hand holding her scarf, her hair in place.

"What about my proof?"

"Here," she said and handed him her phone. "It's a video. Hit Play."

Smith squinted, shielding his eyes from the dust, then watched as the Van Gogh self-portrait filled the small screen, the image frozen a moment, then it zoomed out, the painting growing smaller, someone holding it, hands gripping the sides. Then the painting was lowered, and a man's face, blindfolded, filled the screen.

"The real thing…is on board. You'll see for your…" the woman said, the rest of her words lost under the roar of the plane's engines.

Smith was still focused on the video, something familiar about the blindfolded man though he couldn't place him, when the men in black took hold of him and hoisted him onto the plane.

77

In the distance, Van Straten saw the plane take off. When it was no more than a spec in the sky, she spotted the helicopter coming into view.

Jaager, the equipment in his arms, beside her, Steiner behind them trying to keep up.

A few minutes later, the helicopter was hovering a few inches above the ground, twin propellers like striped claws whipping up dust, the sound deafening as they raced toward it, Van Straten reaching up for Dispatcher's arm and he pulled her in, her body vibrating as she made her way into the cabin. Jaager handed the tracking devices through the cockpit door.

Pilot leaned across Dispatcher and shouted, "You're coming, kid. I'm going to need you to work your tech."

"It is simple," Jaager shouted back. "You can do it."

"But I am *not* doing it. *Get in.*"

Dispatcher hoisted Jaager in.

Van Straten shouted, "Go!"

Steiner, behind them, a hand clamped on his toupee was shouting, practically bawling, "Wait, wait for me!"

It took everything for Van Straten not to leave him behind, but she didn't need INTERPOL on her back. She tapped Dispatcher, who offered Steiner a hand and lifted him in.

Then the propellers and auxiliary engines kicked in and the copter lifted off the ground with such propulsive force Steiner tumbled backward into the cabin and fell.

78

Alex stood beside the graves at the far corner of the cemetery, a small plot covered in low, lush ivy no more than seven or eight feet square, with two simple headstones. She leaned down to read the carved words.

"*Ici repose* Vincent van Gogh. Here rests Vincent van Gogh." The stones were worn and pitted, the dates partially hidden by ivy, which she gently lifted aside. 1853–1890.

"Some people live a hundred years and do not accomplish a thing. Vincent lived thirty-seven and changed the way we see," she said to Finn, but he had drifted a few yards away and was on his cell phone again.

Alex took in both gravestones, Theo's just beside Vincent's, the younger brother who had taken care of his older brother, the troubled genius, until he died, then died only six months later at the age of thirty-three.

"Are you ready?" Finn called over. "Toussaint will be coming."

Alex looked over at him, tall and handsome, hair fluttering in the breeze, and thought, *What an ugly man*. "You are standing on someone's grave," she said.

"Am I?" he said and glanced down at the plot, the headstone a few inches from his feet, but didn't move.

She looked back at Theo's grave, knew he had been sickly much of his adult life, that syphilis had been a contributing factor for both brothers, that he had died in Utrecht, but his wife had had his body exhumed and buried here beside his brother.

"He is coming," Finn said.

Alex looked up to see a man striding across the cemetery toward them, middle-aged, salt-and-pepper hair, handsome.

"Monsieur Toussaint," Finn said, introducing him to Alex.

"*Enchanté*," he said, with a slight bow.

"Toussaint? Doesn't that mean all saints?"

"Yes," he said, and smiled.

Finn cut in. "*Elle a quelque chose à vous montrer.*"

Alex translated in her head, *She has something to show you.* "Yes, I do," she said, found her phone and the photos, handed it to Toussaint, and told him to scroll through while she explained how she had found the painting.

"Incredible," he said.

"Now you understand why I brought Ms. Verde here to meet you," Finn said. "And so you can show her the artwork you have, as you would not allow me to photograph it," he added tersely.

"Are you here to buy my drawing?" Toussaint asked her.

"No," Alex said, surprised by the question. "*Pas du tout.*"

Finn, checking his phone, urged them to get going, already several feet ahead of them.

Toussaint gave him a reluctant nod but offered his arm to Alex and led her out of the cemetery. He stopped to point out the cathedral. "The one Vincent made famous in his paintings," he said, and Alex recognized it immediately, wanted to linger, but Finn insisted they keep moving. Toussaint sighed. "He thinks I will sell him my drawing. But I will not."

"Why are you letting *me* see it?"

"Because Monsieur Finn would not let me see your artwork unless I showed you mine and I was curious." He paused, looking her over. "You are not Monsieur de Jong's girlfriend, are you?"

"Oh God, no," she said, and Toussaint laughed at how emphatically she'd said it.

She explained she was an art history student here to see Van Gogh artworks for her thesis. She did not say she was still hoping to find the self-portrait, though right now she felt she was closer. She and Toussaint walked on ahead, Finn off to the side, cell phone to his ear.

Toussaint led the way across a railroad track and along a country road with pretty, well-kept houses. "My home is just there," he said, indicating a narrow two-story stone house set back from the road behind a metal fence, flowers and plants in the small front lawn overgrown and reaching the sills of tall first-floor windows just a few feet off the ground.

He pushed the front door open.

"You don't lock it?" Alex asked.

"Auvers is a very safe place," Toussaint said.

Inside, Alex could see all the way from the foyer through the living room to the back windows, also tall and open like the ones in front, a warm breeze wafting through the house, the place charming, if a bit of a mess, the furniture old, standing lamps with frayed tasseled shades, bookcase shelves sagging.

"I am afraid I did not change much after my wife died," Toussaint said, clearing things off the dining room table where he made room for a portfolio, Finn crowding beside him.

Using an X-Acto knife, he carefully slit the tape holding a piece of old-fashioned wax paper, raised it, and Alex caught her breath.

It was a pencil drawing on cardboard, a few of the edges frayed, a corner chipped, the sketch pale in some places, sharper in others, but amazing. Alex leaned in for a closer look at the pencil strokes that followed each form, the heaviest ones outlining the nose and defining the eyes, the beard and mustache and hair made of lighter cross-hatching, the shirt collar and vest sketchy and slightly smudged.

But there was no doubt it was a Van Gogh self-portrait. Just like *her* self-portrait, the pose, the angle of the head, the clothes, all of it almost identical, here in pencil.

"Quite like your painting, is it not?" Finn said. "Why I wanted you to see it."

"Where, *how* did you get this?" Alex asked.

"It was given to my great-grandfather, Julien, by the artist himself," Toussaint said, explaining how his great-grandfather, a teenager at the time, had lived here in this house, and in the spring and summer of 1890 had assisted Dr. Gachet. "He would run errands to the *pharmacie* for drugs and herbal remedies the doctor was using to treat Monsieur Vincent."

Finn interrupted with talk of the restoration and a sale, but Toussaint continued speaking to Alex, describing how Julien would go along with Vincent when he went out to paint, to help him with his easel and canvases.

A hand on Alex's arm, Finn leaned in between them. "As you can see, the drawing is in desperate need of restoration, the cardboard could crack further and then what? Really, monsieur, it must be someplace where it will be properly cared for. It is an important piece, and valuable."

"Which is why I came to you," Toussaint said. "For restoration."

"It needs more than that," Finn said. "It needs museum-quality framing, temperature control, a new home. It will not last long here."

"It has lasted here for well over a hundred years, and I will not part with it. It has always been in my family and will remain so."

But Finn would not quit, arguing that the sketch needed to be somewhere safe, and after checking his phone yet again, he said, "I am ready to sell it for you, and I will make you rich."

"I have enough money," Toussaint said. "If you will not restore it, then I will find someone who will." Toussaint asked Alex if she might help, and she said she had contacts at her school who would know.

Toussaint looked at her photos again, scrolling through them. "I can tell you that such a painting existed," he said. "According to Julien, it was laid out with Monsieur Vincent's other artwork at his funeral. This drawing was his preliminary sketch."

"What had happened to it?" Alex asked.

Toussaint produced a small, worn-looking notebook. "My great-grandfather wrote it all down here in his diary. There are several pages concerning this sketch and the self-portrait Monsieur Vincent made from it, and what happened to it after happened he died."

79

Just past the town of Taverny, my Google Map disappeared again, and my phone quit. I drove a mile, pulled over, turned the phone off, waited a minute, then turned it back on. Nothing. No reception. A dead zone. I popped open the glove compartment, hoping to find an old-fashioned map, but there were none, only a manual for the Opel. I was on a highway, cars and trucks whizzing by, trying to think—*go straight, take a turn?* I had been following the GPS step by step, had never looked at the whole route, and now I was lost.

I drove a mile looking for a sign or a name I remembered, but there was neither. The next exit promised gas and food and I took it in search of directions.

The Super U at Bessancourt was a big supermarket with fruit and vegetables, aisles of sauces and canned goods, a fish market, and a butcher, each with enormous signs, LE MARCHÉ FRAIS, LA POISSON-NERIE, LE BOUCHER, the latter the name of an old Claude Chabrol film Alex and I had watched on Criterion about a small-town butcher who might also be a mass murderer, the thought in my head as I perused the mostly empty aisles with only a few shoppers and even less sales staff. I tried the woman manning the checkout, but she didn't speak English. She pointed to the man at the fish market, who, holding fish fillets up to his nose, inhaled deeply to prove their freshness, but had no idea what I was saying, staring at me as blankly as the glassy-eyed fish in his hand.

I was close to giving up when I spotted a woman at the far end of the butcher counter and remembered how Alex had taught me to ask for the bathroom.

"*Où est*…Auvers-sur-Oise?" I asked.

The woman answered in English, "You are not far."

"Oh, that's *great!*" I said with so much gratitude she took a step back, then ushered me outside where she explained the route, complete with hand gestures as if she were speaking to someone hard of hearing. "*Le deuxième* exit, the *second* exit after the roundabout, go toward Avenue Charles de Gaulle and into the town of Méry-sur-Oise," she said, describing how I should drive through the town to another roundabout and I would see signs for Auvers-sur-Oise. "*Très simple*. It is very easy."

She was telling me the drive would be no more than twenty minutes when a man in a bloodstained apron sprinted out of the supermarket, shouting in French and waving a meat cleaver. He snatched a package of ground meat from the woman's hand, a moment before we both realized he was the store's butcher and that the woman had left the store without paying. She explained in French, and he went back to the store, grumbling, the packet of meat in his hand. The woman and I shared a good laugh. I thanked her and apologized for getting her in trouble.

Then, I was back on the road, driving through the first roundabout, my mind racing ahead, and with the idea of strangers following Alex, I sped the rest of the way to Auvers-sur-Oise, my foot heavy on the gas.

80

It took Smith a few seconds before the plane's interior came into focus, the cool lighting and individual leather seats, the people in them.

The woman moved past him, sidled up to the man in the front seat, a striking man with white hair and white eyebrows, his cheeks sprinkled with stubble like snow. She showed him the Monet and he told her to take it to the back of the plane and put it under the black light.

He patted the seat beside him. "Join me," he said to Smith.

Working hard to keep his cool, Smith sat down and offered his hand.

"Sorry," the man said. "I make it a habit never to touch."

Behind him, a young man with a collar of neck tattoos, arms, hands, and fingers inked with letters and symbols, looked up from a comic book and laughed.

"Be quiet, Gunther!" the white-haired man said.

Smith strained for something to say. "Nice plane."

"I am glad you think so, Mr. Lewis," the man said, scrutinizing Smith's face. "I find it is important to look into a person's eyes, particularly a prospective business partner. Your glasses, please." He stretched his hand out, waiting.

Smith removed his glasses and laid them in the man's hand, watched as he lifted his palm up and down weighing them. "Deceptively heavy."

"Yes, I'm thinking of getting a lighter pair," Smith said, fighting an urge to grab them back, but he didn't dare. "*I* find it important to know a prospective business partner's name," he said.

"Trader will do for now."

The woman came back with the Monet. "Nothing showed up under the light," she said.

"Of course not," Smith said. He knew the Monet was authentic and unretouched. "Now, what about the Van Gogh?"

Trader angled his chin at the woman, who went to the back of the plane again. This time she returned with the painting, which she handed to Smith, along with a pair of white cotton gloves.

"Beautiful, isn't it?" Trader said.

Smith slipped on the gloves, and tried to take it in, this painting he was holding in his lap, the lost Van Gogh everyone had been look-ing for, the famous artist giving him a sideways, knowing glance, the blue swirls of the background almost dizzying. "I'll take good care of it," he said. "Until I sell it."

"I am counting on that," Trader said.

The men in black had taken seats facing them, the one with the halt-ing speech trying to stretch out his long legs, difficult in the tight space.

A quick glance out the window at blue sky, then down at a body of water, houses, and cars. Smith could even make out a few people. They were flying low, but he wondered if Jaager's devices would work now that they were in the air. His glasses were still in Trader's hands, and he gently removed them and put them back on. "I'm blind without them," he said, his stomach fluttering.

"Jennifer," Trader said. "Mr. Lewis needs a drink."

The woman jumped up as if on command and once again disap-peared into the back of the plane.

"She makes a very good flight attendant, does she not?" Trader said with a laugh.

Smith said nothing. With his glasses on, he studied the painting more closely, the green shadows, the darker strokes of pigment in the red hair, the knit brows that gave the artist a look of worry.

The woman returned carrying a tray with crystal tumblers, ice, and a bottle of whiskey. She had removed her scarf and what had obviously been a blond wig, her dark-brown hair loose and to her shoulders. Her sunglasses were off too, and Smith had been right, she was pretty, though there was something hard and brittle about her. She handed the tray to Trader and took the painting from Smith.

"Don't want you to spill anything on this!" she said, while Trader poured them drinks.

Trader raised his glass. "To...us, Mr. Lewis."

"To you," Smith said. "So, where are we going?"

"Not far," Trader said. "Something I need to pick up."

"What?" Smith asked. The paintings for the trade were here, the plan being to swap them and that was it, wasn't it? Or were they planning to take the paintings and dump him somewhere? Another glance out the window. His glasses felt a bit cockeyed after Trader's handling, but he made no attempt to straighten them.

Trader did not answer his question. Instead, he said, "Oh, I almost forgot. There is someone I want you to meet." He nodded at Gunther. "Please fetch our guest for Mr. Lewis."

"Who?" Smith asked, turned, and saw Gunther leading the blindfolded man from the video down the aisle. Gunther stopped in front of him and waited until Trader gave him a sign, raising one of his white eyebrows, then he pulled the blindfold off, the guy swaying and blinking, then staring at Smith.

"He seems to recognize you," Trader said, then stood up and slapped the man across the face a few times. "Tell Mr. Lewis what you told me earlier."

The man shook his head, his eyes unfocused, darting, wild.

"You cannot or *will* not tell him?" Trader said.

"I used three of your syringes on him," Gunther said and laughed.

"*Three!* What a waste," Trader said. "All right, I will have to tell you," he said to Smith, feigning ennui. Then, he snatched Smith's glasses, dropped them into his glass, and poured more whiskey over them. "We cannot have your friends hearing this, can we, Mr. Lewis? Rather Mr. Smith. Or do you prefer *Analyst* Smith?"

"I don't know *what* you're talking about," Smith said, trying hard for outrage.

"*Please*," Trader said. "Your friend here, Mr. Tully, has told us everything."

"He's not—"

"Imagine," Trader said, cutting him off. "I hire Mr. Tully to find a painting for me, and he does, then he *steals* it and tries to ransom it back to me!" He leaned in to Tully. "Were you planning to sell it and retire to Buenos Aires?" He laughed, but a vein in his forehead was throbbing. "Of course, once Mr. Tully let me know he had the painting, it was easy to find him and send my people to take it away. I could have left him behind or had him eliminated, but when he identified you, I thought it would be fun to unite two old friends."

"I have no idea who—or what—" Smith said, but Trader stopped him, a hand in front of his face.

"I must say, I am very disappointed in you, Mr. Smith. I was looking forward to our association." He asked Gunther to hold Smith, which he did at gunpoint, Smith hoping, praying, the team was picking this up. "And *you*, Jennifer," Trader said, turning to the woman, then slapped her hard. "You and your...surveillance. I give you one thing to do, to watch and report back to me, and you cannot do it."

"But I–I *did*, Stefan. I did everything you asked. I followed my friend from school, I got the information about the painting, otherwise you wouldn't have known," she said, a hand to her cheek, tears forming in her eyes. "And I lived with that woman for *you*, just for *you*."

"And yet you gave me nothing but this spy. You let this happen, Jennifer. You allowed this spy into our midst, into my business, into my life!"

Jennifer started to speak but he raised his hand again and she jerked back, then he signaled Gunther and the men in black, one of whom wrapped his arms around Smith, the other reaching for the red T on the plane's cabin door.

"Now I need to know: who you are working for?" Trader said. "We have the paintings, so you are of no further use to me. But you can save yourself if you tell me *who* you are working for."

"You already know I work for INTERPOL," Smith said, breathing hard, mind spinning.

"I want the names of the people and the organization you are working for, Mr. Smith. It is that simple, or you will die. Last chance."

Smith met the man's pale eyes, and said, "*Fuck. You.*"

"All right," Trader said and nodded at Gunther, then at the man in black with his hand on the cabin door. "*Auf wiedersehen*, Mr. Smith."

81

"Hang on!" Pilot said.

The wind had become erratic, the helicopter dipping and whirling.

"Tail rotor under control?" Dispatcher asked.

"This is not my first rodeo," Pilot said, working the pedals, then going into a roll, a bumpy maneuver that worked, the copter flying smoothly again. Van Straten sucked in a breath, Steiner had gone green, Jaager shouting, "Awesome!"

Then the tracking screen went blank and Jaager sobered, and Van Straten was no longer worried about the turbulence. "Have we lost him?" she asked, a rare dramatic pitch in her voice.

"We have lost audio and visual," Jaager said. "Something has happened to Smith's glasses, but we are still tracking him from the link in his neck chain. Look." He indicated the other, smaller screen and a small moving blip on the topographic map.

"I am tracking the plane on my radar," Pilot said, and indicated a tiny airplane icon on his screen.

Van Straten asked Jaager to rewind the tape to Smith's last conversation before they lost him.

Trader's voice was clear but tinny through the mic, *He seems to recognize you… Tell Mr. Lewis what you told me earlier… You cannot or you will not tell him… All right, I will tell you…*

"Who is this person Smith is supposed to recognize?" Jaager asked.

"I think you have it backwards," Steiner said. "It is someone who recognizes Smith."

Van Straten's breath caught in her throat. She could not afford to lose Smith—or the paintings—or Trader. Steiner started to say something, but she told him to be quiet, trying to think who this unknown person could be, and if Smith had been identified.

Pilot indicated the airplane's icon on his screen, noted it was reducing its height, probably landing. "Hold on," he said, and the helicopter dipped dramatically.

Dispatcher looked out his window at what appeared to be a field beside a body of water, reading the name off his screen's topographic map, "that's the river Oise."

"The wind is going to make it rough to land," Pilot said.

Dispatcher continued reading the names of towns off the map, "Nesles-la-Vallée, Ennery, Auvers-sur-Oise, Méry-sur-Oise. Any of those sound familiar?"

It took Van Straten only a few seconds to connect the painting to the famous town. "Auvers-sur-Oise," she said.

Steiner, fighting nausea, typed the town's name—the message his contacts had been waiting for—into his tablet.

"What the hell are you writing?" Van Straten barked at him, then Pilot interrupted.

"The plane had landed," he said, explaining he would keep them airborne until he found a place to land, "nearby but not too close."

Dispatcher pointed out a flat area on the map, and Pilot decreased power. But the helicopter was wrenched up by a sudden gust of wind, everyone lurching with it.

Van Straten gripped her seat. Steiner stopped to hold a barf bag to his face. Jaager shouted, "Woo-hoo!"

Pilot caught a headwind and used it to hover the craft down until one of its skids touched the ground, where it balanced for a second until the headwind shifted and the helicopter surged upward again.

"Jesus," Van Straten whispered under her breath. She felt as if she'd left her stomach behind, but she was too anxious to care, afraid of losing the plane, of losing Smith. "We must land," she said.

"In pieces?" Pilot said. "Or will you wait till I can do it safely?"

Van Straten asked Jaager if he was still tracking Smith, and he said, "He is on the ground. That is all I can say for sure."

82

A short ride from where the plane had landed to the center of Auvers-sur-Oise, the man in black, the one with the halting speech, was out first to check the scene before signaling it was all clear, then got back in the car behind the wheel, the car idling.

Then Trader got out and did his own surveillance of the square, the gnarled trees on the perimeter, the stores along one side, a pharmacy, a chocolatier, the Hôtel de Ville, and across the road, the famous Auberge Ravoux. He knew its history, found it ironic that they should have ended up here. He noticed Les Opticiens beside the Auberge, a reminder of Smith's glasses and the man's betrayal.

Gunther was out of the car, gun in hand, staring down the barrel like he was on a shooting range.

"Put that away," Trader said. "We are not here to attract attention."

Jennifer was out too, the wind blowing her skirt up, Marilyn-style, and Trader laughed good-naturedly, though he was finished with her and thinking about what he was going to do about her now that she had failed him. He checked the address and directions Finn de Jong had texted him; the house was nearby. He rapped on the car window and told the man in black to move the car to a side street, someplace quiet. Then he looked in the back seat at Smith, whose hands and feet were tied, a gag in his mouth.

"If we are not back in thirty minutes, kill Mr. Smith," he said to the man in black. "Then pick me up. I have sent the address to your phone. Do not forget."

The man in black nodded and stammered, "I will…not…forget."

Smith's mind was buzzing. He figured they were going to use him as some form of barter before they killed him, though right now he was grateful to his teenage obsession—knowing that it was impossible to open a plane's cabin door in midflight, something Trader obviously knew as well, all of it a stunt. Rather than tossed, he had been punched. He could still taste the blood in his mouth and on his swollen lip. He peered through the window as another car pulled into the square and a man got out, face in shadow. He watched as Trader greeted him, then all of them headed across the square.

83

You follow him as you did the others in New York, watching, worrying, your heart like a cracked glass trying hard not to shatter after the hateful words he said to you on the plane. The way he has been treating you since you arrived in Amsterdam finally falling into place, making sense: he is tired of you, finished with you.

Head down, you trail him across the square, watching leaves scatter and blow away, and you see it clearly, what you have done and given up for him, and how you will be cast off, discarded like some errand boy who has disappointed him. You, who have lied, cajoled, betrayed friends, sacrificed everything because you believed he cared for you, even loved you. Now you see the truth: that you were used, that you were a fool. But you will not let him get away with it.

"Stefan." You call his name, but he keeps walking. You call again, louder, and he looks back.

"What?" he snaps. "What is it, Jennifer?"

You say you want to talk "*now*," surprised by the strength you can muster. Then you soften and affect a smile. "Let them go. We will catch up."

"Be quick," Trader says, an eye on the others waiting at the edge of the square, looking back.

Heart fluttering, mind firing, you say the wrong thing first, apologizing for Mr. Lewis, Smith, how you didn't know, how you are sorry.

"It no longer matters," Trader says, and waves it away. "Even if

Mr. Lewis had been legitimate, I only intended to keep him around for the transactions, then have him terminated. Soon there will be no evidence of a connection to this supposed Mr. Lewis, no evidence of Mr. Lewis at all." He touches your cheek, and you try not to flinch. "If that is what you are worried about, there is no reason. All evidence of Mr. Lewis will be eradicated."

Like you? Is that his intention, to eradicate you? "No," you say. "That's not it."

"What then?" Trader shifts his weight from one foot to the next, restless.

"I have something."

"*What?*" he asks, his tone sharp. Backlit by the sun, his face in shadow, his white hair a halo making of him a demonic angel. "What is it you have?"

And so you tell him about the papers, the bills of sale, the evidence of his illegal business transactions. You say you came upon them accidentally, that you had no intention of ever using them against him. And you wouldn't, "unless absolutely forced." You look at him, feeling strong, empowered. You will not be so easily discarded.

He returns your look, then he stutters a laugh.

"My dear Jennifer. Do you think I did not know you went through my safe, that you stole from me? I know every paper, where I put them, and in what order. When I saw they had been disturbed, I knew it was you, that you had seen them and made copies."

You take a breath and try to remain calm. "Then why..."

"Why didn't I say something? Because I found it amusing to let you think you had something on me, some kind of insurance. What did you plan to do with them?"

You tell him you had no plan because you were in business together, and that you hoped it might eventually be more.

"In business together? *You* and *me*? And *more*? Like *what*? Did you think I would *marry* you?" He laughs again, head thrown back, the veins on his neck standing out in high relief, and you imagine your nails digging into them. The idea that you ever cared for him, allowed yourself to believe you would be his partner in business, in life, now ridiculous, sickening.

He strokes your cheek. "How lovely you are. And how naive. But do not worry, I am fond of you and will never betray you." He drops his hand to your heart. "And of course, you will not betray *me*. If you did, I would of course find you and punish you. You understand that, do you not?" His voice is a purr while his hand tightens on your breast.

"Yes," you say, suppressing a wince of pain.

"Good," he says, his grip easing. "Now let us join the others and finish what we came for. This will all be over soon, in the past, and we will forget it ever happened."

He takes your arm and leads you across the square, and you know for certain that he will betray you. Unless you betray him first.

84

Toussaint had been reading from his great-grandfather's diary, explaining how Julien had regretted not accompanying Vincent on the last day of his life. He described the hot July weather and how Vincent had returned to the auberge late without his easel or his art supplies, and how, only later, they had discovered him in bed, wounded.

"Does he say anything about the painting?" Alex asked. "The one made from the sketch, the one I found?"

"Yes. According to Julien there were two self-portraits in the arrangement around Vincent's body. But after the funeral, only one."

"What happened to it?" Alex asked.

Toussaint began to speak but Finn interrupted. "That is all very nice. And your great-grandfather's story validates the existence of the second self-portrait, the one Alexis found. But right now, we need to deal with that drawing of yours before it rots!"

Toussaint gave up reading and handed the diary to Alex. "Read it yourself, my dear, and return it later." Alex slipped it into the pocket of her jeans.

Finn regarded his cell. "Good news, monsieur. I have found a buyer for your sketch."

"I told you, I will not sell it," Toussaint said.

Finn sighed. "If you will not cooperate in saving a national treasure, I will be forced to take steps."

"I have given you my final word," Toussaint said, and was carefully laying a sheet of wax paper over the sketch when the front door flung open.

85

From the back seat, Smith had watched Trader and his cohorts disappear behind the Hôtel de Ville. He was not sure what they were doing here, but he was certain they would be back; they had left the paintings—and Tully—with the other man in black on the plane. It was only a matter of time before they killed Tully, and him. They'd only kept Tully alive to act out their little drama on the plane for his benefit. It was likely they planned to stage it so it appeared he and Tully had killed each other, neat and simple.

He knew Van Straten's team could no longer see him but hoped the tracker in his neck chain was still working and they knew where he was. He squirmed, could feel the plastic gun digging into his back, the bullet still sewn into the inside of his belt, impossible to reach with his hands tied, though he'd been picking at the rope, loosening it.

The man in black, *Lennie*, as he called him, drove a few blocks. When he parked, Smith kicked the back of his seat, again and again, and muttered through the gag in his mouth.

"S-stop it!" Lennie said, but Smith kept it up, muttering louder, the kicks harder until Lennie leaned over the seat, and waved his gun. "S-stop!"

Smith pointed at his mouth with his bound hands, made urgent noises, trying to telegraph with his eyes that he had something important to say. He could see Lennie thinking, considering, and kept it up until Lennie said he'd take the gag off—"for a m-minute"—if Smith promised to be quiet.

Smith nodded, and Lennie tugged the gag down, and Smith started talking. He figured he had maybe a minute to convince Lennie before the gag went back on.

"I need to *warn* you," he said, sucking in air and talking fast. "They're going to *kill* you. I heard them say it, that you're too risky to keep around with all you know."

"Q-quiet!" Lennie said and waved the gun, but Smith kept talking.

"You *and* your partner, expendable and easily replaced they said, and think about it, it's *true.*"

"W-who said t-that?"

"The kid, the boss's son, Gunther." Smith was making it up as he said it. "I'm trying to help you, man. And here's the thing, if Gunther doesn't take you out, *my* people will. I'm with INTERPOL—you heard that, right?—and they're on their way." One of the rare times Smith hoped it was true. "INTERPOL, as in international police, in every goddamn country, number one crime-fighting organization *anywhere*, right now, here in France, and they're coming to save my ass and get yours!"

"Q-quiet! I'm t-trying to t-think," he said, holding his head with both hands like it hurt, and that's when Smith swung his bound hands up and into Lennie's jaw, then down on the back of his neck. Lennie sputtered, shaking his head and blinking, but a second later he was over the seat, roaring and lunging at Smith, smashing him against the car door so hard it opened, and Smith toppled onto the sidewalk, all two-hundred-fifty pounds of Lennie hurtling toward him. But Smith was faster, a quick feint one way, then the other, and the big guy came down hard, air knocked out of him, gun skittering along the ground, both diving for it, but Smith got there first. Gasping for breath, he pressed the gun into the thick flesh of Lennie's neck, and shouted, "I don't want to shoot you, but I *will!*"

Lennie swatted at him like a sad, captured bear, but Smith easily dodged the blows and kept the gun pressed into his neck. "Get up," he said, and led him around to the back of the car where he popped the trunk and ordered him in.

"N-no," Lennie whined, but Smith cocked the pistol's trigger and the big man crawled in. Then Smith untied the already loosened rope from his wrists, fished Lennie's cell phone out of his pocket, whacked him on the back of the head with the gun butt, and slammed the trunk closed.

Another minute to untie his feet, then to check Lennie's phone. Locked. Password or Face ID needed. Smith opened the trunk, held the phone in front of Lennie's half-conscious face, waited for the phone to open, then slammed the trunk closed again.

There it was, the last text, the address Trader had sent to Lennie's phone. Smith slipped the phone into his pocket, then headed across the square.

86

I'd found my way to Auvers-sur-Oise, then into the center of town. I recognized the Hôtel de Ville and the famous Auberge Ravoux, though right now I hardly cared and did not hang around. I had to find Alex.

But how?

I took in the square and the various stores along its perimeter. Just past it was a bar. I went in and asked the guy behind the counter if he'd seen Alex. "A woman, American, young, and blond."

"*Il y a beaucoup de blondes*," the guy said with a leering smile and turned to his other customers, repeating what he'd just said, all of them laughing.

I headed out. Cut across the street to the Auberge, which was closed, but a sign beside it indicated an entrance with arrows, which I followed past a low stone wall, then along a short path that led to a ticket office, where a young woman was reading a book. This time, when I asked if Alex had been there, I got my cell phone out and showed her a picture.

"*Oui*," she said, then explained in English—*thank God*—that she had shown Alex the house and Van Gogh's room. "She was with a man," she said, and I figured it had to be the curator, but when I asked if she knew where they'd gone, she shook her head.

I was halfway down the path, determined to make the rounds to every nearby inn in Auvers-sur-Oise when she came after me. "I saw them again," she said. "In the square, with Monsieur Toussaint, a local man, who lives nearby." She walked me out to the road and gave me directions to his home, with details and landmarks.

I thanked her, crossed the street, and went into the square. The wind was whipping up, the French flags on top of the Hôtel de Ville flapping like birds of prey, the sun starting to set.

"Past the square," she'd said. "*À droite.* To the right," and I followed her directions to a small road just behind the square into a suburban area of houses, continuing until I came to the railroad track she had mentioned, and the sign, NE TRAVERSEZ PAS SANS REGARDER DANS LES DEUX DIRECTIONS. I didn't need the illustration of an oncoming train and an oblivious man stepping onto the tracks to know what it said. I took a moment to look both ways. No trains were coming. No cars either. It was quiet, the only sounds the howling wind and the loud buzz of insects.

Then, along a street lined with gnarled trees like clenched fists, the light fading fast, and the road growing dark though I could make out the individual houses, one with trim like gingerbread, then two small stone houses in a row. Both were set back from the road and both with metal gates, as the young Frenchwoman had described.

I was trying to figure out which was the right house when I thought I saw something moving in the grass. I wasn't sure if it was real or the dying sun casting shadows and playing tricks on my eyes. Then I looked closer and saw it was a man.

87

The man saw me too, both of us frozen for a moment, then he waved me over and pulled me down to the ground, hand over my mouth.

"Shhh," he hissed, then slowly removed his hand and we both whispered the same thing, "What are you doing here?"

Smith sketched in what had been going down, from a car ride to a plane ride with the art fence. There were plenty of gaps, so I didn't quite get it, but this wasn't the time to ask. He ended with, "I'm hoping they're still able to track me," then asked why I was there.

"To find Alex," I said, and he didn't ask why either, just that he was following the art fence and pointed to the back of a house, the same one I was looking for. "Alex could be in there too," I said, and he nodded as if he was not surprised. Then we scooted across the lawn and hid in the shadow of a house with a sign, A VENDRE, shuttered windows, and a dying vine covering the wall that shielded us from the road. After a minute, Smith gave me a signal and we crab-walked around the house to a large, untended backyard. The sun dipped below the horizon and a few windows lit up, cicadas buzzing, the night electric.

Without speaking, Smith pointed out the back of the house we were both looking for, and we slithered across the backyard and stopped when we reached the gate and a hedge that served as cover.

From where we were, we could see the back of the house clearly, two stories and narrow, the windows open and lit up, shadows of people moving within.

We huddled there a minute, sheltered by the hedge, and Smith gave me a gun.

"It's a Glock 29," he whispered. "Took it off one of the thugs, too long to explain. But it's loaded, ten rounds."

"Ten rounds? Fuck, what are we going up against, an army?"

"If I'm right, they're all in there, and at least one of them is armed, probably more." He showed me how to hold the grip and told me to aim high. "It's got a kick."

It had been a long time, but I'd handled a gun before.

Smith tugged another, odd-looking gun out from his under his shirt, tore something off his waistband and loaded it. "Looks like a toy and only fires once but it's lethal," he said. "You think you can handle this?"

"Getting over the fence? Yeah."

"No. That's the easy part," he said. "I mean whatever we find inside."

I put an image in mind, myself at sixteen, breaking into a house, and nodded.

We helped each other over the fence, then crept through grass leading to the back door. On either side of it were tall windows maybe two, three feet from the ground, both open.

It was only a few feet to shrubbery where we hid and waited. One of the windows was lit up like a stage. In it, the young guy with the tattooed neck was pacing, gun in hand.

"Jesusss," I hissed. "I know him."

Smith didn't ask how but shushed me, and with my heart thudding and mind spinning, I heard the tattooed guy say, "We need to do something with them," and a man in the shadows said, "We will, after we get the paintings." Then a woman said, "Does Mattia know you have the painting or are you planning to cut your partner out of the deal, like you do everyone else?" And the man said, "Shut up!" and slapped her so hard she staggered out of the frame.

Then I heard Alex.

"I can't believe it's you," she was saying. "I just can't believe it."

And another, different man, one I couldn't see, said, "You don't understand."

The tattooed guy said, "We have what we came for, Father. Let's finish them off now and get out of here!"

I was ready to charge but Smith held me back, his hand on my arm. Then he raised one finger, then two, then three, then took a few steps and leapt, scaling the ledge, and I followed right behind him, the two of us in midflight vaulting through the open window.

88

For a few minutes everything was a blur, bodies in motion, shouts, and screams, then I fired a shot at the ceiling and everyone froze, and the scene came into focus: Alex, with a man on either side of her, all duct-taped to chairs, Smith pressing the tattooed guy against a wall, a gun in his back.

"Are you all right?" I called to Alex, and she nodded but I couldn't get to her. My gun was trained on two other men half-standing, half-crouched, looking about to pounce or run. Then they straightened up, and I knew them. "That's Stefan Albrecht," I said to Smith. "An art dealer I just met in Amsterdam."

"He's Trader," Smith said. "The one we're after."

"The other one is Richard Baine."

"Hello, Luke," Baine said, unruffled, or at least acting it. "I've gone straight. I'm working for Uncle Sam."

"You are working for *them*?" Albrecht said.

"Sorry," Baine said, flashed a smile and reiterated that he was working for Smith's team, and that the State Department had brought him in.

"It's true," Smith said. "But you're not supposed to be *here*, Baine."

"Oops," Baine said.

"He's here for the drawing," Alex said. "They all are." She angled a look at the table. On it was a pencil sketch. "So, it was all about the painting," she said to Baine. "Was that it, Father?"

"No, my dear. I sincerely wanted to see you, my only daughter."

"You're a liar," she said.

Smith and I exchanged anxious looks, the volatility in the room palpable, up to us to contain it, and I knew he only had one shot. The rats were accusing each other of disloyalty and deceit, the woman joining in, telling Albrecht she was going to ruin him. Then, she swiped an X-Acto knife off the table and held it to Alex's neck.

"Drop the gun," she said.

I did. At the same time the tattooed guy grabbed Smith's gun and they struggled, then someone must have pulled the trigger and the gun fired and the tattooed guy fell, a hand to his neck, inky-blue tattoos flecked with blood.

"Gunther!" Albrecht cried, and kneeled beside him, pressing his hand against the wound.

Smith had the gun again, though I knew he'd fired his only shot. "Drop the knife," he said to the woman.

"Jennifer, *please*," Alex said, the knife pricking her flesh, a thin line of blood running down her neck.

"Don't do it!" I said, but in an instant, she'd overturned Alex's chair and as it crashed forward, she raced to the back door, and Albrecht and Baine made a run for it too. I fired my gun, then Smith took it from me, fired another shot, both of us too late, then he headed off after them while I helped Alex up.

"I'm okay," she said. "But he's not." She nodded at Gunther on the floor, blood seeping out of his neck and pooling around his head. She handed me a scarf and I tied it around his neck. "They've taken the sketch. Albrecht and my father."

"*Mon dessin*, my drawing!" the Frenchman cried.

I cut him loose and the other guy too, the curator.

"You're a part of this, Finn," Alex said to the curator, the guy rubbing his wrists, his eyes darting.

The Frenchman joined us, called for help but there was no answer. He advised us to get Gunther to the nearby Hôtel de Ville, "where there are always police."

I wasn't sure Gunther would make it and asked the guys to help, but the curator took off, and I couldn't stop him without a gun.

Then Alex and I and the Frenchman managed to get Gunther to his feet and, with him wavering and unsteady between us, headed out into the night.

89

The moon was hidden behind clouds, and without streetlamps it was dark, but we made our way to the railroad crossing, then along the country road toward the square.

"I'm sorry," Alex said.

I knew she was referring to having brought her father into this—or had that been me? "It's okay," I said.

It was only a few minutes' walk, but Gunther was practically unconscious by the time we reached the edge of the square. Then it opened in front of us, the perimeter ringed with police cars, ambulances, gendarmes, and men in camouflage with rifles across their chests, a helicopter above, blades thwacking the air, its beacon bleaching the scene black and white.

But it was oddly still, as though we had arrived too early or too late, like a director had just yelled, "Cut!" or was about to call, "Action." The only real movement was us, cutting across the square with Gunther between us, calling out to emergency workers who loaded him into an ambulance.

Just beside it, Van Straten and Smith were huddled with a few civilians and cops in a small circle, and in the middle was Albrecht, his face a mess, split lip, swollen eye, Jennifer beside him, everyone's guns trained on them.

The police tried to keep us back, but I cut in just beside Smith, and he signaled to the cops that it was okay. He looked a little beat up too, his face and arms scratched, lip bleeding.

"Are you the one who did that to Albrecht?" I asked, and when he smiled and nodded, I said, "Good work."

"They didn't get far," he said.

"What about Baine?"

"I have my two best men on it," Van Straten said. "They will catch him, or they will kill him."

I felt Alex shudder beside me.

"I would've killed Trader," Smith said, and I could see he meant it. "But Van Straten here wants him alive to stand trial."

I scanned the square, asked what all this was, the police and the soldiers.

"All thanks to an asshole agent on the team who alerted INTERPOL to have local militia standing by. Overkill, much?" he said, cool, in his element, a new Smith.

Van Straten leaned into him, whispered, "I need to get them talking," then, to a young guy beside her, added, "Make sure you get this," and she moved into the center of the circle as cops were putting cuffs on Albrecht and Jennifer. "Hold on," she said to the cops. "She will not need those." She took a step closer, raised Jennifer's face with her hand. "Tell me why you did this."

"Do not be a fool, Jennifer. Do not talk to her," Albrecht said.

"For *him* you are willing to go to prison," Van Straten said. "Willing to throw your life away?"

"She is using you, Jennifer," Albrecht said. "Just keep your mouth shut. They have nothing."

"*Nothing?*" Van Straten said. "We have your plane, the paintings, your deposits in a Swiss bank account, we have James Tully, we have Smith's eyewitness accounts, and we have tape recordings."

"You and your kind," Albrecht sneered, the helicopter's beacon highlighting his curled lip and eyebrows like whitecaps. "You think you are so smart, so clever."

"My *kind*?" she said.

"We will *bury* you," he said.

"We will see who buries whom," Van Straten said coolly. Then to Jennifer, "Be smart, talk to me, let me help you."

Jennifer started to say something, but Albrecht told her to shut up. Then the cops started to cuff her and lead her away, and she looked back at Van Straten and said, "Anika," plaintive and pained. "Will you really help me? Because I have things I can tell you about him, show you too."

"Shut up, fool!" Albrecht said, and tugged against his cuffs, but Jennifer was already talking. "Fine," he said. "Listen to her lies. She is a nobody with nothing to offer other than sex, and frankly she is not very good at that. Wouldn't you agree, Anika?" The sneer back on his lips.

"I have proof," Jennifer said. "Papers, bills of sale going back years, all you need to put him away, Anika."

Albrecht shouted, "Shut up!" and tugged out of the cop's grip just enough to ram into Jennifer and knock her to the ground. But when she looked up, half raised herself, she had taken the cop's gun and it was aimed at Albrecht.

"*No,* Jennifer," Van Straten said, "we will deal with him. Put the gun down."

"Useless, worthless, slut," Albrecht said. "A nobody. A *liar*!" Then to the cops, "She is going to shoot me. You must stop her."

"Get him out of here!" Van Straten shouted at the cops, who had their guns drawn. The militia had joined them, their rifles aimed and ready. "Give me the gun, Jennifer," she said quietly and took a step forward, her hand outstretched.

"*Liar! Whore!*" Albrecht shouted, and Jennifer fired, and he fell back, and the cops and militia let loose a barrage of gunfire, Van Straten screaming at them to stop while Jennifer's body jerked and shuddered until she lay still, and they finally put their guns down, and Van Straten stopped shouting and went to her and put her arms around her.

"Oh my God," Alex said, and buried her face in my neck.

"Jesus Christ," Smith said. Then to the young guy beside him. "You get all that, Jaager?"

"Every word on tape," the guy said. "And here." He raised his cell phone to show he'd taken a video.

Smith laid his hand lightly on Van Straten's back. "She's gone," he said, and helped her up, then the medics descended on Jennifer's body.

Albrecht was hit, his shoulder bleeding, a couple of medics attending to him too.

Alex and I were shell-shocked but still watching, listening to Van Straten speaking to Smith.

"Albrecht will stand trial," she said letting out a breath, sagging a bit but resolved. "And we have the Van Gogh, one of the most important Nazi-looted artworks, and that's what matters. We did our job."

"And that makes it all worth it?" Smith said to her.

"Have you learned nothing, Analyst Smith? I thought you understood that *this* painting, *every* stolen work of art represents a *stolen* life." Then she turned to me and Alex and spoke plainly. "It will fall to you as the ones who discovered the painting to publicly return it. You will not be questioned and none of this ever happened. You understand?"

I nodded as the attendants loaded Albrecht into one ambulance, Jennifer's body into another.

"I am going with him," Van Straten said, resigned. "He is the one who needs watching." Then to Smith, "Go home. Someone will be in touch."

I put my arm around Alex, and with Smith beside us, we watched Van Straten get into the ambulance with Albrecht, followed by two cops. Then an attendant closed the door and it drove away, its siren cutting through the night like a cry.

90

Van Straten was right. Alex and I were not questioned. It was as if nothing had ever happened. We took the train to Paris, then a plane to Amsterdam, where we stayed several days waiting for the restitution ceremony, filling our time with museums and restaurants and walks, looking without really seeing, talking though we were still in shock.

Smith called one night and asked me to meet him, this time without urgency. I asked Alex to come but she was too tired, and I went alone.

Smith had chosen the place, a small, local bar, Café de Spuyt. He told me it had some special significance but didn't say what and I never got around to asking. He ordered a whiskey, and I got a nonalcoholic beer, but no one made a toast.

We were both quiet, then I asked if he was coming to the restitution ceremony, and he said no. Then he told me how the painting had been delivered to Albrecht.

"By Tully," he said. "He had it all along, tried to ransom it back to Albrecht, his client. Not a smart move. He's lucky to be alive. He could be charged as a coconspirator in international art theft, obstruction of justice too, but I'm guessing he'll get a slap on the wrist, pay a fine, and lose his PI license. Van Straten said she'd find a way to put in a word for him, said the poor slob had suffered enough."

I asked why she would do that, and he said because they got the painting back. "That's all she cares about. She's a crusader, you know. Her code name is *Hunter*, for Christ's sake."

I had a dozen questions, and he answered some of them. He told me he was pretty sure Van Straten was Mossad, and the helicopter pilot and another guy who'd helped them with the op called Dispatcher, were Kidon.

"Which is what?"

"A unit within Mossad, assassins, very exclusive and a well-guarded secret, no one will admit they exist…but they do."

I asked if there was any word on Baine.

"Not yet," he said. "But if those guys are after him, and Van Straten confirms they are, they'll not only get the sketch back, but Baine's a dead man."

I was quiet again, thinking of Alex.

"You and Verde can never talk about this," he said. "None of it. Van Straten's anonymity is essential, crucial to her work. Her life depends on it."

I told him I got it, then asked what was next for him, and he said he was taking a few weeks off, staying in Amsterdam to do some work for INTERPOL. Then, a striking woman with a mass of red hair came in, sat down at our table, and Smith introduced her.

"Municipal Police Tess Vox. My personal shopper," he said, pointing out his cool black shirt. "Bought for the job, but I got to keep it." She flashed Smith a smile and put her hand on his and I got why he was staying in Amsterdam, at least partially, and when I started to feel like a third wheel, I said I had to get going, and though Vox politely protested, Smith said, "See you round, Perrone."

The ceremony was at the Van Gogh Museum, the self-portrait donated by the heir, whose grandfather had owned the painting.

His only request was that his grandfather's name be on the wall plaque when the painting was installed. Right now, the painting was propped on an easel, Vincent in shirt and vest and jacket, a three-quarter view, his haunted blue eyes staring out at the viewer against a swirling blue background, two odd little cows painted in a bottom corner. The painting looked as if it was waiting for Vincent to come in and add a few last-minute touch-ups.

The gathering was small but impressive, the museum's director and a few curators, the mayor of Amsterdam, and a representative from a Netherlands restitution organization.

Alex had dressed up in a black pencil skirt and a sweetly sexy halter top by Rosette. Other than the new white shirt she'd insisted I buy, I wore my black jeans and my Chelsea boots. I had shaved off my beard at her request and felt oddly exposed.

It was just before the ceremony that Alex and I got pulled into a conversation between the representative of the Netherlands restitution organization and one of the museum's curators, a Dutch woman who looked to be in her sixties, clad in a sober-looking suit.

"The current list of paintings being repatriated is a long one," the restitution rep said to her. He was young, late twenties or early thirties, bearded, wearing a suit with socks and sandals. "A Monet from a museum in Zurich. A Franz Marc from a German museum. A mass restitution in France, fifteen artworks by artists like Chagall and Klimt, from such respected museums as the D'Orsay, even the Louvre."

"Yes," the curator said softly. "But the museums did not know what they were acquiring."

"In some cases," the rep said, then turned to Alex and me. "Currently your Metropolitan Museum of Art in New York is embroiled in a lawsuit to return several Nazi-looted artworks."

"And now they must identify all such work," Alex added, citing a recent law that required New York museums to put up signage identifying artworks looted by the Nazis.

"As well they should," the rep said in a righteous tone, then went on. "A Mondrian in the Philadelphia Museum of Art under investigation, *twenty-nine* artworks from a museum in Bern, all of them donated by Cornelius Gurlitt, now being returned to the Jewish heirs."

"The son of Hildebrand Gurlitt, one of Hitler's appointed art dealers," Alex said.

The rep gave her an approving nod.

"My fear is that one day soon the museums may be empty," the older Dutch curator said.

"But what is the choice?" the rep said. "To keep artwork known to be stolen?"

"It is a difficult issue for museums that collected artworks they thought were legitimate."

"But once they know the truth, it is simple. They must return the objects, without question."

"I agree. In theory," the curator said.

"In *theory?*" the rep said. "Keeping artworks that were stolen from fleeing and murdered people?"

"Several institutions have come to agreements with heirs that allowed them to keep the artwork," the curator said, trying to defend herself, and I saw her point. I saw the rep's point too. It was a thorny issue, complicated by time, and I was glad the conversation was cut short when the ceremony began.

The museum director and the mayor each said a few words, then the heir, a well-dressed and well-groomed man of late middle-age, spoke of his grandparents.

"From all accounts they were kind and generous people," he said. "Philanthropists and art collectors who, like so many others, were brutally stripped of their identity, their possessions, and finally... their lives." He swallowed and cleared his throat. "Though nothing can undo the crimes of the past, it is important that this painting, by one of Holland's, one of the *world's* greatest artists, something that belonged to my grandparents and is a part of their legacy, has been rightfully returned. It partially closes a wound that has remained open for too long." He thanked the museum, then me and Alex, and I realized, possibly for the first time, what this was all about. I imagined that Vincent would be happy, too, that his self-portrait had come home.

There was no acknowledgment of Smith or Van Straten; it was assumed Alex and I, who had found the painting, simply returned it. We didn't make a speech but did say a few words to the heir, who thanked us again sincerely and profusely. Like us, he had made no money off the painting's return. We slipped out, using our flight home as an excuse, feeling contented that the painting had been discovered and repatriated, but with dashed dreams of it ever being ours.

On the plane, I fell asleep and had one bad dream after another—Alex bound, people being shot, falling out a window over and over—until I jerked awake. There was something under the dreams too, something I was trying to remember, but whatever it was, I was too tired to get at it.

91

The Bowery
New York City

It was spring, that rare two-week event in New York City, trees in bloom, outdoor restaurants packed, people running, biking, the city thrumming. I was back to teaching and Alex was hard at work on her dissertation. There'd been no news of her father, and we assumed he was still at large with the Van Gogh sketch, not the prize he had been after but enough to warm the cockles of his art-thief heart. Until he was caught.

As usual, Alex went upstate to see her mother, and with the pressure of my exhibition, I got back to painting, windows open, the spring breeze commingling with exhaust fumes, garbage, and enough weed to get me high.

I worked on an unfinished painting, sketching a frame within the frame. When I realized I'd created a window, I drew figures inside it, shadowy and faceless, and while my brush moved across canvas, it came to me that I was recreating the open window of Toussaint's house that night in Auvers-sur-Oise when Smith and I crouched in the grass watching people and hearing their conversations, which I now heard again. At first, it was just a few disjointed words, then it came back to me in full sentences and I was forced to put my brushes down.

———

Mattia Beuhler was wearing a peach-colored shirt and a blue linen suit, everything about him, as always, perfect. He brought me into his private office and asked about my trip, if I'd gone to the galleries he'd suggested and met the dealers, something I was certain he would know by now, but I said yes, and asked my question: "Have you heard that Stefan Albrecht was arrested?" I made an effort to keep my tone light and newsy.

"*Really?*" He seemed shocked, his two-colored eyes widening. "What on earth for?"

I didn't sugarcoat it. "For selling Nazi-looted art."

"Oh? You must be mistaken. Stefan Albrecht is a very honest man, above reproach."

I explained it was in the news, which he said he had missed.

"You've worked with him, haven't you?" I asked.

"We have had some...dealings," he said slowly as if measuring his words. "But they have been few...and far between."

"Here's something weird," I said, still affecting that newsy tone. "A woman, an associate of Albrecht's, asked if he had told his partner, *Mattia*, about a painting he was selling." I pictured the moment I'd heard it outside of Toussaint's window. *Does Mattia know you have the painting, or are you planning to cut your partner out of the deal?*

"How did you hear *that?*" he said.

"I...overheard it," I said. "She wasn't referring to *you*, was she?" I shifted from newsy to incredulous.

"*Me?*" His tone even more incredulous than mine. "Why, there must be dozens of Mattias."

But no other Mattia in the New York art world; I had checked. I waited a moment, wanting him to deny it, wanting him to shout his innocence, to say I was a fool, to prove me wrong.

But what he said was, "I suggest you be careful, Luke," and stood up and came close to me, his face only inches from mine. "You would not want to make trouble for the gallery, not with your show coming," he said. "You must have misheard." He slid his arm over my shoulder and walked me to the door, his grip tightening, his face so close to mine I could smell his cologne and something off about his breath. "Now go home and make beautiful paintings and forget we ever had this conversation."

I slipped out of his grip hearing the threat and knowing it was probably true: that he was Stefan Albrecht's partner.

Back home, I paced the loft a dozen times before I made the call.

"You know what time it is?" Smith said, sounding groggy. "This better be good."

I apologized for having forgotten the time difference, then told him about my encounter with Beuhler and what I suspected.

"And what do you want me to do about it?"

"Get in touch with Van Straten?"

"Not me," he said. "But *you* can." Then I heard him rustling around and a woman in the background asking who was calling and Smith saying, "Go back to sleep, Tess." Then he gave me Van Straten's number and hung up.

She was surprised to hear from me. I told her about my conversation with Beuhler and what I'd heard that night in Auvers-sur-Oise.

She said I should have called her before I'd confronted him but that was all the reprimand I got. Then she said her people had known for a long time that Albrecht had a U.S. partner, and she was not surprised to hear it might be Beuhler.

"We have been watching several U.S. art dealers, Beuhler one of them," she said. "If it is true, I am quite certain we can get confirmation of Beuhler's involvement out of Albrecht. His lawyers are anxious to cut a deal. But I will have to move fast. Time is our friend, and on occasion, so is publicity."

I asked what she meant, but all she said was to lose her number and hung up.

The next day there was a small piece in the *New York Times* about Mattia Beuhler being questioned in regard to Nazi-looted art and a few things on social media. The day after, it was everywhere.

Time is our friend and on occasion, so is publicity.

Of course, Beuhler was denying everything through his lawyers, who were, according to another *Times* article, mounting a defense.

I wondered if I'd hear from him, but it was one of his assistants who called to say the gallery would be suspending a few forthcoming shows, mine among them.

No surprise, but it was a tough blow, my fantasy of fame and fortune over before it had begun.

92

A few days passed like a month. I tried to paint but couldn't. I read Van Gogh's letters for inspiration, even found a quote, "'If something in yourself says, *You aren't a painter*, it's then you should paint…and that voice will be silenced.'" I printed it out and pinned it to my studio wall. It looked good but didn't help.

Instead of painting, I listened to music, cleaned my studio, washed my brushes, and arranged paint tubes according to hue.

I had drinks with my friend Jude, who apologized profusely about bringing Beuhler to my studio in the first place. If anything, he was even more shocked about the art dealer than I was.

There was more news about Beuhler, "mounting evidence" according to a follow-up article in the *New York Times*, and an "unidentified witness" ready to testify to the art dealer's involvement in selling "hundreds of looted artworks."

When the unidentified number flashed on my cell, I debated answering but finally did.

"Have you shaved off that dreadful beard?" was the first thing Wil Kuhr said.

I laughed and said I had, and she dove into the "Beuhler scandal" with a kind of relish and giddy excitement, then asked if I had made plans for the paintings I was going to show with Beuhler, and before I could answer said, "How about showing them with me?"

It took a moment to get past my shock, then I agreed, and she gave me the dates and told me to book my flight. "I cannot wait to see your handsome face without that beard," she said, trilled a laugh, and that was it.

I was dying to tell Alex, but she was at school, so I jogged up to Twenty-Third and Fifth, ducked into Eataly, and loaded my cart with focaccia and olives that Alex loved, then into its connecting liquor store where I bought prosecco for Alex and sparkling cider for me. I spent more money at the Union Square Greenmarket, then dashed across the street to Breads Bakery for a dozen chocolate rugelach.

Alex was there when I got home, and when I told her the news, she said she never doubted for a moment that I would get another gallery, and we drank the prosecco and cider and ate half the rugelach before dinner, then made love.

Afterward, we picked at the focaccia and ate olives and Alex rummaged through a bag and came up with a small, tattered notepad, something she had totally forgotten.

"It was written by Toussaint's great-grandfather, Julien," she said and explained he'd been a teenager who had assisted Dr. Gachet with Van Gogh those last months in Auvers-sur-Oise. "Toussaint gave it to me to read just before all hell broke loose," she said, then she curled up on the couch and began to read.

93

I joined Alex on the couch, and looking over her shoulder could see the yellowed pages and the small print, all in French.

"It was a warm day, a Sunday, the twenty-seventh of July," Alex said, translating and paraphrasing. "Vincent had eaten lunch at the Auberge, then headed out to paint. 'How I regretted not going with Monsieur Vincent that day,' Julien writes, but Dr. Gachet had assigned him errands and chores, and he didn't see Vincent until later that night."

I was immediately hooked by what she said and the tone of her voice and the look on her face. The lamplight caught her profile, the slightest down on her cheeks that I loved, her full lips moving slightly as she read to herself.

"Go on," I said.

"He says the owners of the Auberge, the Ravouxs, and their guests were having dinner outside due to the heat when Vincent returned, that he came back without his easel or his art supplies and went directly to his room, and that it wasn't until later that Monsieur Ravoux heard moaning and went upstairs." Alex ran her finger up and down the page, then another.

"*What?*" I said, and she told me to wait a moment, then went on.

"Monsieur Ravoux found Vincent in bed, wounded," she said and reached for my hand, then read another page to herself, occasionally repeating a phrase in French aloud. "Apparently, a doctor was called, one who was visiting for the summer, and he inspected Vincent's wound and described it as *about the size of a small pea*, with not much bleeding, and by the time Dr. Gachet arrived, Vincent was sitting up, smoking his pipe, and demanding the doctors remove the bullet."

"What then?"

Alex squeezed my hand and told me to hang on while she skimmed another page. "Neither that doctor nor Gachet felt equipped to do it, something about the shot being at an awkward angle. Oh, and listen to this, it was as if it had been fired from some feet away."

"Like someone else had fired it?"

"He doesn't say." Alex turned a page and read to herself, and I asked if she was deliberately keeping me in suspense. She patted my cheek and I tried to be patient.

"Okay," she said. "So, Dr. Gachet sent a hand-delivered letter to Theo, in Paris, and urged him to come, saying Vincent had '*wounded himself.*'" She made air quotes around those words. "Julien stayed with Vincent for several hours, refilling his pipe, occasionally gripping his hand when Vincent grimaced in pain, so it apparently got worse. But when Theo arrived the next day, Vincent was sitting up again and smoking his pipe."

"Incredible," I said. "So, what then?"

"I thought you read the biography. It's all in there, isn't it?"

I admitted I hadn't finish it yet. "Plus, I like it better when you tell it," I said. "It's more exciting."

"And *easier*," she said, and read a few more pages to herself. "So, a search was made for Vincent's easel and paints and canvases, but they were never found. And listen to this, a townswoman reported having seen two teenage boys visiting the town for the summer— Rene Secretan and his brother Gaston—with their rowdy friends drinking at a bar at the bend in the Oise River right where Vincent had been seen painting. And later, when people took stock of who in town owned a gun, the only gun unaccounted for belonged to Rene Secretan, but he and his brother Gaston had left town during the night."

"*Whoa.* So, they shot Vincent?"

"Julien doesn't say that, though the gun wasn't found for a hundred years, *if* it was *the* gun."

"So, they cleaned up the scene!"

"You've been watching too much film noir," she said. "If they shot him, *if*, it could have been an accident. Julien writes that the boy, Rene Secretan, used to show off with his gun, and it was known for misfiring." She paused, and I asked what she was thinking. "Well, we know that a part of Vincent must have welcomed death, with his depression, and his fits of darkness."

"So, you're sticking with suicide?"

"I don't know," she said.

"But Vincent had so much to live for," I said, "his art, the shows he'd recently been in, and more were coming. It's a myth that he was unknown. By that time, he was getting attention, and had he lived another year, he would have seen his success."

Alex said I was speaking rationally in the face of the irrational and the unknown, but it seemed to me the evidence was simply not there for Vincent intentionally taking his life. I thought about the books and movies, all the immersive experiences, even a song, of the culture and romance of suicide that had grown up around Van Gogh and how much we had all invested in the idea of the tortured genius who could not go on living, and I said so.

Alex wasn't so sure. "We'll never know for sure who fired that fatal shot," she said, closed the diary and asked me to remind her to get it back to Toussaint. "One thing we know for sure is that Vincent died

in his brother's arms, and his last words were, 'I want to die like this,'"
she said, with tears in her eyes. I put my arms around her, and she
leaned against my chest, and we sat like that a while, and I thought
about Van Gogh and all he had gone through in his short life and all
we'd gone through, taking the trip, all the unknown risks, and how
we'd gotten past our own suspicions and lack of faith in each other,
and I felt happy.

"I love you," I said, and Alex said the same, kissed me, then curled
back against me.

"It was something, wasn't it?" she said, "having the self-portrait,
if only for a day."

"Yes," I said, reliving the moment when I'd scraped away the paint
and we could see the face below and Vincent's piercing eyes. "But
something that great, that important, it was never ours to keep."

Alex sighed and agreed. "I guess we'll never know what happened
to it."

"But we do know. It's on the museum's wall, safe and sound."

"No," she said. "I mean we'll never know who took it from the
funeral, or why."

94

July 30, 1890
Auvers-sur-Oise, France

It had been easier than she imagined, leaving the funeral, slipping into the Auberge, the mourners eating and drinking just next door, her boy standing guard. At first, she had considered a landscape of fields and puffy clouds, then one of a tall cypress, but finally, it was the portrait, its swirling back-ground and the funny little cows in the corner, and Vincent's piercing eyes on hers, that face she had known and caressed and loved.

In one fast move, she had it off the wall and under her coat. Then, she forced herself to walk at a normal pace so as not to attract attention, though no one was watching the tall woman in the shabby coat and bonnet with the young boy beside her as they made their way to the train station, how they had arrived just a few hours earlier.

With arms folded across her chest to keep the painting in place, she boarded the train and found them seats in the second-class compartment, the cabin so hot she was sweltering but did not dare remove her coat. Then she sat back and closed her eyes, picturing the graveyard on the hill, how she had kept her distance as the casket was lowered but watched and listened, hearing someone say, The abbot has refused the use of the church... they are saying it was suicide, *something she refused to believe—Vincent had always sworn he would never take his own life.*

Then, the young artist friend speaking of Vincent's painting, The Red

Vineyard, *how it had been sold for four hundred francs, and when he mentioned the name of a Paris gallery, she committed it to memory, deciding in that moment what she would do.*

Sien opened her eyes and looked over at her son, Willem, not Vincent's son but bearing his middle name, a shy, fatherless boy. Then she closed her eyes again and did not open them until a conductor was shaking her awake.

Paris was big and bustling and hot, men in suits and jaunty hats, women in tight corseted dresses, hats with feathers and flowers, twirling parasols to protect themselves from the summer sun while Sien felt her pale Dutch skin going pink. Swept into a crowd, she grasped the boy's hand, and they hurried along wide avenues lined with buildings that looked like palaces, horse-driven carriages kicking up great clouds of dirt and dust.

They stopped for a moment in a wide plaza and sat on the edge of a fountain where she dipped her handkerchief into the water and the boy cupped his hands to drink, and she did the same, her throat dry. Then she wiped the dirt from her face and dabbed at the back of her neck, and pulled herself up, feet aching in high-buttoned shoes, heels worn down, but they had to keep moving, she had to find the gallery. She had no idea how, the city was enormous and unknown to her, but she was determined.

Finally, it was a worker hauling his cart whom she dared to approach, and when she gave him the gallery name, he ventured a guess, a posh street of art galleries where he sometimes made deliveries.

"Viens," he said, indicating his cart, and offered her his hand. Then he hoisted the boy up and they took off down the street, bumping over ruts and furrows, the boy laughing in a way she had rarely heard, while she took in the splendors of the city she had never dreamed she would see.

He dropped them on an elegant street, and she found the gallery, paintings, silver candlesticks, gilded frames in the window. But she was paralyzed, intimidated, and kept walking. On the next street the galleries were less grand, and she noted one on a second floor above a bookshop and mounted the staircase where she took off her bonnet and shook her hair free. Then, she unbuttoned her coat and removed the painting.

For a moment, Vincent's painted gaze stopped her, and she thought of their two years together, of the many drawings and paintings he had made of her—sometimes naked, sometimes with the baby, or sewing, or peeling potatoes, or smoking a cigar—and she recalled the illnesses they had battled and how they had tended to each other, and her excruciating pregnancy, Vincent by her side and the tenderness he had shown her. In the end he had betrayed her when his brother insisted and threatened to cut him off, but she understood now he'd had no choice, that without Theo's support he had no way to care for them, or himself, or to paint, which he loved above all else.

She looked into Vincent's painted eyes and whispered goodbye, then climbed the steps, took a deep breath, and opened the gallery door.

The art dealer, overweight with thin hair lacquered across his scalp, took off his glasses and stared at the painting.

"How did you get this?" he asked.

Sien did not hesitate. She told him the artist was a good friend and produced envelopes addressed to her with Vincent's name and address, and letters with sketches in the margins and Vincent's signature at bottom.

Eyes glistening with greed, the art dealer offered her a hundred francs.

"Do you take me for a fool, monsieur?" she managed to say in her best French. She knew that Vincent's Red Vineyard *had sold for four hundred francs and told him that.*

Now, back on the street, sun low in the sky, she counted the money again, six-hundred-and-fifty francs. She was certain the greedy art dealer would sell it for a lot more, but it was enough, more than she would have asked of Vincent's brother, though he owed her at least that much, having robbed her of marriage and a home.

She folded the bills and slid them into a small tear in the lining of her coat, and they headed back to the train station. This time, when Willem said he was hungry, they stopped at a sidewalk café where she had a glass of wine and a baguette with cheese and the boy devoured an omelette with fresh herbs, and a few blocks later when they passed an ice cream vendor, she bought him one and felt happy and no longer cheated. She had taken the painting knowing it was not hers to keep.

AUTHOR'S NOTE

What you have just read is a novel that mixes fact and fiction.

These are just some of the facts:

Simone Segouin, also known by her *nom de guerre*, Nicole Minet, was an actual French resistance fighter.

The 1937 *Entartete Kunst* exhibition, made up of 650 artworks confiscated from German museums, attracted more than two million visitors.

Nazi-looted art was stored in Paris at the Jeu de Paume.

Hitler was planning to build an art museum, the Führermuseum, in his hometown of Linz, Austria, to be filled almost entirely with stolen art.

Descriptions of Carinhall and Reichsmarschall Hermann Göring are based on actual texts and photos.

Descriptions of the Anne Frank House, the photos on Anne's bedroom walls, the videos, and excerpts from Otto Frank's dialogue, along with the facts of Anne and Margot Frank's death at the Bergen-Belsen concentration camp are true.

Curt Valentin was a German-Jewish dealer who dealt mostly in "degenerate" art stolen from European museums by the Nazis. He emigrated to the U.S. in 1937 and opened the Buchholz Gallery, which changed its name to the Curt Valentin Gallery in 1951.

The 1939 Fischer auction of Nazi-looted art was held at the Grand

Hotel National at Lake Lucerne, where Curt Valentin bid on looted art on behalf of Alfred Barr, the director of New York's Museum of Modern Art.

Nazi art-looting programs, such as Alfred Rosenberg's ERR and the Dienststelle Mühlmann, were real.

The 2012 raid on the Munich apartment of Cornelius Gurlitt, son of Hildebrand Gurlitt, one of Hitler's approved art dealers, in which more than 1,500 pieces of Nazi-looted art were recovered, is true.

Almost all the artworks described in this novel are real, i.e., *Merde d'artiste* by the Italian artist Piero Manzoni, the duct-taped banana, titled *The Comedian*, and the "Hitler" sculpture *Him*, both by the artist Maurizio Cattelan (the latter piece sold at a Christie's auction in 2016 for $17.2 million), as well as pieces in the MET by Manet and Courbet, the Van Gogh double-sided self-portrait, etc.

Stefan Albrecht is a fictional character, but art dealers like him, ones who buy and sell Nazi-looted art, *Fluchtgut*, exist and operate today in the international art world (above- and underground) and on the dark web.

Scholars continue to debate Van Gogh's death as suicide, accident, or murder. Rene Secretan and his brother Gaston were real people, living in Auvers-sur-Oise at the time, and possibly at the scene of Vincent's death.

THE AUTHOR'S SKETCHBOOK FOR
THE LOST VAN GOGH

A page of pencil sketches I made from Vincent's various self-portraits. The portraits have all the same elements (mustache, beard, hair), but I was struck at how differently Vincent saw himself in each, distorting his face without vanity.

Sketches made from
Van Gogh self-portraits

The church at Auvers-sur-Oise that Van Gogh made famous in his painting. Here, in pencil, along with Vincent's and Theo's graves. In actuality, the graves are a ten- to fifteen-minute walk from the church, though I sketched them on the same page.

Vincent and Theo. Here, replicated in ink-wash. The younger Theo over Vincent's shoulder, keeping a look out for his troubled older brother.

A typical canal bridge with the omnipresent bicycles one sees everywhere in Amsterdam, in ink-wash.

Just one example, in ink-wash, of the many houseboats lining the Amsterdam canals, which I loved.

My pencil sketch of the light box containing photos of the eight residents in hiding at the Anne Frank House, which struck me and stayed with me. It was like previewing the cast of a tragic play.

Otto Frank

Edith Frank

Margot Frank

Anne Frank

Hermann van Pels

Auguste van Pels

Peter van Pels

Fritz Pfeffer

The Eldridge Street Synagogue, which feels somewhat out of place on New York's Lower East Side, like a Gothic church that has lost its way. The exterior and interior sketched in ink-wash.

A self-portrait I made in pencil looking into a reflecting sculptural cube in front of the Van Gogh Museum in Amsterdam.

READING GROUP GUIDE

1. What is John Washington Smith's relationship to his job? What does he want from his career? What is he willing to do to get that?

2. Many valuable works of art were coerced from Jewish collectors though they are recorded as legitimate sales by the Nazi party. When evaluating provenance and assessing rightful ownership, how should museums and auction houses accommodate these dubious sales?

3. Many characters in the book have secrets, conceal the truth, or lie. Do you think it is sometimes necessary to misrepresent the truth? What are the consequences of lying or evading the truth?

4. Most art dealers avoid looted art entirely, but some are willing to buy and sell it from a remove. How do you feel about this? Should art dealers be allowed to buy and sell works with dubious provenance?

5. The three main characters, Luke, Alex, and Smith, take great risks to attain what they are after. How are their aims and attitudes toward risk different?

6. Why would Alex continue to have a relationship with her father, and how does it benefit either of them?

7. What power does Jennifer hold throughout the book? Does her eventual outcome change the way you relate to her story?

8. How do the various theories about Van Gogh's death affect your interpretation of his art?

9. Luke makes a moral decision that seriously affects his art career and his future. Would you have done the same in his position?

10. The path of the lost painting in this story is just one explanation of how a Nazi-looted artwork survived. Do you think many works of art took similar routes to be recovered?

A CONVERSATION WITH THE AUTHOR

Alex and Luke's Van Gogh is partially invented but based on a real-life rumor. If that rumor did prove true, what would the effects be in the art world?

It would be tremendous news, extending well beyond the art world, in every newspaper, and all over the internet. The recent discovery of a modest pencil sketch Van Gogh made on a bookmark was big news. Imagine what the discovery of a late self-portrait painting would be. As one of the world's most beloved artists, any new discovery relating to Van Gogh causes a stir.

Was your writing process for *The Lost Van Gogh* significantly different than the way you wrote *The Last Mona Lisa*? What is most difficult about returning to existing characters?

My writing process has not really changed. I write a draft, then rewrite many times. I am an obsessive rewriter. When writing a dual story—one in the past and one in the present—it's difficult but exciting because one story informs the other.

As to writing existing characters, it's both fun and challenging because as the writer, you get to learn more about them, expand who they are, show how they are growing and changing as people. With characters in a series, it's always a balance between the information given about them in a former book and what you are adding to that.

You can never assume someone has read the earlier work, so your characters must exist fully in each book.

Repatriation of looted artwork is an important part of the book, and Luke counts himself grateful that he doesn't have to decide who is right about the issue. In your opinion, how should museums and collectors handle works of dubious or coerced sales?

I purposely had Luke say it was a difficult and tricky issue because it is. But if there is evidence that an artwork was looted (and this applies to all works of art and artifacts), they should be returned to the country from which they were stolen or to the heirs of the people whose work was taken during war or under duress.

Despite a veneer of legitimacy, some of the art dealers in the story turn out to be involved in illegal activities. What did you want readers to take away from these characters?

I think it's often the case that if you strip away a veneer of legitimacy you may find something unsavory in a character's past. I wanted these discoveries to put Luke in a moral dilemma, knowing his career would suffer if he told the truth. Like many of us, Luke is flawed and has his own personal demons, but at heart, he is morally decent. It was important to me that he make the right decision even if it hurt him. That reflects a larger theme in the book—making difficult, even life-threatening moral decisions. A group of Otto Frank's employees risked their lives to hide and protect the Frank family from the Nazis. I hope I would have the courage to do the same.

In both timelines, people relinquish the self-portrait with the sentiment that it hadn't been theirs to keep. Who *should* keep art, and what responsibilities does that entail?

I used that specific idea—that the painting was not theirs to keep—as a way to connect the characters in the present, Luke and Alex, to the characters in the past, Sien and Vincent. But who should keep art is a bigger question without one answer. Stolen artworks should be returned, but what about an important piece of art by a world-famous artist? Should it be in a museum so everyone can see it or in a collector's home because they can afford to buy it? I'll let my readers answer that one.

Beuhler's name opens many doors for Luke. How does the networking-heavy structure of the art world stymie new entrants? Could Luke have found folks like Wil Kuhr without Beuhler's intervention?

I do not think the art world stymies new or young artists. It's true, once an artist is in a big-name gallery, doors open for them, but I'd say today's art world is quite welcoming and that gallerists are always looking for exceptional artists.

Luke might not have found his way to Wil Kuhr without Beuhler's influence, but good artists usually find their way. Of course, there are plenty of talented artists who do not make it because they can't navigate the system. When I taught in art school, I tried to imprint on my students the idea that taking care of their work—that is, getting it out there to be seen—was part of their job. They may not like that part (I never did), but they need to do it to the best of their ability. All artists have a responsibility to their work beyond making it. Van Gogh was not the unknown, unconnected artist people think. His brother Theo was an influential art dealer, and Vincent hung out with many important artists of his generation, which ultimately helped his work get seen.

What's next for Luke, Alex, and Smith? Do you see their paths crossing again?

If I have my way, the unholy trio will surely be teaming up again. Luke and Alex and Smith have a mutual attraction and bond that draw them to danger (my fault, not theirs). What I like is that they encourage each other to pursue what they want and take risks. I was recently in India and kept seeing Luke or Alex or Smith on a Mumbai side street or at an Indian wedding or lost in a dicey neighborhood. Believe me, I didn't invite them, but they came along anyway. I can't seem to go anywhere that one of them is not whispering in my ear.

BIBLIOGRAPHY

While researching and writing this novel I read many books, but these continue to resonate:

Hitler's Art Thief, Susan Ronald, St. Martin's Press. An incredibly well-researched, totally accessible, and fascinating look at Nazi art looting.

Goring's Man in Paris, The Story of a Nazi Art Plunderer and his World, Jonathan Petropoulos, Yale University Press. This, and the other book by Mr. Petropoulos, *The Faustian Bargain, The Art World in Nazi Germany*, Oxford University Press, were tremendously helpful to my further understanding of Nazis art plunder.

The Orpheus Clock, The Search for My Family's Art Treasures Stolen by the Nazis, Simon Goodman, Scribner. An affecting book on the search for a family's lost art.

The Diary of a Young Girl, Anne Frank, Everyman's Library, Alfred A. Knopf.

All About Anne, Menno Metselaar and Piet van Ledden, Anne Frank House, Amsterdam.

Van Gogh: The Life, Steven Naifeh and Gregory White Smith, Random House. A brilliant biography of the artist that reads like a great novel; all you ever wanted to know about Vincent Van Gogh.

Van Gogh's Finale, Auvers & the Artists Rise to Fame, Martin Bailey, Frances Lincoln publisher. I read several of Bailey's beautifully illustrated books on Van Gogh, and though he will disagree with some things I say in my novel, I am indebted to him and to his ongoing column, *Adventures with Van Gogh*, in *The Art Newspaper*.

ACKNOWLEDGMENTS

More than once I have described writing a novel as falling into a pit, then clawing my way out. Here then, the people who made it possible for me to get out of the pit.

The patient and perceptive Shana Drehs, who takes what I write and makes it so much better.

Cristina Arreola, Molly Waxman, Anna Venckus, and the rest of the Sourcebooks team, all of whom obviously take their cue of excellence from the top, the amazing Dominique Raccah. To Laura Klynstra, who has created two beautiful book covers for me.

Thanks to writer friends like Megan Abbott (who planted the seed for this book even though it grew into a different plant), along with Janice Deaner, Joyce Carol Oates, and SJ Rozan, for their advice and inspiration. For providing writing homes away from home, Jane Rivkin and Susan Crile. And to Judd Tully who always connects me to the most incredible people wherever I go to research my books.

To Michele Leblond, who just may be the reason that Paris is still the City of Light.

In Amsterdam, my thanks to Christine Koenig for her hospitality, Easter dinner, and guided tour through the red-light district; Erika Prins and Menno Metselaar; Fabian Handschin and the inspiring Café de Spuyt.

In NYC, Donna Brodie and the quiet oasis of the Writers Room.

My gratitude always to Elaina Richardson and the Corporation of Yaddo, which has sustained me and so many artists for years; that it exists is a miracle and a gift.

The team at Aevitas, Erin Files, Allison Warren, Kate Mack, Mags Chmielarczyk.

To Billy Wilder for his thoughts on art and entertainment, which I took to heart.

And to the amazing Jane von Mehren, my agent at Aevitas, who does it all. This book would not exist without her.

ABOUT THE AUTHOR

Jonathan Santlofer is a writer and artist. His debut novel, *The Death Artist*, was an international bestseller, and his novel *Anatomy of Fear* won the Nero Award for Best Crime Novel of 2009. Jonathan has taught both art and writing, and his artwork is in many museums and private collections. Along with his writing, he has been creating "legal forgeries" of famous paintings for private collectors for the past twenty years.